You are made to live
in the center of God's
love.

Emma Watson

The Other Side
of Silence

A Novel

Lauren Martinez Catlin

The Other Side of Silence

A Novel

Lauren Martinez Catlin

Double Pixel Publications, Saint Paul, Minnesota, U.S.A.
First Edition, January 2012

THE OTHER SIDE OF SILENCE

ISBN: 1-62083-000-0
ISBN: 978-1-62083-000-0

www.DoublePixelPublications.com

Cover illustration by Jamie Winter Dawson
Photo of the author by Justin Horton

To Ben.
You are my clearest sign that God loves me
more than I can understand.

Table of Contents

A Thousand Voices Raised in Song

Today, I was gonna talk Celeste into letting me move back in with her and our kid. Five years was about five times longer than I thought Celeste'd keep me away just 'cause I drank some, but the woman had a stubborn streak I couldn't touch. Living apart from Celeste made my heart forget how to beat like it should, jumping and thumping in the middle of the night, or leaving long empty spaces when I thought I'd freakin' die. All that was gonna stop now, because I hadn't had a drink in six long months. Sometimes it was hard to think about anything else, but I was a strong man and I wanted to be with my woman and my kid.

I sat in my truck for a few minutes, feeling a little more at home just in Celeste's parking space. She didn't have a car anyway. I liked being almost close enough to touch Celeste. It gave my heart some time to find its rhythm before I went inside, which kept me from being a jackass to my girls.

An old woman banged on the driver's side window with her cane and I cringed. Sitting here helped my heart remember how to beat right, but I always forgot about Mrs. Krantz. Angrily, I cranked the window down.

"Hey, Mrs. Krantz."

"Vai embora, vai embora! Ouça-me! Ninguém quer te ver aquim, você comprende?" Mrs. Krantz not only hated my breathing guts, but took a sick pleasure in bawling me out in my mother tongue.

"I speak English, Mrs. Krantz. I've been in the States since I was five years old."

"Você não sabe como se comportar, né?"

"We have good manners in Brazil, Mrs. Krantz."

"Se você é um exemplo não acredito."

"Can I get out of my car, Mrs. Krantz? I want to see my family."

"They are not your family! You're a bum, you hear me? You haven't even been here in weeks. You're nothing but a tourist in that house, and don't think I don't know it." She backed away from the door, but continued to swing her cane for emphasis.

They were my family, no matter what that old bitch said. I wanted to be there every day, wanted to live there like a normal family. Every time I had to go back to my own apartment I wanted a drink so bad I could taste it. I saw them as often as I could stand it. I grit my teeth and tried to smile.

"At least you know I can understand you now."

"I thought some Portuguese might make it through that thick Latin skull of yours. Maybe if you heard what your own grandmother would say if she could see what a disgrace you are to her."

I snatched the toy I'd picked up for Ellie, pushed past the old woman and turned without breaking my stride. "I never knew my grandmother, Mrs. Krantz. Sorry."

"You watch yourself, Miguel. I've got my eye on you. I've seen your kind before. You might not be drinking, but you're as much of a drunk as ever. I can see it in your eyes."

"Leave me be, lady. Celeste wanted me to stop drinking so I did. I'm doing the right thing for my family, and it's none of your goddamn business."

"I'm the one taking care of that poor child every day while poor Celeste works double shifts."

"I help when I can, what do you want from me?"

"Mrs. Krantz!" Celeste shouted from her porch. "Leave poor Miguel alone."

The old woman hobbled away muttering in Yiddish.

"Come on in, Miguel. Sorry about that." Celeste smiled, and that made everything perfect.

"That's okay, baby. It's good to see you."

"You staying for dinner?"

"Nope, I ate already." Mrs. Krantz had already given me enough shit for eating Celeste's food. I didn't care what the old crank said, but Celeste was looking pretty skinny these days.

"Daddy!" Ellie came scrambling down the hall and barreled into my legs. Ellie had all the best parts of Celeste; her magnificent eyes, her grace, and her unbreakable will to forgive.

"How's it going, querida?"

"I got stars at school, come look!" she cried and started to run away. Something stopped her, and she came back with a shy smile. "What's that?" she asked, pointing to the toy under my arm. It was a stuffed rabbit. I smiled.

"This? Oh, this is just something I picked up today. I was looking for a good little girl to give it to. Do you know any?"

"I'm a good little girl! I'm so good, Daddy. Mommy, tell Daddy how good I've been. I got stars at school and everything." She bounced impatiently.

"Yes, Ellie's been a very good girl," Celeste said with a small smile.

"Well, I guess I'll have to give this to you, then," I said, holding the rabbit out. Ellie snatched it, hugging it to her chest before even giving it a once-over.

"I love it!"

"I can tell."

"I'm going to call her Paddy, because Paddy sounds like Daddy and you gave her to me. The P is for puffy or padding, because that is what this little bunny is like."

"Ellie likes to name things these days," Celeste explained.

"I know," I said, feeling defensive. I couldn't keep it up though, those luminous eyes melted me. "That's a great name, Ellie. Did I hear something about stars?"

"Oh! Yes, come see my stars, Daddy." Ellie ran off towards the bedroom and I followed.

There was only one bedroom in the house, and Celeste and Ellie were sharing the double bed in there. On one side of the bed were some prescription medications, magazines, and a physician's desk reference. The book was a gift from Mrs. Krantz when Ellie was born. On the other side was shelf with a few kids' books, some textbooks, and some little toys and trinkets, mostly things I'd brought her.

Ellie was petting the stuffed rabbit and talking quietly when I walked in, but looked up when she heard me.

"I was just telling Paddy what it's like here, so she won't be scared. Sometimes it's scary moving into a new place, but it's not so bad if you know what to expect."

"That's true. It's nice of you to tell Paddy what to expect. Where are the stars?"

"Up there!" Ellie said, pointing at the ceiling. There were four stars cut out of yellow construction paper, emblazoned with glitter, and hanging from pieces of yarn that were tacked to the ceiling. "Those are my stars, and I got them for being extra smart."

"Wow, those are great, Ellie."

"Will you stay to tuck me in tonight, Daddy? I want to hear the rest of the story, and I'll try extra hard to stay awake so I can hear it all."

"No problem, kid. If it's okay with Mommy I'll stay all night." It'd be so great to sleep next to Celeste again. It'd been years, but I still remembered how her body fit mine, how it felt when her muscles relaxed and her breathing slowed. My body stirred.

"I thought that couldn't happen for a long, long time," Ellie said.

"It's been a long, long time, Ellie." It'd been forever, if anyone asked me. Ellie's black eyes sparkled and her chubby limbs danced with excitement.

"Can we go ask her?" Ellie was facing the door.

"No, Ellie. Let me ask her. She might be mad if she knew I was getting your hopes up. It's not for sure, 'k, kid?"

"Okay, Daddy. But you'll stay to tuck me in?"

"Yep, no sweat."

"And you'll tell me the story? The one in Portuguese?"

"That's the only kid's story I know."

"Yay!" She jumped up and down.

"Ellie, come eat dinner, sweetie!" Celeste called. I followed the bouncing ball of joy to the kitchen where Celeste handed her a plate of chicken nuggets and some ketchup. Ellie spread a ratty towel in front of the television and sat on it with her dinner.

"I told her we could watch the Disney movie of the week, since it's not a school night," Celeste explained.

"You're the boss."

"You look pretty good, Miguel. Is work going well?" Celeste sat on the couch and invited me to sit with her. My body hungered to be near her, closer even than wrapping my arm around her shoulders, but I'd take what I could get.

"Work sucks, same as always."

"Hm." Celeste looked tired, and she let her head fall against my shoulder. When she didn't move right away, I took the chance to kiss her head. She smelled like Ivory soap, sweat, and something else that was just the scent of the woman I needed.

"I've got good news though, baby."

"Yeah? I could use some good news."

"I got six months today," I told her, swelling with pride.

"That's great, hon." She looked up at me and smiled, patting my stubbly face with her smooth brown hand.

"Mommy, the movie is starting!" Ellie said, holding a pudgy finger to her lips so we wouldn't distract her from Puff the Magic Dragon.

"Ellie, try to say that nice, please," Celeste said.

Ellie made a visible effort to control her impatience. She was such a plucky kid, and I was proud of her. "Mommy, could you please not talk during the movie, please?"

"That's better."

Ellie settled down and ate her chicken nuggets, dipping each one into the ketchup pile three times, once after each bite. The movie dragged on, pretty boring stuff, but Ellie was glued to it every second. Celeste fell asleep against my chest, and I held her close to me. It was worth being here just to feel her breathing against me. If I could have this every night, maybe I could really give up booze for good.

By the time the credits were rolling, Ellie was almost asleep. Celeste stirred, and I grudgingly let her go.

"Come on, Ellie. Time for bed," Celeste said, holding her arms out.

"But Mommy. Daddy said he would tuck me in and tell me that..." she paused for a wide, pink yawn. "That story."

"It's a little late for a story, but I bet Daddy will tuck you in."

"Sure, kid. Let's go." I lifted her into my arms. Ellie was getting heavy. I wondered how Celeste managed with her skinny arms. Ellie was already leaning heavily against my chest by the time I got her into the bedroom; her limbs were limp as I got her into her pj's. Still, I talked to her the whole time in Portuguese.

Talking to Ellie was about the only chance I got to speak my mother tongue anymore. The distant relatives who took me in moved to Florida years ago and we hadn't kept in touch. They never liked me much anyhow, and the feeling was mutual. But I wanted Ellie to be able to talk to her grandparents, and my sister Tasía too, if they ever met.

When Ellie was tucked in and sound asleep I went back to the living room. Celeste was asleep on the sofa, so I took the remote and flicked off the tv.

"Hey gorgeous, time for bed," I said, shaking her lightly.

"Hmmm?" she mumbled. I was feeling like a big man, so I slid my arms under her legs and around her neck and picked her up.

"Jesus, Celeste. You're losing weight again." She didn't feel much heavier than Ellie.

"Mmm," she grumbled. "Thanks for tucking Ellie in. It was good to have you with us tonight."

I kissed her, took in that wide beautiful mouth, that salty delicious flavor. She let me, giving into me like we used to do before Ellie was born, before she made me leave.

"I love you, Celeste," I whispered.

"I love you too, Miguel." She smiled. "Come back soon okay? You don't have to wait two weeks to see us."

My chest stirred uneasily. "Let me stay, baby. I want to stay with you."

Now she moved, wriggling to stand on her own.

"Not yet, Miguel." She tried to sound cheerful, but she was setting up for a fight. I'd give her one too.

"Come on, Celeste. It's been six months, what do you want from me?"

"A year."

My stomach tightened. "A year? Seriously?"

"Keep it down, Miguel. Ellie is sleeping."

"I know Ellie's sleeping, I just put her to bed!" My muscles felt the strain of too many months of not getting what I wanted, always putting it off to the next day. Why couldn't she see that? Didn't she care that I was busting my ass just so I could be with her?

"Go," Celeste said. She pushed me back to the living room, away from the bed, away from where I would feel my heart beating strong for a whole day together.

"I've been sober six months, isn't that enough to show you that — "

"Listen, this is not a deal. If you're going to live with us you're going to have to be sober forever, so six more months won't kill you. You can come over whenever you want, but you can't live here until you've been sober for a year."

Her eyes pleaded for me to let it go, but I couldn't. I didn't want to go back to my crappy apartment again, knowing that it'd be summer before I could have all the things I wanted. All the things I'd sacrificed for. I wanted to stay. I told the kid I'd stay.

"It's like you don't want this to work, Celeste. You're just waiting for me to fuck up."

"I am not. Miguel, please. This was a good night."

"Why can't it keep being good? I'm not dangerous, I'm not a criminal, and I've cleaned up. You know I have."

"I'm not doing this. You're doing great, and when you've been doing great for a year then you can live with us. Go home now." She pushed me. Pushed me away like a piece of garbage.

"Fine, I'll go. You can tell Ellie why I'm not here in the morning. You better tell her the truth too, that you didn't want me to stay. Tell her that you don't want us to be a family."

"Oh," Celeste whimpered. Two tears streaked her soft brown face. Fuck, now I'd made her cry.

"Celeste, I – "

"Go. Just get out." She pushed me again and turned away.

"I didn't mean that Celeste. I just want to be with you. I want to be with you all the time." Now she was going to have me crying like a damn baby. "I'll just go, then."

I waited for her to say something. I wanted her to say she'd changed her mind, or at least that she forgave me for being a jerk. She didn't say anything, just went back to the bedroom, leaving me behind.

The door slammed behind me louder than I'd meant. I'd never make it a year like this. I'd never be welcome in that house. Why couldn't I just live with my own family, my own woman and my kid? Was that so fucking nuts?

It was less than a minute from Celeste's place to my crappy apartment, and I needed air before I could face that empty room. I decided to drive. Neon signs beckoned me as I drove. Happy people sat in restaurants, went into bars, and sipped cups of coffee. Everyone had someone; not one goddamn person was alone.

I couldn't remember how the bottle found my mouth, but I sucked it down and told myself it was just this one time. After that, I didn't have to tell myself anything. I could feel alcohol burning through my system, numbing the memory of Celeste's body, of Ellie's joy, of my failure, of everything, everything, everything.

··

My heart throbbed once and stopped. Twice, and stopped

again. In the thick gray of early morning, I rolled over on my cheap mattress and grabbed a fistful of my shirt. The shirt felt gritty in my hand, and I remembered that I'd fallen onto the mattress with my clothes on. I wasn't sure what I'd done last night, but the sour taste of cheap tequila coated my tongue and teeth. Great.

I checked the clock, and it wasn't even six yet. I had a couple more hours to sleep it off before I had to get up for work. If only my damn heart would calm down. When my cell phone vibrated against my leg, I wasn't surprised.

"What?" I demanded as I snapped the phone to my ear.

"Miguel? Is that you?" The voice sounded familiar, but I couldn't place it.

"Yeah, it's Miguel. Who's this?"

"This is Mrs. Krantz, Celeste's landlady."

"I know who you are. How did you get this number?" The last thing I wanted in the world was Mrs. Krantz with my cell phone number.

"It was in Celeste's phone. I have to tell you something, Miguel. It is important that you are calm."

"Is Ellie okay?" My heart throbbed again, painfully. I sat up in bed and started putting my shoes on.

"Yes, Ellie is fine, she is here with me."

"What's going on?" I asked, relaxing a little.

"Celeste's been in an accident, Miguel. It's very serious."

"Accident?" Images started flicking through my head like a slide show on crack; everything from jack-knifed semi's to glasses of spilled milk.

"She was hit by a car while she was waiting for the bus this morning. I'm at the hospital with her."

"Hit by a...I don't understand. Is she okay?"

"No, she isn't. You should come right away if you want to see her."

"If I want to see her? Are they moving her somewhere?" I already had my car keys in hand and was picking my way towards the door.

"Miguel, it was a…it was a drunk driver. They were going very fast."

"What hospital are you at?"

"HCMC. Come quickly, Miguel."

"I'm out the door." I hung up as I leapt into my truck and it roared to life. Anyone else would need directions to the hospital, need to know which wing she was in, need instructions on where to park and possibly Celeste's room number. Not me. There was a connection between my heart and hers that would lead me to her anywhere. Celeste was part of me; finding her was like finding my right hand.

My heart's wild throbbing worked like radar, getting stronger and louder the closer I got to Celeste, and I followed it without question. I double-parked outside some sliding doors and went inside. Colors and people swirled around me, but I followed the vibration in my chest, the pulse I knew was Celeste. Celeste's heart beating, Celeste needing me, Celeste waiting for me to arrive, to give her heart the strength it needed.

People talked to me, a few hands touched my shoulders as I searched through the series of curtains and people with tubes sticking out of them. The pulse led me to a room with a huge glass window, but the room was locked. Mrs. Krantz was sitting in an ugly orange chair just beneath that glass window, holding Ellie in her lap and whispering in her ear.

"Daddy!" Ellie cried when she saw me. As she barreled into me, I picked her up, but focused on the window.

"Is she in there?" I pointed to the glass. Mrs. Krantz nodded.

"They had to start surgery. I thought you should see her first, but they said it was urgent. I didn't…I didn't know what to do."

I'd never seen Mrs. Krantz look so soft before, like she might cry. Her cane, always a weapon, was leaning against the wall next to the orange chair like an assistant waiting to be needed.

"What kind of surgery?" The glass window had a curtain over it on the other side of the glass, but I could just barely make out figures moving inside of it, crouched over something delicate.

"I'm not sure. They said she has internal bleeding, and a collapsed lung. Something about the liver or…I don't know. They're trying to fix it."

"Daddy, you're hurting me," Ellie whined in my ear, wiggling from my grasp. When I released her I saw the white imprint of my hand on her arm. I was squeezing her tighter and tighter.

"Sorry." I set her down and she ran back to Mrs. Krantz.

I drew close to the window, not really wanting to see what was happening to Celeste inside, but needing to be near her. The curtain was white, making the faint figures inside colorless shadows, but to me it looked like red. Red everywhere. Red on the doctors and nurses, red in the bag hanging from a thin metal pole, red in the tubes, red on the table, red on giant swabs of cotton at the end of metal tongs. No trace of Celeste in there, just a mass of bones and flesh and red. Still, I couldn't move. My radar ended at this spot, and this is where I had to stay.

"Sit, Miguel." Mrs. Krantz patted the chair next to her, shifting Ellie's wiggling body to her other knee.

I sat, more out of obedience than anything else. I wasn't tired. I wasn't edgy, agitated, or even worried. I was numb, dull, and empty. I said nothing, just sat listening to the steady beat of my heart.

"Why does Daddy look like that?" Ellie stage whispered to Mrs. Krantz. The old woman shushed the child and tried to pat my hand for comfort. My skin felt like cold leather.

"Why does he?" Ellie insisted, trying to get a closer look at my face. I felt her gaze, but I couldn't return it.

"He's just worried about your mom," Mrs. Krantz said, pushing Ellie back to the other side of her lap. "Don't stare, dear."

I sat there for a long time, not moving, not blinking. I stared ahead, listening to the bleeping of the heart monitor behind me in that room full of red. The bleeping matched my own heartbeat, so I knew it was connected to Celeste. Ellie chattered to Mrs. Krantz, a bubble of life in a cold, dead sea. I was a discarded anchor, heavy and immovable.

Something happened and I jerked back to life. The beeping smoothed into one long tone, and I jumped out of my chair. When I turned to the window, the figures inside were in fast-forward, jerking in panicked motion. A small explosion made the lifeless body on the table jump, and the beeps resumed for a moment before falling back into the endless tone. Another explosion, and another, but no lasting effect.

"Miguel," Mrs. Krantz was pinched with fear, and I realized that I was grunting with pain at each explosion. My heart was shot through as the doctors tried to jerk Celeste's body back to life.

A hard, hallow banging sound rang through the hallway, and a soft-looking man in blue scrubs was pushing my arms away from the window. I was banging on the glass, dying to get through to where Celeste was fading away, but they wouldn't let me. A thicker curtain was drawn across the window, but I knew what was happening inside. My heart told me, as it was gasping out its last words.

I could hear her inside, drifting away. *I love you, but...I love you, but...* I loved her, but I hadn't been there for her. I loved her, but I couldn't stop drinking. I loved her, but I couldn't keep her alive with my love.

The beeping stopped. A roaring, gnawing silence filled the hallway. The soft man stared at me as I fell against the wall, curling around myself. Ellie's tender hands touched my tense forearms.

"Don't cry, Daddy. Don't cry," she begged. She was confused, the blue people in the blue scrubs were confused. Mrs. Krantz pulled Ellie away from me with the same firm urgency that she would have pulled her away from an open well.

Words swirled above my head, but they couldn't make a dent in the silence, the awful silence that pushed through my ears and crushed my insides. A horrible pain was building in my chest. When I laid my hand against it, I felt nothing. She hadn't known I was here, hadn't told me good-bye, hadn't warned me she was leaving. Now there was nothing left of me, just an empty shell that needed to be filled.

People were asking me questions and talking about Ellie, Ellie who looked up at me with wide black eyes, frightened. She wanted me to comfort her, but I was scared too. I knew if I just stood here looking into those deep black eyes that I would crumble to dust. The poor kid had been through enough already.

Mrs. Krantz was speaking in a concentrated voice to the blue shapes around us, gesturing with her free hand. Her other hand was griping Ellie's soft arm. She pointed to me and I heard the words "not suitable."

"Sir? Sir?" Someone was talking into my face. I squinted and backed up, unable to deal with people who call me sir and a bitchy old lady who said I wasn't good enough.

"Sir, have you been drinking?"

"What?" He might have asked if the sky was up or if the moon was made of cheese. Who the hell cared about drinks? He was a damn doctor; couldn't he see that I was dying?

"I will take care of the girl. She is not safe with him."

The words struck me across the face like a wet piece of leather. I saw why they were asking me about drinks now. They wanted Ellie.

"Forget it, you fucking bitch. Nobody's taking Ellie away from me. No fucking way."

Everything fell silent, and all the blue shapes became still. All the doctors became crystal clear, and they were all looking at me, all wondering how they hadn't noticed a gorilla standing in the hall.

"We'll have a social worker come and evaluate the situation." The man who said this was much younger than me. He had lily-white hands and round glasses.

"Ellie, come with me." I held my hand out to my daughter, because she was mine, and I wasn't going to wait around and see if they decided to take her away from me.

"Ellie, you stay here with me. We have to make sure you are safe, first." Mrs. Krantz was holding Ellie in her arms, speaking in her softest voice. She looked like a demon, clutching my beautiful girl, tricking her into giving up her home.

Ellie looked up at me, tears brimming in her eyes. She looked at Mrs. Krantz, who smiled warmly back at her. The bitch.

"Daddy, can you stay with us?" she asked in her tiny squeaking voice. Mrs. Krantz grinned at me, claiming her victory. She had my Ellie, and Ellie would rather stay with her than go with me. A yawning, gaping void was opening up in my stomach, and I could feel contorted sounds sneaking up my esophagus; sounds that would break the world.

"I…I have to go. Just…just take care of her."

As I stumbled out of the hospital, the voices behind me picked up speed and raced around in crazy chipmunk form. I knew I had to get out of there before pieces started falling off me.

I drove to the nearest bar and drank until they kicked me out. This was the end of everything, the black hole of life. They took my keys, so I walked to the nearest liquor store and spent all the money I had on big bottles of precious gold and clear liquids. Between missing my truck and losing track of where the sidewalk met the road, I couldn't find my way back to my shitty apartment. The bridge I slept under was almost as comfortable anyway.

·•·

If I'd thought about it, even for a second, I would remember the dark green glow of this emerald necklace against my mother's collarbone, before she died, when she was still beautiful and strong. I didn't think about it, I just handed the necklace to the pawn shop guy and took the cash. I needed a drink worse than I needed a fuzzy memory of Mamí right now, just like I needed a drink more than I needed food, more than I needed a coat in the snow, more than I needed anything.

If I thought of anything at all, I tried to think about how fucking mad I was that my sister hadn't told me she'd brought a fortune in heirloom jewels to the states. I'd been living in a rat hole for…well, for a long damn time before Tasía even came to the US. She just appeared, expecting me to take care of her after Papí got into some kind of trouble. Fucking bastard, assuming I would take care of a middle-aged woman without even being asked.

Tasía scrubbed toilets for three months before she moved us into this cheap-ass apartment, cheaper even than the one I'd had before the rat hole. The woman wouldn't even buy toothpaste for Christ's sake, and all the while she had a butt-load of money stashed away. As I felt the anger rising up in my chest, I also felt a mild discomfort trading the cold green glimmer for the warm glowing liquid I started drinking before I was all the way out of the liquor store. That discomfort was a fly on my shoulder compared to the reasons I had to down this bottle.

The frosty air felt good on my face, but I stumbled back to the apartment. Since…well, since things got really bad I'd had a problem with getting lost. Tasía never said anything when I didn't show up for a couple days, but even I could tell she worried. No reason to sleep outside and deal with the freakin' cops if there was a clean piece of carpet to sleep on back at the apartment. So I went back and drank there, making sure I hid the bottle nice and tidy before Tasía came home. She'd freak if she found booze in the apartment.

After a couple good gulps of the burning gold liquor, the warmth of the apartment wrapped around me. I had no trouble falling asleep on the cheap carpet. Tasía had an air mattress in her room, but she'd threatened to kick me out if she found me sleeping on it. Pretty sure she was more worried about me puking on it, but the thing made me seasick anyhow.

I was deep in a murky sleep when I heard Tasía shouting, her voice muffled, but pushing against my body.

"Miguel! You're sleeping against the door!" She shouted at me in her perfect, angry Portuguese. She was a dead ringer for Aunt Nanita. Maybe that's why I obeyed, shuffling into the tiny living room.

"Miguel!" she shouted again. God, why was she always shouting?

"Just let me sleep, Tasí," I moaned. My head reeled. I didn't want to waste my buzz, so I tried to zone her out. Her voice was thick and blurry, so it wasn't too hard to ignore. I mumbled answers, but she just kept after me. When I cracked one eye to look at her, she was standing over me with her hands on her hips, glaring at me like a piece of shit she had clean up.

"Do you steal?" she demanded.

"No, I don't steal," I mumbled. Sometimes I stole, but Tasía didn't need to know that. I never stole from her, anyways. Then I did remember how the emerald looked on my mother's neck, and how it looked in the rough hands of the pawn shop guy. Well, it wasn't my fault Tasía hid those jewels. If she'd told me about them then maybe we'd have talked about how to use them, but…well…my head throbbed.

A sharp whining started in the kitchen, hurting my ears. Now

Tasía stood over me again, holding Aunt Nanita's embroidered bag where the jewels had been. She shouted so loud it was almost a scream. I didn't hear her, blocked out her screechy words, but I caught just the last one. *Ellie.*

That word pulled me off the ground and flung me forward, the floor swinging dangerously. "I...I warned you not to mention them!" I shouted, trying to be bigger, stronger, and meaner than my sister so she would shut the hell up. Fuck, the only reason I drank now was so I didn't have to think about...about...

"Watch your step, girl!" I roared as loud as I could, wanting to push her away, but afraid to touch her. I'd hit her once, and I still couldn't believe it. While I was straining every muscle not to lose control, she shoved me. She shoved me hard against the counter. I blinked.

Tasía was yelling, shouting, screaming, calling me names, saying Papí was ashamed of me. Her face looked different, not like Aunt Nanita anymore, or like Mamí. She was shaking with rage and full of righteousness like a warrior angel. I was a big, strong man, but I was scared of my sister.

"Get out of my house!" her voice broke and squeaked, but I knew she meant it. "Forget about me! Don't ever come back here! Get out!"

She expected me to fight, I could see it in her glittering eyes. I was too tired. My last piece of family in the whole continent, and I'd pissed her off so bad she never wanted to see me again. Only took four months.

A year ago I had a good job, family back in Brazil, Celeste across the street, and Ellie dying to see me every time I came. If I thought about it I would break down and cry like a little baby. Looking into Tasía's flaming eyes, I knew she wouldn't give me another chance even if I did break down in tears. I'd blown it, really blown it, again. I should just go die.

I stuffed my wallet in my pocket and walked to the door,

keeping my eyes on the ground. I couldn't look in Tasi's eyes; they would burn me up. Near the door there was a huge splatter of orange puke. So that's why she got pissed. Tucking my head, I mumbled an apology and left.

·•·

When I woke up, half my face was wet. As I shifted, I found half of my whole body was wet. My jeans reeked, my shirt felt days old, and I had a distinct puke-taste in my mouth. Something blunt was shoving one of my shoulders, and I rolled over to get away from it, getting my other side wet. Looking around, I realized that I had been sleeping on a large piece of lawn that hadn't been mowed in a long time. The long green leaves were covered in dew, and that dew was also covering me. My face hurt.

"That's some black eye you got there," a far too cheerful voice said. The blunt thing pushed me again.

"Cut it out," I moaned, futilely trying to push the object away with a limp hand and a limper arm.

"Sorry, friend. We're trying to put a tent up here. You're gonna have to move." Again, the cheerfulness. It made me sick.

"Fuck off." I rolled over again so my back was to whatever was shoving me and tried to go back to sleep. The grass didn't bother me; the wet didn't even bother me. The shoving bothered me though, and so did that sunshiny voice.

"You're welcome to come inside the building while we're setting up the tent. Would you like some coffee?" Instead of the blunt thing, which I think was a shoe, a warm hand touched my shoulder.

"Got any whiskey?" I asked.

"Nope, sorry. We do have real good coffee though. It's a beautiful morning, it'll help wake you up."

I glared at the source of the voice. He turned out to be an older man in overalls, shielding my face from the sun with his hand. I despised him. If only because he was clearly a morning person, I felt he deserved to die.

"I don't want to wake up, jackass. Why do you think I'm sleeping here?"

I honestly didn't know why I was sleeping on the grass. I had no idea where I was or how I'd gotten here. Weeks, months, maybe even years had passed by in a fuzzy blur of demanding people and bottles of liquor. For a long time I hadn't been able to remember what it was I'd wanted to forget so badly, which was just how I liked it. Now, with this chipper morning person nudging me, and the night's sleep I'd had, and who knows how long since my last drink, it was coming back to me. The room full of red, Ellie screaming for her daddy, my sister's pinched shouting, the dead stillness in my chest.

"When's the last time you had a good meal, friend?" His cheerfulness was turning into sympathy, which I liked better because it was quieter.

"I don't know." I didn't care much either.

"Tell you what. You come on inside and you can sleep on a couch 'til you're ready to get up. I'll fix you up something in the kitchen and you can get back on your feet." He clapped me on the shoulder, which I resented. But a couch was a lot better for sleeping than wet grass. If I slept long enough, maybe I could remember how I'd gotten here, where I'd left my truck, and what my plan was to get my next drink.

"Sure."

"Let me help you up there," the man said. He offered me his hand, rough with calluses. His eyes had the dark murky quality of someone who'd enjoyed a few nights in the bars himself. The smile was deep and sincere, the hand strong enough to pull me up. So I took it.

I don't know how long I slept on the couch I was offered, but it was getting dark outside when I woke. Waking up on the grass had the dreamlike quality that all my experiences took on lately, but now my body was starting to come alive again. I couldn't remember the last time I'd been this sober, but I was glad I'd blocked it out. My chest ached where that horrible stillness was, and I put my hand to the spot instinctively. My entire body screamed for a drink, even dead things like my hair and fingernails. Nausea ruled over everything, and I had to clench my stomach muscles to keep from heaving right there on the couch. Everything seemed so bright, so clear. It hurt my eyes.

"Are you awake, friend?" an eerily familiar voice asked brightly.

"A little."

"I got some hot dish for you here. Some of the ladies brought some stuff over for the meeting tonight, but they won't miss one little bowlful. And I got you some of that real strong coffee, 'case you still wanted it."

Something brownish with toasted tater-tots on top was offered to me in a pink plastic bowl, and a coffee mug full of thick, black liquid was placed in my other hand. I struggled to get up.

"Even brought you a spoon," the man in the overalls said, proudly handing me the plastic utensil.

"Thanks. I don't know if I can eat this." I don't know why I was trying to be polite, but I didn't say "this makes me want to puke."

"Just try a bite. Lotta times you need a little something in your stomach to set you to rights."

"Yeah." I knew that, but I didn't want whatever was in this bowl. Setting the coffee aside, I took one bite, for show. The cheesy, meaty mixture was like heaven in my mouth. Despite how disgusting it looked in the bowl, my stomach growled that it'd been waiting for something like this for years.

"Thanks, man." I said, devouring the rest of the bowl.

"I can get you some more if you like."

"That would be great."

I finished off the bowl in seconds and handed it back to the guy, who went to fill it up again. My stomach was happy, and the nausea faded a little, but my chest ached all the more. Although I was grateful for the hot meal and a soft place to sleep, I resolved to get out of here as fast as possible to get my next drink. Where was my truck anyway? A cursory search of my pockets proved that I had no keys.

"Here you go." The man handed me another bowl of hot dish; this one was nearly overflowing.

"Thanks." I started to dig into the meal with fervor.

"What's your name, friend?"

"Miguel," I answered around a huge bite.

"What a great name. There's strength in that name," the man smiled. I scoffed.

"There isn't much in the man."

"Some food will help you out." The guy seemed so sure that a bowl or two of hot dish would fix my entire life. I laughed bitterly.

"Not enough."

"I'm Charlie, good to meet you." He offered me his hand.

I looked into his murky eyes suspiciously. What was this guy's problem, anyway? Wasn't it obvious that I was a drunk, that I would eat the food he gave me, drink the coffee, have my nap on the couch, and then go get fucked up again?

"I don't think we're gonna be friends, man."

"Why not?"

"I'm a drunk, okay? I don't have friends."

"Sounds kinda lonely." The smile hadn't left his face. He acted as if he liked me on sight, like there was some golden halo around my dirty head. "You got family?"

"No," I all but growled. "Well, I've got a sister in town, but she doesn't want to know me anymore." I didn't blame her either.

"I bet she's worried about you."

I blinked at him, took another bite of the delicious meal. "Can't you hear me, man? I said she doesn't want to know me."

He shrugged, still smiling. "Once I told my father that I hoped he'd die. Left the house and didn't come back for ten years. Wasn't one day I didn't think of him, though."

I shifted uncomfortably in my seat. "What kind of a building is this, anyway?" I asked, looking around. Big double oak doors lined one whole wall. To my right was a counter that looked like it might be a café or a coffee shop. The carpet was red and cheap, and everywhere I looked there were little plastic containers full of menus.

"This is a church, friend."

A wave of rage swept over my body. "Well fuck that." I stood. Dizziness pushed me back down again, but I wavered, trying to work through it. The horde of black dots rushing at my eyes won over, and I sat down again, hard. "I don't have time for churches."

Charlie shrugged again. "We got time for you."

"I'm not getting into any programs or anything like that, you got it? I am not interested in the 12 steps, rehab, or any kind of exorcism."

Charlie laughed, not seeming one bit bothered by my contempt for churches and programs. "We ain't gonna make you to do nothing you don't want to."

"Uh-huh." I was suspicious. I wondered if eating the hot dish somehow obligated me to do something here, or if there was something in it to make me compliant. Looking down at the coffee, I nudged it with my foot.

"We're having a big old meeting out on the grass in the tent there tonight. That's why you had to move. You're welcome to stay for the service if you like."

"No thanks," I said automatically. "I hate churches."

"Why?"

I looked at him carefully; that question sounded weird. After a moment, I realized that it was weird because it sounded like he really wanted to know why I hated churches. What was even stranger was that I really wanted to tell him, and I hadn't wanted to tell anyone anything in a long time.

"They're full of hypocrites. I'm not going to pray to any god who made the world, 'cause the world is full of shit. I tried to give up the damn bottle and be with my girl, with... with our daughter. There's something in me that couldn't let go. If someone made me, they put that in me, and I hope they fucking die."

Charlie nodded, the smile finally fading from his face. "That sounds pretty awful. I'd be mad, too."

I stared at him. "You aren't going to argue with me?" That's what church people did. I'd seen them before, everything from calm men in suits and ties to crazy long-haired hippies standing on boxes and shouting.

Charlie laughed. "Argue with you? I ain't gonna argue you outta your pain, friend. I still think you outta try the service out, 'cause if there is something that bad in you, maybe if we pray for you it'll go away. I've seen it happen before. But I ain't gonna argue with you."

I shifted in my seat. He made me uncomfortable for some stupid reason. I should have just told him to fuck off in the first place and gone back to sleep on the wet grass.

"I don't know where my truck is," I said lamely.

"What does it look like?"

"It's green, a Ford. Kinda beat up. You seen it?"

Charlie thought for a moment. "Nope, sorry. I'll keep my eye out. Sometimes people park at the grocery store across the way; maybe it's over there?"

"Sure. I'll go look."

"I'll take you around to look for it. I got a truck myself. But I gotta stay until the thing tonight is over; I'm helping out."

"Thanks, Charlie." I paused. "You're a pretty cool guy."

He waved his hand. "Ain't nothing."

"Okay if I wait here?" I looked toward the door where the tent would be constructed by now.

"Whatever you want, friend. Sleep some more if you want. Might be kinda late when we're finished."

"Sure."

"I gotta get going. There's more coffee behind the counter in that pot. Help yourself."

Charlie left, going out the big front doors. As the large door swung open, I saw light glowing from the white canvass tent. Upbeat music was playing, it sounded live even. A girl about ten or eleven carried a rainbow-striped flag past the door as it was closing. They looked like they were getting ready for a rave, not a church service.

I shook my head, wondering what kind of reality warp I was in. After lying back on the couch, I found I wasn't sleepy anymore. Steadying myself against the couch, I got up really slow. After a moment, the dizziness cleared and I was able to walk around.

I picked up one of the menus from the plastic holder. *Confused?* The front asked, sporting a glossy picture of a beautiful woman holding her hands up in a helpless pose, a quizzical look on her face. This looked fishy. I opened the pamphlet and saw information about a class that was supposed to answer all the questions of life. I put it back, disgusted. Another one had some green leaves with dew on them on the front, and big white cursive letters that said *Creation Care*. That one was about some environmental bullshit. Like recycling your pop cans was going to save the world or something.

This was a mistake, staying here. Charlie seemed nice enough, but I had a feeling that he was tricking me into staying by promising to help me find my truck. Besides, finding the car wasn't going to help me much if I didn't have the keys. I should just get out of here, find the nearest bus stop and high tail it back to... well, to somewhere else.

When I stepped out of the church, something had changed. The tent was bursting with people; all the flaps were lifted to allow the maximum number of people inside, and they still oozed out all the openings. A band played a song that seemed to move inside of me, like the bass was pumping my blood for me. All the band members had their eyes closed and their heads lifted to the sky, like they were all in their own worlds, playing the best songs of their lives, and they just happened to be on the same stage.

The sea of people facing the stage were all on their feet, waving their hands in the air. They looked like seaweed or something, the way they all swayed together, pumping with life but still peaceful in a weird way. Three or four of those rainbow-striped flags were waving back and forth, swung by people with strong arms and huge grins. Right in front of the stage a knot of people were dancing like there was no tomorrow, jumping and twirling and flailing. They were in total abandon, total freedom. In hundreds of people, I couldn't find one who was holding anything back, not one with a trace of worry or embarrassment.

I wanted it. Whatever was sweeping through this crowd, I wanted it. Stepping to the edge of the crowd I looked around for a way into this wild, communal dance. The pulse of the crowd drew me in, but there was something missing. I tried holding my hand up to the air like I saw other people doing, but I felt stupid. No one else looked like they felt stupid, so I put it down again. *Maybe I should just leave*, I thought. Maybe there was something special I had to do or go through to be admitted to this kind of experience. Maybe only the sober, straight-arrow people could be that loose and free. Still, I could try. Gathering a little courage, I tapped a blissful man on the shoulder. He was wearing khakis and a white business shirt, so I half expected him to ask me to leave after a look at my dirty clothes.

"I-I'm sorry to bother you," I said. I had to shout over the music and the crowd.

"Do you need something?" he asked. His whole face, his whole body was glowing. His hands shook with energy, the smile on his face was wide and firm.

"I...how do I get into this?" I asked. I could only hope he understood.

The smile on his face widened. He slapped the palm of his right hand against my forehead and held it there. He spewed some kind of gibberish, talking a mile a minute but not making any sense. I was about to tell him thanks, but I'd leave without drinking the Kool-Aid. Then something happened.

My heart beat. Not a weak fluttering, but a good strong beat that pumped blood into my veins. My body grew warm and felt light, like I was floating towards a gentle sun. Closing my eyes, I let the sensation wash over me, just feeling alive. It wasn't the burning warmth of alcohol, and it didn't make me numb. Instead, I felt like I was waking up, muscle by muscle, nerve by nerve, cell by cell. Everything that was hibernating, sleeping, or dead was coming back to life. My skin tingled, overwhelmed with feeling. All the sensations that tickled the thousands of nerve endings in my skin were sheer delight, pure ecstatic pleasure. Suddenly the beat of the music made sense, the swaying of the people was inside me, rising from deep within.

When I had the courage to open my eyes, I saw that my hands were shaking like they were electrified, only it didn't hurt. It felt warm and full, like I was being shot through with life. The last little piece of me that thought all these people were fucking nuts gave in to the pulse. Who cared if they were? This was better than anything I'd ever felt, even being with Celeste. This was the only moment in my life I wasn't drinking or miserable. This was something new, and

I loved it.

Before I knew it, I was swaying with the rest of the crowd, feeling the warmth pour through me in waves of joy and freedom. Here I was in the grip of something more powerful than alcohol, something that made me higher than any drug I'd ever taken, something that filled every ounce of my being with a sensation more satisfying than sex.

In my mind I saw a picture of myself floating in a dark sea full of pain and death, but I was being pulled up, up, up. As I reached the surface the light of the sun revealed something dark that was wrapped around my whole body, stuck like a growth to my skin. As I watched, the warmth of the sun dried the black stickiness and it fell off of me in flakes, like ash. I knew the picture was only something in my head, but I could tell that something real had happened in my body. I knew because, for the first time I could remember, I didn't want a drink.

..

I stayed in the canvas tent until the very last moment. I didn't want to miss one drop of whatever it was that touched me. I felt light, weightless, and stronger than ever all at the same time. When the band stopped playing, I wanted to beg them to keep going, feeling that I could spend the rest of my life in this spot, dancing and singing.

Charlie approached me as the crowd filtered out of the tent.

"Do you have somewhere to sleep tonight, friend?" he asked.

The question seemed so totally irrelevant, I didn't even know how to answer it.

"Did you...I mean...have you been here the whole time? Did you feel...did that...I don't even know how to talk about it!" I cried. Charlie smiled, still calm.

"You got some of that Spirit, friend. I thought there might be something for you here."

"I don't want to drink. That's... I've never not wanted to drink, not for as long as I can remember. I fucking lost my girl and my daughter 'cause I couldn't stop drinking. I should try and find them, and apologize to my sister. I wonder if I can get my mom's jewelry back or – "

"Hang on, friend. You're going too fast there." Charlie laid his big hand on my shoulder to stop my words, but his smile was still pleased. "You're free of your chains, but you're gonna need some help to keep 'em off. If you've had a drinking problem, you should get into a rehab program, work off some of the physical stuff, get a sponsor."

I shook my head. "You don't understand, I don't think I need any of that. I really don't want a drink at all. It sounds disgusting. Disgusting, how awesome is that? It is gross, but I just never could get away from it." I laughed out loud.

"Right now you don't want a drink. Tomorrow when you wake up and you still don't have a place to sleep and you have trouble finding your daughter, then it'll be harder. You can't do this alone, friend. You need some community, that's what the church is for. Besides," he paused for a second, looking deep into me. "You're gonna have an easier time getting by in life if you can honestly say you've been through the program."

His words made sense, but I didn't want sense right now. What had happened to me didn't make any sense at all.

"Is there a program here at the church?" I asked. I might give it a shot, after all. These people were pretty amazing; maybe going to group here would be different.

"Not here at the church. A lot of our people go to a program over on the West Bank though."

"Great. I used to live in Seven Corners."

"Hey, that works out well. Meeting's at seven, I'll see you

there."

"You're going to be there?" I asked. If Charlie was going to be there I'd really have to go; he'd know if I was bullshitting him. I had a feeling he knew already.

"Yep. Four years sober, another meeting will only do me good."

"I'll see you there, then."

"You got somewhere to go?" Charlie asked again. In the midst of my joyous oblivion, I thought Tasía might take me back. Maybe not, though. After all, it didn't matter what had happened inside of me, to her I would just be a drunk promising not to drink anymore. I told myself that I was being mature by deciding that she might need some more time before she could forgive me. The new light inside me knew that I was afraid of being rejected by the only family I had left.

"Not really, man. I don't think my sister's going to want to see me yet."

Charlie nodded. "I know a good shelter, and it's close to the AA meeting. Here," he gave me a card with an address on it. "Here's a couple bucks for the bus." He dug two grungy dollar bills from the pocket of his overalls. I clapped him on the shoulder in appreciation.

"You're a lifesaver, Charlie."

"Nah, I'm just a janitor with a couple bucks," he shrugged.

• • •

I had to change busses on the University campus, and I'd already been riding for forty minutes or more by the time the bus pulled up to that stop, surrounded by brick walls and concrete stairs. I knew I wasn't far from the shelter based on the address, so I decided to walk the rest of the way. It was early morning now, and the cool air felt good after the stuffy bus ride. I watched all the college kids rushing around with their backpacks, all looking like they were sorting out the cure for cancer. A girl who couldn't be older than eighteen bumped into me on the stairs.

"Sorry," she muttered. I caught a glimpse of her face, the eyebrows bent together, the mouth drawn into a knot, white earplugs stuffed in her ears, worry gripping every bone in her body.

"Hey, don't worry about it," I said with a smile. I hoped that whatever happened to me in that tent was making me look and sound like Charlie, that maybe she would see that life was going to go on even after this semester. Without a second glance she plunged ahead at double-speed. After she moved on, I thought how distracted she must be to bump into a guy like me. I knew from experience that my wide shoulders and brown skin made white women nervous, and I probably smelled bad too.

As I walked along, seeing more students caught up in a world of intensity, I wished I could share the joy that was brimming in my chest with all of them. They had no idea how complicated life could really get, how much more things could suck than just not passing a class or whatever college kids worry about. I could tell they also didn't know how incredibly awesome life could be. Hell, I'd just figured that part out myself.

I cut across the big empty lawn, passing in front of a huge building with columns where students were coming and going like ants in a farm. In the midst of all the activity, there were two guys sitting on the stairs up to the building, just sitting. One of them, the darker one, had his head down between his knees. His buddy wrapped an arm around him and was silent. All the other kids were just walking around him. The kid looked so sad. If Charlie had seen him, I was sure he would say something encouraging. College kids already thought I was some weird dude on campus, so I didn't have much to lose.

I walked right up to the two guys and tapped the sad one on his shoulder.

"What?" he asked. He sounded angry, but he'd been crying.

"Hey, I don't mean to bother you man. I just felt like I should tell you that God loves you just the way you are."

I smiled, proud of myself. Charlie might have followed up, but I was still a beginner. So I went on my way, hoping that my words hit home with the kid. After all, if God could care about someone as lousy as me, there was no way he'd reject a smart, good-looking kid like that.

A Stunning Revelation

"Sorry, man." A friend of my new roommate, Jed bumped into my back, which was curled protectively around my chest. I responded the way I imagined a clam or a hedgehog might respond if disturbed; cling to my position and maintain camouflage. Jed and his friends all ignored me, which was both what I wanted and feared.

At some point, I wanted someone to notice me. Just not those guys. Not the guys punching each other, playing bloody knuckles and taking swigs of Jack from the bottle. These guys were too good for red party cups. I shook my head and turned back to my homework.

During the first week of classes, Jed mocked me for doing all the assigned reading, then further proving my geekdom by taking notes on the assigned reading. "The first week is get fucked up week!" he shouted. We didn't shout in my house. My parents believed in corporal punishment, dinner at five o'clock, and speaking in a calm tone of voice.

"Dude, don't you do anything but study?" Jed asked, punching me in my shoulder. I tried to see if his bloody knuckles had left a mark on my sweater.

"Not really," I mumbled.

"Dude, don't you have any friends?" one of the other guys asked. He was already drunk and his voice squeaked painfully.

"Not really." I could hear the anger in my voice, but I was sure it was lost on the dufus brigade that was clogging my personal space.

"Lame," someone said.

"Yeah," I muttered to myself as I turned back towards my book.

It was lame. My friendlessness was lame. Tony, my best friend from high school, decided to work in his dad's machine shop instead of coming to college with me, which pretty much shot my plans for a social life. For years, Tony was the only person I could hang out with without feeling ten kinds of awkward. Sometimes I was okay with having one totally awesome friend instead of fifty mediocre ones. Other times I envied Tony for all the groups of people he could melt into. If he came to the university with me, we would room together and I would have had someone to talk to. As it was, I could choose between the drunken goons my randomly assigned roommate brought into my room, and the plastic cheeriness of the one Christian group I had tried.

I could still feel the gross vibe of that group. Guys in khaki's, girls in sweaters, huge smiles all around. I was sure they were all really nice people. Yet, that very niceness made me feel out of place. I couldn't smile that huge, welcoming smile and pretend like I'd finally found my clan in this vast institution. I still wore almost all black clothes and constantly scribbled in a notebook. They thought I was the next Unibomber.

My alphabetized shelf of CDs came crashing to the floor, spreading out like fish scales on the cheap carpet. One of the guys stumbled over them, crushing two of the plastic cases on his way. I jumped up, and suddenly everyone in the room knew I existed. I didn't like it at all.

"Why don't you go to a bar and drink?" I demanded, picking up the two broken cases.

"It's only eleven. We're pre-drinking," Jed said. He sounded slightly apologetic, and stooped to pick up a couple of the cases. "Who is this?" The offending case was held up for me to defend.

"It's Skillet. They're a Christian rock band." My head dropped instinctively.

"Dude! Are you a Christian?" one of the guys asked.

"Yeah. Could you move?" I tugged at a CD case that was partially covered by the Converse of the guy who called me "dude."

"No wonder he's so lame," one of the other buddies whispered too loudly.

"Yeah, that's probably why," I said, piercing him with my eyes. Jed intervened.

"Hey, guys, let's head out. It's mug night at Sally's."

Sally's. I'd never been there, but I'd seen the hordes of students crowding beneath the sign sporting a cartoon bunny in pink lingerie. The guys bumbled out of the room, the one who had knocked my CD's over muttering something like an apology. I closed the door behind them, hoping the whole dorm would dissolve around me, leaving just this little box of light intact so I could finish my homework.

No such luck. Thumps and bumps, crashes and shouts, echoed around my room. Part of me wanted to scream that it was a freaking Thursday night, and didn't anyone have classes the next day like I did? In three weeks of college, I had learned one thing; most people drew the line at drinking on a Wednesday night. Thursdays had already been forsaken.

After a few minutes of relative silence, I gave up on biology. I'd already read over the material, I just didn't really understand it. Usually I didn't feel comfortable going into a class like that, but tonight I was frustrated and distracted. No one would know the difference anyway. Pulling out the tattered Bible that went with me to Mexico or Red Lake five summers in a row, I turned to the Psalms and started to read.

God is our refuge and strength, an ever-present help in trouble. Therefore we will not fear, though the earth give way and the mountains fall into the heart of the sea. The familiar words washed over me, smoothing the tension in my shoulders and neck. Slowly, I felt my body uncurl from its protective posture. From long habit, my mind began to trace the meaning of the words, forming them into my own prayer. *God, you are near me always. You have been and will continue to be a help to me in anything that I face. I will put aside my anxiety about fitting in and making friends, because you are always with me and I'm comfortable with you.*

After a few psalms I was sleepy, so I picked the late-night playlist on my iPod and plugged in my earphones. One of the freedoms I really did appreciate about college was being able to fall asleep with my earphones on. My mom was convinced this habit would give me cancer. If she caught me, she would pull off the earphones while I was mid-doze and keep them for a couple days. I liked to think of a tiny band inside the soft muffs, playing just for me as I drifted off to sleep.

··•·

The empty hallway echoed with my smallest movement. I sat cross-legged in front of my biology class, my notebook resting in my lap as I recorded a conversation I'd heard in the student union. My hand moved smoothly over the page, painting the space between the blue lines with loops and swirls of black ink. I learned shorthand in elementary school and adapted it to my own tastes over the years. I took morbid pleasure in the thought that no one would ever be able to decipher my personal notebook. Knowing that while I was sitting here on the hard linoleum floor, I was invisible to the entire student body gave me a similar feeling of warmth inside. After years of watching groups from the sidelines, I knew how easily that warmth could turn into despair.

"Hey, you're in Kayson's biology class, aren't you?"

Shocked, I looked around to see who the voice might be addressing. In front of me another college guy stood looking intently at me. He had blue eyes and sandy-colored hair that was long and floppy. One of his pant legs was rolled up to his shin, marking him as a proud biker. My dad would call him a tree hugger. Besides this rather interesting character, there was no one else in the hallway.

"Yeah, I meant you," he said with a smile.

"Oh." I fumbled. Quickly, I tried to finish off the thought I was recording in my notebook. "Y-yeah. I'm in that bio class." My eyes stayed on my notebook. He collapsed to the floor beside me and held out his long hand for me to shake.

"I'm Nate," he said.

Still confused, I swallowed hard and lowered my eyebrows before looking up and returning his handshake. "Isaac," I replied.

"Am I bothering you?" he asked. His mouth curved into a half smile.

"No." He wasn't. I just didn't want to accidentally ask him how he could see me. Students had been pushing past me for weeks now, as if I was some odd collection of matter in the clear air.

"Are you a bio major?" he asked.

"No."

He paused. "Have you picked a major?"

I cleared my throat. "Yeah. I'm doubling in English literature and religious studies."

"That's a mouthful." As he spoke he leaned his head against the wall, as if he was weary and was hoping for a nap before class. I hoped he would stay awake; I was intrigued by this person who could see me and would talk to me, too.

"What about you?" I asked.

"Environmental science," he answered, smiling with his eyes still closed. Definitely a tree-hugger. "You know that class doesn't start for another hour, right?" he asked.

"Yeah, I know." My eyes fell back to my notebook and I

scribbled a few notes about Nate's appearance, the way his long arms seemed loosely attached to his shoulders.

"Don't you have anywhere else to be?" he asked.

"Don't you?" I shot back, too quickly.

"Whoa, I didn't mean anything by it. The class I have before this got canceled and it's in the same building."

"Oh." My purpose for studying in the hallway suddenly felt lame. "I just... if I come here first, then I don't have to guess how much time it'll take me to walk here, and I get more study time that way."

Nate laughed. "I hadn't thought of that. What are you studying, Sanskrit?" One of his long fingers motioned towards my notebook, which I instinctively closed against his gaze.

"No, that's just kind of a journal. It's shorthand."

"Are you a writer?" he asked. His head lifted now and he leaned forward in interest.

"Kind of." This was a bigger confession than I had made to anyone besides Tony. I felt this guy had just zeroed in on my hidden identity, the same way he inexplicably noticed my presence.

"Then I guess a 'kind of a journal' is perfect for you."

I laughed. "Sure."

"What do you write?"

I cleared my throat again, feeling lame before the words even came out of my mouth. "It's not... it's kind of personal."

Nate shrugged as if this was no obstacle. "Of course, it's your work. Do you write poetry?"

"Well... some poetry, I guess. Nothing I would show anyone," I added quickly. "I do some short stories too, and there's... a book I'm kind of thinking about." As long as I defined "kind of thinking" as spending hours every Saturday slaving over plot points and character profiles, this was a true statement. "D-do you write?"

"Yeah, I write some. Not fiction so much, but I'm working on this compilation of independent research I've been doing on endangered species of birds and the effect it has on the food chain."

I said nothing.

"Not as catchy as short stories, I'm sure," he laughed, and I realized I'd paused too long.

"No. I just...what year are you?" All I could manage were bumbling, stupid questions. Meanwhile, this complete stranger was cutting right to my most passionate secrets.

"Sophomore. I know it's early to be doing research like that, but I'm doing a UROP project with a professor in the biology department. He's a friend of my father's."

"Sure," I said, feigning comprehension.

"Hey, me and a couple guys are going to see this documentary on the African pelican at this little independent theater tonight. You want to join?"

I stupidly repeated "African pelican?"

"It's an endangered species in Nigeria, something to do with their habitat being destroyed for oil refineries."

"Yeah, okay." Never mind that my parents and my pastor and even Tony had something to say about the manipulations of the environmental lobby. Why was this random guy asking me to go to a movie with him and his friends? "Do you ask everyone you meet to go to these things?"

He laughed. "No. I thought it might be some good material for a 'kind of' writer. Plus, I'm hoping you're going to give me your notes for Kayson's lecture on Monday."

"Oh, yeah. I mean, you can have them, but they're in short hand. There are slides on the class website though, and you really didn't miss much if you did the reading." I tried not to sound sarcastic on the last bit, since Nate seemed like a good guy. He didn't seem like the homework type though.

"No problem. This class is cake anyway."

"Yeah, it's not real complicated." Not like my class on Jacobean revenge tragedy, which had taught me not to overreach.

"So, are you coming?"

"Is it on campus?"

"Yeah, it's near Harvard and Washington Ave, just a little ways down from Espresso Exposé."

"Oh, I know where that is." I was more pleased than I should be, but it was the first time someone had mentioned a landmark that I recognized. "Sure, I'll come."

"Awesome. It's at seven."

"Awesome." The word sounded strange in such a mundane context. Awesome was a word I used for God, not for a documentary that I really wasn't interested in. Yet, when I had been preparing myself to spend my entire college career as a phantom in the halls, being invited to a movie seemed like it might be an act of God.

.•.

Six weeks into my freshman year at the University of Minnesota, I was attending my first college party. Nate had a friend who lived in a house with five other students, all concerned about global warming, endangered species, and lead paint. They were having a party to celebrate a policy initiative that had gone through to restrict mercury levels in water reclamation plants or something like that, and Nate invited me.

Jed laughed for two solid minutes when I told him that I'd be back late because I was going to a party. I tried to tell him that it wasn't *his* kind of party; it was more low-key.

"Are these your hippy dippy friends?" he asked.

I shrugged, not wanting to confirm or deny. "They're some of Nate's friends."

"You know there's going to be pot there, right? Probably some other choice drugs too. Aren't you afraid you're going to get your halo dirty?"

"No."

Honestly, I hadn't been worried at all before Jed mentioned drugs. I knew nothing, absolutely nothing about drugs. Once when I was ten years old there'd been a commercial on tv encouraging parents to talk to their kids about drugs. My dad grabbed the shoulder of my T-shirt and said, "Don't do drugs or I'll kill you." I knew there were kids at my high school who smoked pot and sometimes got into heavier stuff, but that crowd intimidated me and I stayed away from them.

Nate was going to meet me in front of the union so we could walk to the house together. After my chat with Jed I was nervous, so I lingered in my dorm room, wondering if it might be more fun to just stay in and listen to my headphones. Pacing back and forth, I decided that it would be wrong to stand Nate up. So, with the firm resolution that as soon as anything funky started happening I would just leave, I headed out for the union.

As promised, Nate was leaning against one of the huge concrete columns, reading a large paperback book that looked older than dirt. I wondered what my parents would think if they knew that we'd been hanging out so much.

"Hey, Isaac. Thought you might've bailed on me," he said with that same casual smile, as if he knew I would never leave him hanging.

"Just had to finish up some homework."

"I gotta start hanging out with some dumber people, man. You're making me look bad."

"I doubt it. Should we go?"

"Yeah, let's get going. This thing was supposed to start like an hour ago, so it's probably warming up by now."

"Right," I said, pretending that made sense to me.

Nate became a sort of cultural guide for me, but he probably didn't know it. Without much effort, I could watch and emulate him and find myself mostly fitting in with his friends. Once I confessed to him that I really didn't have a passion for the environmental lobby, and he'd laughed. "So it's good that you're hanging with us," he'd said. I balked at the idea of being that inclusive. If I went home and said that I wasn't so sure about this Jesus stuff, the reaction would be a lot different.

"It's about a mile and a half. You've got good shoes on, right?" Nate asked as he started ambling along the crowded sidewalks. His height gave him an advantage over the teeming crowds trying to get to the express campus shuttle. I didn't have that edge, so I tried to move in his wake.

"Yeah, my shoes are fine." I couldn't help noticing that Nate was wearing plaid hightops that were so worn that the heel was the only place where the fabric was physically connected to the rubber soles.

"Are you excited? This is your first party, right?"

"Not ever, just my first party at college." I doubted if the punch and pie affairs the youth group threw would be parties to Nate, but I decided to let it slide.

"High school stuff doesn't count, Isaac. This is going to be fun, and you need to have a little more fun."

"Oh, really?"

"Sure. All that studying can be bad for the brain if you don't release the steam once in a while. You wouldn't want to go all the way through college and do nothing but study, would you?"

"Isn't that what college is for?" This is what my mom would have said, and I cringed to find her words in my mouth.

"Sure, but it's also for finding yourself, experiencing the world, widening your vision a bit. It's good for a writer."

Every time we talked, Nate referred to me that way. It was as if he had set my main attribute down in his mind after our first conversation. I'd never referred to myself as a writer. My first definition of myself was always a Christian.

"Is it good for an environmentalist too?" I asked.

"Aw, are you worried about me, Isaac?" He nudged me with his elbow.

"No. You seem to have everything figured out."

"Not everything, my friend. Not everything. How did that quiz go for you yesterday?"

"Fine."

"Just fine? I thought it was kind of hard," Nate said.

"Science seems pretty easy to me. They tell you the information, you read the information, you review the information, and then they ask you for the information on a test. It's pretty simple."

"Sure, if you can remember all that stuff."

I shrugged. "It's my English class that's driving me up a wall. I feel like I need psychic powers to figure out what my prof is looking for."

"The liberal arts can be like that," Nate said. "At least you're doing something you like in those classes."

"I do like the reading," I admitted.

"Not me, man. I like doing my own reading. Have you been to May Day books?"

"Is that the place over on the West Bank?" I asked. I'd seen the sign, but I hadn't been inside.

"Yeah. It's run by a bunch of these crazy anti-war Vietnam vets. I'm pretty laid back, you know, but those guys freaked me out. It's pretty awesome."

I laughed. "What's awesome about that?"

"I like people who are passionate about what they believe in. They've got this drive, this momentum behind them. It's inspiring, you know? I've never been that way. I love birds, but I'm not like some of the activists. They are so sure about what they're fighting for, it's kind of…divine, I think."

"Divine?" Another word that I was familiar with being used completely out of context.

"Yeah. The stuff of the gods."

I jotted down that definition of divine in my notebook.

"Isaac, you know it freaks me out when you write down stuff I say," Nate said, glancing at my coded scribbles.

"Then stop saying interesting things," I muttered. Nate just laughed.

Spring hadn't fully bloomed in Minneapolis, so it was a bit of a relief to arrive at the house and the cozy warmth of the living room. All the furniture was mismatched and damaged in some way, but it was soft and comfortable. The people seemed pretty much the same as the couches - dirty but friendly. They greeted me with eye contact, not casting sidelong glances at my open notebook or scanning my black sweater and loose jeans to see if I fit in. I did not fit in, but that didn't seem to matter.

"You want a drink?" a small girl with bright green eyes and a thick head of carefully rolled dreadlocks asked. She introduced herself as Natalie.

"Um, water?" I said with a sinking feeling in my stomach.

"Sure, no problem. Nate?"

"Got a good hefeweizen?" he asked casually.

"Are you kidding? Vick just got back from Germany last week." Natalie perked up, and Nate smiled his bland smile.

"Awesome."

Natalie left to get the drinks

"Are you dating her?" I asked.

"No. Natalie and Vick are kind of a package deal. Nope, I'm single for the moment."

I had an intense desire to ask how long the moment had been. I couldn't quite picture the kind of girl that would fit Nate. He seemed so unflappable, I couldn't imagine him in the hyped-up testosterone stupor I'd seen Jed and his friends exhibit in the presence of pretty girls.

An odd smell caught my attention, and I turned to see two guys smoking in a corner. I wasn't familiar enough with cigarettes or weed to tell the difference, but I felt my pulse start to race.

"Hey, Nate?" I asked, eyeing the smoking guys suspiciously.

"Yeah?"

"Um, can I ask you something?" I did my best to maneuver him we wouldn't be overheard.

"Sure, what's up?"

"Are there…well, are there going to be drugs at this party?"

"I don't know," he answered with a shrug. He didn't seem to care much.

"I'm kind of…I guess I should have mentioned it before, but I'm not really okay with drugs." Somewhere my dad was cringing at my wishy-washiness.

"So don't do them," Nate said. There was something immutable about that suggestion.

"But I mean…if other people are doing them, will it be…I'm just not sure, I don't have a lot of experience with it. Is it…safe?"

Nate laughed at me, but it didn't feel like it did when Jed laughed at me. Nate's laughter was bathed in warmth and affection, like he would probably laugh at a little kid trying to fly a kite indoors. "No one's going to get messed up on drugs here, Isaac. It's not that kind of party. Some people like weed, 'cause it's kind of fun, but it's a very mellow drug. Worst they're going to do is hug you, I promise."

Now, I had been coached about this kind of situation. A Christian's very attendance in the presence of unsavory behavior was considered condoning. What I should do is tell Nate that I would have nothing to do with him or his friends if they had no respect for the law or their bodies. That's what my pastor would call "shining for the Lord in the darkness of this world."

I didn't want to leave. The way Nate explained the situation, it didn't seem so bad. I didn't have to do the drugs just because they were there, which was a good point that had never been brought up at youth group. Maybe it would be better if I stuck around and provided an example of partying without drugs. That sounded right. The truth was that these people were really kind and welcoming, and I wanted to be more like them.

"You look pretty deep in thought there, Isaac," Nate said, looking amused.

I shrugged, unconsciously taking on Nate's casual smile. "Jesus hung out with prostitutes, right?"

"Whatever you say, man."

Natalie approached us with one large glass of cloudy water and one chilled bottle of beer.

"You boys having fun?" she asked.

"Sure," Nate answered, taking a swig of his beer. "That is awesome, Natalie. You gotta tell Vick to go to Germany more often."

"Only if he'll take me with him," Natalie replied cheerfully. "Have you ever traveled abroad?" she asked me.

"Oh, um. Not really. I've been to Mexico several times, but it wasn't like...touring."

"Were you smuggling immigrants across the border or

something?" she teased.

"No. They were, um, mission trips."

"Mission trips? What kind of mission?" she asked. The question seemed genuine, and Nate nudged me to tell me to relax.

"I went with my church to help out an orphanage down there. We'd do some construction, painting, that kind of thing. Then we did a program for the kids with skits and Bible lessons and stuff."

Her eyes widened. "Wow, that's pretty cool. Nate, you didn't tell us you were bringing a church-boy over."

Nate shrugged. "I don't think of him that way."

Natalie laughed and punched him in the shoulder. "Just make sure that Vick has a couple drinks before you introduce your friend. And maybe Bart too."

"Is it a problem?" I asked, ruffling slightly.

"Oh no, not at all. I just thought you'd rather relax and have fun than spend the whole night debating the legitimacy of the resurrection. Vick's Jewish."

"Oh. Yeah, I wasn't going to get into that." I kept my Republican tendencies quiet around Nate and his friends, and I kept my distaste for apologetics on the down-low around my church.

"Hey! Here's to cleaner water in the Twin Cities!" someone called from the staircase. He was a heavily tattooed and pierced man with a muscular build but a very compact body. His black hair looked dyed, and his expression was fierce.

Everyone raised their glasses and shouted in unity. I half-heartedly followed along, and the tattooed man seemed to pick out my lack of enthusiasm from the crowd and zero in on me. Nervously I touched my forehead as if I could remove the bull's-eye.

"Hey, you're new," he said.

Natalie smiled, putting one hand on my arm and one on the scary guy's.

"Vick, this is Nate's friend Isaac. You should be nice to him."

"I'm nice to everyone today, we finally won one," Vick said, brushing her off his arm and offering me his hand. "Nice to meet you Isaac. Are your parents Bible-beaters?"

I gulped. "Excuse me?"

"The name. It's from the Bible, isn't it?"

"Um, yeah. Does Vick mean anything in particular?"

"I'm named for Victor Hugo. My mom's a French literature freak."

"So you just assume that all children's names come from their parent's freakishness?" Nate asked with a slow smile.

"Pretty much," Vick replied. He wrapped his arm around Natalie and turned back towards me. "Are you going to try to convert me?"

"Vick," Natalie reproved.

"No." I answered, failing to add that I didn't have the first idea how to convert anyone.

"Well, now that's settled. Tell me about how you got the policy initiative through," Nate asked.

"I don't think my story is going to help with your bird issue," Vick replied.

"Couldn't hurt."

Throughout the night, Nate effortlessly deflected attention away from me. What impressed me was how he knew I didn't want a lot of attention at a party. Although no one really talked to me, I could have engaged if I'd wanted; they were open to me, and that was a feeling I hadn't experienced before. At the first opportunity I found a comfortable corner, broke out my notebook and scribbled down as many notes as I could about the setting. Tonight I didn't want to engage, I just wanted to watch. This was a new world, and I wanted to commit every detail to the page.

Political debates sparked up at the slightest provocation. Names like Saul Alinksky, Susan Faludi, Bobby Seale, and Cesar Chavez were thrown around as if they were part of the group. Unlike the bleeding heart liberals my dad complained about, these students weren't just complaining, they were taking action. Some of them were studying political science and plotting a life in politics, while others were practically professional protestors. In youth group I'd been taught that kids who drink, smoke, do drugs, and have sex before marriage were the shame of society. They wound up in prisons or with babies they didn't want, and their minds were rotting away. So I was surprised, genuinely surprised to find that even the guy with the dyed green hair and a suspicious hand-rolled cigarette hanging from his mouth was engaging in a tightly wound debate with Vick as they discussed what the next move should be on the clean water campaign.

My watch told me that it was well after midnight when Nate and I left the party and headed back to the center of campus.

"Did you have a good time?" Nate asked.

"I really did."

"Don't sound so surprised," Nate laughed.

"Sorry. I am a little surprised."

"Well, I'm glad you enjoyed yourself. You're a bit of a curiosity to my friends, I think."

"They are curious to me."

"Yeah, we picked up on that. Bart thinks you work for the CIA. I told him that a CIA agent wouldn't be so obvious about taking down every word we said."

"Yeah? What did he say?"

"He said I was putting too much faith in the competence of the US government."

Laughter bubbled up and shook my chest. Nate laughed along with me, more casually of course.

"Glad to know you can laugh, man."

"Sure. I can."

Amused, Nate just shook his head. We were approaching the union, where we would part ways.

"Hey, Isaac. Can I ask you something?" Nate looked around to see if any strangers were within earshot. Suddenly, he seemed very serious. At least, he seemed very serious for Nate.

"Sure. What is it?"

"I don't know if you'd be into this. I know you're a Christian and all that. I respect that, man, I really do."

"I know."

"So it's totally cool to say no, but I thought maybe we could go out sometime."

"We go out all the time. We just did go out."

"Um, yeah. I meant like, out, as a couple."

Nate was gay. Nate was gay. My mind would not let any other thought enter for a solid minute as I stood there staring at him. Of course, it made sense that Nate was gay. A sinking feeling of stupidity was pulling on my stomach. My father would have pegged Nate as a homosexual in seconds.

"Man, don't worry about it. I just – "

"Just give me a minute." I held up a hand to stop him.

"That's cool."

Through my mental haze, I felt him step away from me, felt the drop of his head, felt the pain I'd inflicted on him. My chest hurt.

"I just…I didn't know that…"

"You didn't know I was gay?" Nate asked. So quiet, his voice barely rising through the screen of his hair that fell in front of his eyes.

"I don't mean it like that. I hadn't thought."

Drawing himself up, Nate resumed his casual posture and smiled in a reassuring way. Until that moment, I hadn't realized that his nonchalance was a defense of some kind.

"Don't worry about it, man. I just thought you might like to try it out with me, but it's no big deal. I don't want to lose you as a friend, not because of that."

"Just… just wait. I can't process this."

"Dude, I can tell I'm stressing you. That's not what I wanted to do. Just forget it."

The pounding of my heart was drowning out all my reasonable thoughts. I could feel the distance widening between Nate and me. My mouth went dry with panic.

"I… I would like to. I just… I think it's wrong."

Nate just looked at me. Unless I was wrong, there was a trace of pity in his eyes.

"Please understand, please just try. It's not part of my life; it hasn't been part of my life to even think that way. I really like you. You're kinder to me than just about anyone, even Tony. Tony's a great friend, but he leaves me behind to hang out with other people, when you bring me along. It doesn't bother you that I don't fit in or that I'm weird."

"I kind of like it, actually," Nate said with a sidewise smile.

"Okay. I just…" Every bone in my body was telling me to say yes, to try. In my life at this moment, Nate was the only bright spot. He made me accepted and valuable in a way no one had before. Going on a date with Nate, just the idea of it was so compelling I had to bite my lip to keep myself from accepting.

"I can't give you an answer right now," I said finally.

"Okay."

"I have to… um…"

"Ask your pastor? He's not going to be stoked," Nate said.

That was the closest I'd ever heard him come to sarcasm.

"I was going to say pray about it. Is that better?"

Nate shrugged. "I'm not going to tell you not to pray, man."

"I know." My intention was to clap him on the shoulder in a very manly way, but he caught my hand and held it in a way that shot tingles up my arm. Before I could think, he was kissing me.

"Sorry. I shouldn't have done that," he was already backing away.

"I'll call you," I said to his retreating form.

"See you in bio class," he returned, waving as he turned away.

For a moment I just stood there, looking at where he used to be, trying not to cry.

··•·

Please help me, God. Please help. My mind raged, pleading all the way back to my dorm, feeling heat on my lips even in the freezing cold. My heart swam in concentric circles like a panicked goldfish, finally narrowing down to one humming spot that burned as I walked.

A slow, inevitable drag was pulling deep inside. A desire, a deep wanting that was awakening from a long sleep. The pull was not physical, although my lips were still hot to the touch. The long draw within was to know someone; someone who would know me like no one had ever known me. No person, anyway. Before I'd said a word, before I'd thought it through at all, I knew that I wanted Nate to be that person. Nate, because he could see me, because he was kind, because he actually wanted me around. Nate, because I didn't have to change to be part of his world.

I took the stairs two at a time, dying for a safe place to collect myself, out of pressing crowds. *Please don't let Jed be home, please, please, please.* My room was empty and dark. Sitting on my bed, I looked up at the peeling paint on the ceiling.

"Thanks for small favors," I muttered. After that I felt bad, so I looked at my shoes. Those scuffed black Sketchers carried me through the long lonely years of high school, and here to this spot. The shoes I'd been wearing when I left home, as my mom tearfully packed my last pair of socks. Now here, at a moment that could change my whole life over again, or be absolutely nothing at all.

"But I want it to be something," I found myself saying to the shoes. I'd hoped that college would somehow fix my social life, make it an actual life for once. A month watching Jed and his buddies taught me just how silly that thought was. Now there was this, this other chance at something different, a life I could live with someone else, not just with God and my notebook. "It can't be, though, can it?" I let the question hang in the air.

God and I, we'd been here before. When I'd felt a strong impulse to come to this huge university instead of the woodsy, Christian safety of Northwestern College. When I'd posed the question just like this, back in my bedroom at home, I'd gotten a strong internal sense. It was as close to a voice as I'd ever heard, saying gently, *I will be with you there, too.* So I'd come, and because I'd come, I'd met Nate. So I waited.

I heard laughter in the dorm above mine, and someone running past my door. A toilet flushed. Below me, a girl was crying. I closed my eyes, I focused. *Can it?* I asked silently, the question pulsing in my skull. Patient, certain that God loved me and cared about my life, I waited.

Time passed, but I held steady. My arms started to hurt and I realized that I was bracing them against the mattress. I relaxed my elbows but held my concentration. The crying got louder. My feet fell asleep, but I was determined. I shifted on the bed, driving a fist into my tingling feet to wake them up. When I finally glanced at the clock, an hour and fifteen minutes had passed.

At that moment, I knew I wasn't patient or determined. I was in shock, stubbornly refusing to acknowledge the long minutes marching past, circling dark and silent. The significance of that hour was its silence. I was facing the biggest crisis of my life, and God said nothing.

"Seriously?" I demanded of the empty air. Empty air is what it felt like. Not like when I usually prayed and the atmosphere filled with an unknowable but undeniable presence. Tonight I was alone in this room, alone like I'd never been before.

It was possible that I already knew the answer, I reasoned. I knew well, better than most, the passages that my parents and pastor and fellow-churchgoers would use to answer my question. I had heard that if you're not willing to read the Bible and follow what it says, God will leave you alone until you figure it out.

That's not the relationship I had with God. I didn't believe that he, like my father, would send me away until I'd submit. Certainly I was dead wrong about stuff before and God was there to correct me. I was more than willing to accept that, because his correction never made me feel small or stupid. I believed, truly believed he could do that because God actually liked me. But if God really liked me, wouldn't he have an answer at this most important of times? Couldn't he at least be *around*?

My breath caught in my throat as panic and despair began to creep over my shoulders. Before this aching void swallowed me whole, I quickly decided to go home for the weekend. Silly, and stop-gap at best, but if I couldn't feel spiritually close to God, I might feel better being physically close to my parents. I could go do something with Tony. Maybe being home would settle the questions that were whirling out of control. If I remembered why I did things the way I did them, maybe the memory of Nate's lips on mine wouldn't be so tempting. Maybe I could reset my life by going back to the source. Maybe this way I could put off dying of solitude.

· • ·

My mom unabashedly hugged me for forty-five seconds while I

was still standing in the doorway, a giant bag of laundry slung over my shoulder. She'd begged me to come back on the weekends since I left school, but until now I had resisted. At first I hadn't wanted to be that kid hanging out in his parents' house on a Saturday because there was nothing to do on campus, then I had things to do on campus. Even though I pushed her away with my "I'm too cool for you" look, there was a mystical comfort in her soft arms and unquestioning love.

"It's about time you made a visit home," Dad said from his La-Z-Boy. The smile was genuine, though.

"School's hard, Dad. Okay if I use the washing machine?" I asked, pushing my bag of laundry onto the brown shag carpet.

"Oh, I'll do that for you." Mom whisked the bag away before I could protest, but I wasn't going to protest. "I'm making broccoli cheese hot dish for dinner, I thought you would like that."

"Thanks, Mom." The prospect of spending the weekend eating hot dish and watching my mother fold my underwear filled me with a sense of shame so deep I felt physically ill. "After dinner I'm going to go out with Tony, is that okay?"

"Sure, honey. Go out with your friends," Mom said, patting my arm.

"Where are you going?" Dad asked, looking over from the television.

"I don't know."

"Well. Be back by midnight, I don't want you to wake your mother."

I rolled my eyes and my mother gave me a warning look. Probably nothing would happen if I turned up at twelve-thirty, so it wasn't a big deal. Still, it was so ridiculous that he had to give me a curfew after I'd already gone to college.

Retreating to my room, I picked up the phone and called Tony.

"Hello?"

"Hey, Tony. It's Isaac. Are we still on for tonight?"

"You bet. Are you coming by the shop or what?"

"Could you pick me up? I don't want to have to ask my dad to borrow the car. He's already getting on my nerves."

"You've been home for like five seconds."

"Yeah, that's all it really took."

"Sure, it's no problem. I'll treat you to some Krispy Kremes so you can feel rebellious."

"Donuts are rebellious now?" I asked, laughing.

"I don't know. We'll eat them anyway."

Tony picked me up just as I was finishing dinner. Although I knew my mom would be hurt that I was rushing out and grabbing an extra roll on my way, I really needed to talk to my friend.

Tony's car was from the early eighties and was practically held together with bubble-gum. Since he got it he spent most of his weekends fixing it, but he loved it almost as much as he loved his mother.

"Did you bring one for me?" Tony asked as he watched me shove the rest of the roll in my mouth and slide into the car.

"Oh. Sorry," I said with my mouth full.

"I'm kidding. Did you think I wasn't serious about the donuts?"

"They're good rolls." I shrugged. "How is the machine shop?"

"Well, it sucks. I'm going to be deaf before I'm thirty, but I'm already making more money than you're ever going to." He grinned before looking back at the road.

"You don't know that," I quipped.

"Oh yeah? What lucrative careers are you qualified for with degrees in religion and literature? A lot of CEO's with those qualifications?"

"Not everything is about money, Tony." As I spoke these words

"Nope. Something on your mind?"

"Yeah. It's awkward."

Somehow this warning excited Tony and he perked up. "Oh yeah? Girl troubles at college?"

Maybe this was a bad idea. "No."

"Hm, college roommate a bust? I told you to apply for a single room. You should hear the stories my sister comes home with."

"No, he's fine. Loud, a little rude, but he doesn't bother me much."

Tony shot me a look as he pulled into the drive through of the donut shop. "As much fun as this guessing game is, there is a way to cut to the chase here. You want anything special?"

"No, I'm good."

Leaning half his body out the driver's side window he shouted into the drive through receiver, ordering our usual box of glazed donuts. When I fumbled for my wallet, Tony waved me off.

"I said it was on me. I know you're a starving student."

"Thanks."

He pulled into a parking spot under a streetlamp and we dug into the warm, gooey treats.

"So what's your deal?" he asked around a mouthful of glaze.

"A guy asked me out," I said. Somehow the donuts made this admission a lot easier. Plus it sounded so simple, so factual.

"Seriously? That's crazy."

"Crazy?" I didn't like that word.

"Yeah. I mean, I knew it was a liberal campus but you've only been there like what, less than two months, right?"

"Yeah." I ate another donut.

"Are you hanging out with a gay crowd? Isn't there a campus crusade group or something there?"

"There's intervarsity, but I don't like that group. They creep me out."

"You don't like any group, Isaac, but I don't think it's a good idea to be hanging out with the GLBT crowd. That's just asking for weird problems."

"That's not true. I went to a party last weekend with some really great people. I don't think they were, you know, like a gay crowd. They were political activists."

"What, like a pro-life group or something?"

"N-no. Can I have the last donut?" I asked, keeping my eyes down.

"Yeah, sure." He paused. "I'm glad you're making friends though. I knew it would be hard when I decided not to go with you. I wouldn't want to be on that huge campus all by myself, and I make friends easier than you."

"Yeah. It's my best friend at school, and he's a really amazing person. He's um... well he's gay, and he wants to... you know."

"Are you telling me that your best friend at school asked you on a date?"

With a sigh, I nodded. Tony stared.

"What are you going to do?" he asked.

"I'm not sure. I'm really confused. He's a really great guy and he really likes me."

"Dude, seriously. You have got to distance yourself from this person. He's obviously gotten the wrong impression."

My stomach growled, wanting another donut to cushion my discomfort. "I'm not uh... totally sure that's true."

The comfort with which Tony and I were sitting together and sharing a box of donuts instantly evaporated. He physically leaned away from me, like I'd just told him that I had the plague.

"Um... um... well wait." Tony jerked himself out of his shock.

"You're not saying that you're thinking about dating a dude, are you?"

"Not...exactly. It's just weird, okay?"

"What's weird about it?" His voice was a little louder, just enough to notice.

"I mean, I'd never thought about it before. I always figured if I ran across someone who was gay they'd be kind of...I don't know, gross or something. I just...I really like him, and it...I don't know, it sounds like it might be fun."

"Fun? To be gay? Are you kidding?"

"That's not what I meant. I meant it sounds like fun to be in a relationship with this particular person, not to jump into the whole lifestyle or whatever."

"I don't get it. You want to date a guy but you don't want to be gay? I don't think it works like that, Isaac."

"I just...could you let me talk?" I demanded. I could feel the pressure of his assumptions weighing on me.

"Yeah, go ahead. Talk."

For a second, I was silent, feeling like I needed to test his ability to give me verbal space. Really, I was trying to feel out how much I was going to weird out my best friend, what the possibility was that he would reject me.

"Nate is...he's special. He's different from anyone else I've known, and I really like him. He likes me. He liked me before he was thinking about dating me, so it's not just about that. When he asked me, I...I wanted to say yes. I've never felt that way about anyone before, not anyone. You know that I know all the reasons I shouldn't feel that way, but I do. I feel like...like if I just reject Nate out of hand I'll be missing something that could be really amazing."

For a long time, Tony didn't say anything. Slowly, he nodded. "Okay. I can't help you with this. This is way over my head. If you want my opinion, you should talk to John."

John was our pastor, and a really nice guy. But if it was that hard to explain the problem to my best friend, I wasn't expecting it to be any easier with my pastor.

"I don't want to do that."

"You can do whatever you want, but that's the best suggestion I've got. I think...I mean I can't be sure, but I don't think John will be really insensitive or anything. He must have dealt with this kind of thing before at some point; he's been in the ministry a long time."

"I guess."

"Let's give him a call." Tony already had his cell phone out.

"Hang on, I don't want to call him. It's seven o'clock on a Saturday night. He's going to be writing his sermon or spending time with his family."

Too late, Tony was already dialing.

"You're going to chicken out if you don't talk to him now. I'm sure he won't mind."

"Since I haven't decided to talk to him yet, I can't really chicken out." I made a grab for the phone, but Tony easily deflected me.

"Shhh, it's ringing."

"Damn it, Tony!"

"That liberal college sure has changed you, my friend." Tony's smile was wicked, but I saw what was behind it. He couldn't deal with thinking his best friend might be gay, so he had to make a joke out of it. Only his joke was putting me in a really bad position.

"Hey, John, it's Tony Rollins, how are you tonight?"

"Tony, I really don't want to talk to him, okay?" Another grab at the phone, just as ineffectual as the first one.

"Hang on a second, John." Tony put his hand over the mouthpiece and gave me a half-serious look. "What are you going to do if you don't talk to John?" he asked. Caught off guard, I fumbled.

"That's what I thought," Tony said. "Hey, John, sorry about that. Isaac and I were just talking, and he's having kind of a crisis. Would you be available to have a chat with him while he's here for the weekend?" A pause. "Yeah, he's all for it."

Now it was my turn to shoot a look across the car, but there was nothing half-way about mine.

"Really? Great. We'll be right there." He hung up. I glared. "He said to come right over. He just finished his sermon and Janet took the kids to the grandparents tonight."

"You're pushing me, Tony." I said darkly.

Unperturbed, he shrugged. "You knew I was going to do that; you wouldn't have told me if you didn't need a little pushing."

Although I hated to admit it, even to myself, he was right. If someone didn't make me do something, I would waver from side to side forever, hoping that the Holy Spirit would eventually nudge me in the right direction. Unfortunately, this wasn't a decision I could leave for a couple months. Nate wasn't going to wait forever. My heart tugged.

When Tony pulled up to John's house, I felt I'd arrived at my execution. There were no doubts about John's opinion of homosexuality. Yet even now, I was missing Nate, missing his peacefulness.

John's house was warm and full of pleasant smells. Residual aromas from the dinner he had eaten with his family, the vanilla candle Janet had in the living room, and that faint essence of baby that clung to everything. John was a large man, wide across the shoulders, dark colored and always never without an authentic smile. John's determination to always be glad to see everyone he saw was a big part of what kept me at the same church since kindergarten. Now he greeted me with a warm handshake and offered me a seat on his sofa. As conflicted as I felt about rejecting Nate, I felt almost as much turmoil about disappointing John. I was glad Tony let me go in alone.

"What seems to be the problem, Isaac?" John asked as he sat across from me. Everything about his posture and tone assured me that we could work this out before I left. He had confidence in me. I squirmed.

"I'm uh...having some trouble at school." A strong twist in my chest told me that was the wrong thing to say on like five different levels. The statement was vague, and inaccurate, not to mention that I didn't want to refer to Nate as "trouble."

"You didn't bust in on me on a Saturday night over some bad grades, did you?" John laughed.

"No."

"If I remember correctly, you were pretty close to the top of your class coming out of high school."

"Pretty close," I repeated.

Patient as always, John waited for me to tell him the real issue. Nothing could ruffle him, not even the two solid minutes of silence that followed as my heart thumped and my palms sweated.

"I um...well..."

"You know that anything you say here will stay between you and me," John said calmly.

"I might be making too big a deal out of this." *Or Tony might,* my mind hissed bitterly. "A friend of mine asked me out on a date."

No visible reaction registered on John's face. "Well, I know you didn't really date in high school. Is this the first time you've been asked?"

"Yeah, mostly." Girls flirted with me in high school. Girls who thought they could bring me out of my shell, who thought I was mysterious and therefore interesting. Unfortunately for them, the mystery of my personality was a banal case of shyness, and I never held their attention for long.

"Okay. Do you like her?" John asked. Even John was showing a little confusion at why a freshman romance needed his immediate attention.

"Nate's a guy," I said. Comprehension dawned on John's face, and he nodded slowly.

"That's a risk that you run going to a secular university. I know that you are serious about your prayer life, so I'm sure that you're where God wants you to be, but there are benefits and costs to every choice we make."

I found myself nodding with him. The words rolled out of him, assured and wise. Maybe this wasn't such a bad idea after all; John didn't seem surprised or uncomfortable.

"Have you responded to him yet?" John asked, pulling me back from my train of thought.

"I asked him to give some time. I wasn't…wasn't really sure what to do."

"That sounds like it was the best thing to do. I can understand that you must have been taken off guard. Better to spend some time thinking over how to respond than to just blurt out the first thing that comes to mind. I've always admired that about you, Isaac."

"Thanks."

"So, I think the most important thing is that you are respectful and loving towards this person. What was his name?"

"Nate."

"Nate, right. You should make sure you treat Nate with the respect he deserves as a man made in the image of God. Don't forget that."

"Okay."

"You also have to be clear, and firm. People who engage in that lifestyle are likely to have some kind of trauma in their lives and might not understand healthy boundaries. You don't want to deceive him, even a little bit, about your intentions."

I blinked. "Yeah...but..."

"Do you understand what I'm saying?" John asked, eager to make himself clear.

"Yes, I understand what you're saying. I just think...um...I don't think I've made myself clear."

"Oh, forgive me. I thought I knew what the issue was. Please, go ahead." So sincere, so accommodating. My stomach felt like it was twisting around my windpipe.

"Nate is a really...a really amazing person. He's made me feel like I belong in a way...well, in a way I've never really felt before. I know...I mean, I never caused trouble at youth group or anything, but even church can be a lonely place for me."

John nodded, a crease forming between his dark eyebrows. He was letting me know that he was listening, slowly assimilating the information I gave him.

"College hasn't been...hasn't been what I thought it was going to be. It's been very difficult to make friends. I mean, I've always had that problem, but I thought maybe it would be better in college. Nate's befriended me in a way that makes it...easy for me. He doesn't seem to mind, or to require a lot of effort to be his friend. That's...new for me."

"Well, Isaac, it sounds like you're afraid that Nate won't want to be friends with you anymore if you turn him down."

"Yes, I am." That was part of it, and that mattered.

"I would say that if Nate isn't going to be your friend unless you date him, his friendship might not have been very sincere in the first place."

"I'm not sure that's..."

"I know it might be hard to contemplate, especially if you've already formed an emotional attachment. A lot of people, men and women, feel that it's best to begin a romantic relationship with friendship. That's not a bad idea, and there's nothing insidious about it. However, if those people aren't willing to settle for true friendship, that relationship was never going to be anything but romantic."

"I suppose."

"Does that help?" John asked.

"A little."

"There's something else?"

"Yes, there is." *I want to say yes*, my mind screamed.

Again, he waited, patient and honest.

"Well, there's kind of an assumption about my answer that I'm not sure I'm ready to make." I fidgeted.

"Oh? Can you explain that?"

"It's just…well, you said it yourself. I didn't really date in high school. Most high school relationships were stupid, and I didn't want to waste my time on them."

"A wise choice."

"Sure, but I'm starting to realize that it was easy for me not to spend time and energy on that mess because I never…I never wanted to. I never really wanted to be…that way with someone. Not that I haven't had…certain kinds of thoughts."

"Naturally."

"But the whole relationship thing never interested me. I know it's easy to assume, given my background, that I'd be disgusted by Nate and his…offer."

"I hope not disgusted. I hope that being in our church your whole life would teach you to be compassionate and sympathetic towards those who live without the knowledge of God's unconditional love to sustain them."

"That's not what I meant. I meant…this is the first time I've been interested in someone…romantically." I waited for the shock to register, but there was none. The only sign that John heard me was the silent reappearance of the wrinkle between his eyebrows. "I can guess what you're going to say about that, but it feels…significant in some way. Like, if I just ignore this feeling, if I just move on without thinking about it, I might be missing out on something. Not just anything, but something that could be…great."

John nodded; the wrinkle stared back at me. "Just so I have this clear. Your friend Nate asked you out on a date, and you're conflicted because you're not sure that you want to say no. Is that right?"

Lowering my eyes, I paused and nodded silently.

"Isaac." He was pleading with me, and I bit my lip. "I don't have to tell you what the church's stance is on homosexuality."

"No, you don't." I said.

"The biblical standard is very clear on this point. If we stray from that, there isn't anything else to lean on." He was concerned, worried. Because he wasn't yelling at me, I gave him the respect of meeting his eye.

"I've always found my personal relationship with God more beneficial than trying to translate words written two millennia ago to my own life. I can lean on God, and I believe that he would guide me, even if there were no Bible."

John's eyes widened, and I saw that I had managed to surprise him. "The Bible is a gift to us from God, it is a big part of how he guides us."

"I understand that."

"Then I don't understand what you're saying. You understand that the Bible is a guide for us from God, and you value the relationship you have with God, but you want to just throw some of it out so you can date this Nate person?"

"I didn't say I'd decided on anything, I'm just thinking about it,"

I said. There was no way this indecisive hedging was going to dissuade John.

"I don't understand what there is to think about, Isaac. There is so much in life that we can't grasp, so much of God's will that has to be searched out in order to be understood. In this area, there isn't any ambiguity. I know it might be difficult, but the choice is clear. Will you follow God or will you follow your desire?"

The twisting sensation in my chest was starting to become warm with anger. "There's no ambiguity?" I challenged. John was not ruffled.

"No, there isn't."

"There's a lot of division in the church over this very issue. How do you explain that?"

"The power of desire is strong, and threatens to overtake devotion to the truth of The Word."

"That's all? So everyone who thinks that gays were born that way, that they deserve all the rights and privileges of straight people, they are all just bowing to desire? Churches are splitting because the congregations can't keep it in their pants? Is that what you're saying?"

John spread his hands. "Isaac, I can't tell you what is going on in each church, or break all the political issues down into a simple paradigm. I know for you, a man who believes in the truth of the Bible and claims to live by its message, this is not a negotiable area."

Maybe because his words were partly true, they stung me. Before I felt uncomfortable, even penitent in the presence of John's wisdom and certainty, but now I was filled with rage. Despite all his words of compassion, his kind smile, he was willing to condemn me to a life of solitude because the one person who noticed me was gay.

"You don't understand," I said, feeling my hands start to shake. John noticed.

"Isaac, I'm not speaking against you as a person. I value you, and I admire a lot about you. We all get a little turned around every once in a while, that's why we need the church to support us."

"Your church hasn't been much of a support," I spat at him.

"It's not just my church, Isaac. It's yours too."

"Nobody knows me there. If I never went back there are maybe four people who would even notice." I couldn't help it; the accusations were spilling out faster than I could sort through them.

"Now, that's just not true. If you – "

"You know how I spent most of my time at youth group? Leaning against that temporary wall, hoping that someone would talk to me. No one ever did. No one ever approached me. Nate approached me, Nate befriended me, Nate could see me. You want me to give that up, to reject the only person who – " I sputtered, feeling tears rise in my throat.

"Isaac, please. I'm so sorry. I didn't know how isolated you felt. We all love you; we just didn't know how to show it. The church is full of humans, we can only do our best."

"That's what I'm going to do too. I'm going to do my best to be faithful and happy. I don't believe God wants me to be alone for the rest of my life, to be ignored and lonely. Didn't you always say that God was a God of relationship, of connection?"

"I did, but there are certain kinds of connections that – "

"This is the only one I have, do you get that? I feel…I feel something like God in this. I know you'll say that – "

"Feelings can be deceiving."

"Yeah, I knew you would say that, exactly. I have prayed my whole life; I have cultivated an intimate relationship with God. The coldness, the freaking emptiness of the days I spent in church, in your church, are nothing like what I feel when I'm in the presence of God. Being with Nate is like that, and that's what I want out of life."

Somewhere in that speech I had risen to my feet, and the warmth had left John's face. Without his smile, he looked like a stranger.

"Isaac, if you pursue this lifestyle, I have to tell you that you will not be able to lead at church anymore."

This simple statement, something I should have guessed already, took the stinging heat out of me and I felt cold.

"What?"

"If you are unwilling to conform to the standards of the Bible, at least the ones that we can be sure of, I can't permit you to work with the jr. high this summer. Your influence can't be trusted in this state of mind."

I blinked at him, feeling stupid. "What?"

"I think I'm making myself clear. You've been helping out with the junior high group during the summers, and I think you've enjoyed it. I can't let you continue if you choose to be gay."

"I'm not choosing anything, John, I'm just thinking. Are you going to throw me out of the church for thinking?"

"Of course not. You're always welcome at church. However, you cannot be in a position of leadership in our church if the Bible isn't a guide for your life."

"That's not what I'm saying at all."

"That's what I'm hearing from you, and I have to lean on my own judgment in these matters, not yours."

"You are unbelievable," I said, preparing to storm off.

"Isaac, let's be civil at least. I have to follow the dictates of my conscience and protect my church the best I can. This isn't a rejection of you as a person, I simply cannot condone this choice."

"Fine. If you don't want my free volunteer work, then I'll find something else to do with my time."

Despite this flippant response, I knew that being banned from the leadership would open a gaping hole in my summer. Tony and all his friends would be tied up with that group, going on camping trips and facilitating overnights at the church. It was a lot of work, and none of us got a lot of sleep, but it bound us together in a way hanging out and watching movies didn't.

"Were you going to help with the bake sale this Sunday?" John asked, rising from his seat, supposedly to help me to towards the door.

"I was," I said.

"Probably better if you just buy some brownies this time."

Standing the doorway, I gave him my scariest, darkest glare. "Are you serious? You don't feel comfortable letting me collect money for the Mexico Mission? You think my dangerous influence is going to affect the cookies?"

John shook his head. He looked so sad, like a compassionate father forced to spank his child. The look only made me angrier. "Your attitude is not conducive to service at this point. Come talk to me if you'd like to be involved in another event and we'll go from there."

"Yeah, I think I know how that conversation will go."

John shrugged. "I'll pray for you, Isaac. I really want the best possible life for you."

His sympathy grated on my raw nerves, inflaming me with more rage. How dare he pretend like he was the reasonable one?

"You realize that you're forcing me to pursue this. If you can't accept me when I'm just considering a different direction, how I can choose yours? If you're going to cut me off from the community for thinking about leaving it, what choice do I have but to leave it?"

"I told you that you're always welcome at church."

"I feel bathed in the warmth of acceptance already." I took the trouble to wrest the door from his grasp so I could slam it shut in his face.

What sucked is that he would forgive me for that. He would forgive me for all the things I said and all the accusations I'd leveled against him, but he wouldn't let me be with Nate and take part in church. He wouldn't even consider it.

Tony's car wasn't in front of the house anymore. I figured he looped around the city block to get some air. So I sat on the curb, pressing my knees against my chest as if the tension of my muscles would release the pulling sensation that hadn't left me since Nate's kiss.

I did what I always did when I came to the end of what I knew how to do. Closing my eyes, I turned my spirit to heaven. *What do you have to say about this?* I asked. After a long pause of silence and stillness, I took a deep breath and tried again. *I'm not going to give Nate up because John told me to. I'm not even going to give him up because of that verse in Romans, and I'm sorry if that's wrong. But if you tell me that you've got something better for me out there, I'll let it go. You are still the ruler of my life, no matter how crappy things get, and I trust you to show me the best way.* Another long pause, longer than I would have liked.

When I opened my eyes, I saw the stars glittering above me in the dark navy sky. In the suburbs, it was pretty amazing to see the stars at all, but now those little white dots seemed like they were aching to explode out of the blackness and rain down on the earth. God, in his infinite wisdom, did not feel it was necessary to give me an answer to my question at that moment either. Yet somehow, I felt calm and steady by the time Tony's car pulled up.

．•．

My parents were asleep by the time Tony dropped me off at home, despite the fact that I arrived a full twenty minutes before my dad's silly curfew. I'd never been much of a night person anyway. I didn't know it when I climbed into my childhood bed and drifted off to sleep with my jeans on, but there were unintended consequences for returning after my folks turned their lights off.

At about nine, I wandered downstairs looking for some coffee and Coco Puffs. There they were, sitting straight as boards in the uncomfortable wooden chairs in the breakfast nook, both clutching their coffee mugs as if they were their only points of gravity.

"Did someone die?" I asked, still rubbing sleep out of one eye. My mother looked from my father to me and back again, her anxiety so painfully clear it could have been written on her forehead.

"Seriously, what's going on?" I asked.

"Pastor John gave us a call last night," Dad said. The set of his shoulders, the depth of his tone, and the white-knuckled grip he had on his mug told me more than his words.

"Oh. I guess confidentiality is only for the pure in heart," I said, trying my best to play the part of the indifferent rebel. The last thing I wanted was for my parents to catch a whiff of the cold fear trickling down my throat.

"I'm sure he meant well, dear," Mom said, shifting her mug.

"Yeah. So I assume you know what we talked about last night," I said.

"I don't know exactly what you talked to Pastor John about, but he did have some concerns about how that college is changing you," Dad said. There was no shifting for him, and there was no need for him to keep speaking. John was delicate, sensitive, and nuanced compared to what my father thought about gays.

"That college is a prestigious university that's giving me a great education. You might as well blame anything you're unhappy about on me, it'd be more honest."

My father opened his mouth, but Mom placed her white hand on his arm. "I think we're getting off to a bad start," she said. "Honey, why don't you have a seat? Would you like some coffee?"

"I'd rather stand. I would like some coffee, though," I said, breaking at the end, knowing how painful this was for my mother.

So I took the steaming cup of black coffee that she handed me and sipped it submissively while she settled herself at the table again. "Why don't you just tell me what you think is happening, then I can clear anything up that's inaccurate," I said. That seemed fair, especially considering I'd only woken up five minutes ago.

"That sounds reasonable," Mom said, looking hopefully at Dad, who frowned.

"Fine. My understanding is that there's some kid at that school who's convinced you that you're gay. Is that true?"

Mom closed her eyes in pain, and then looked at me, pleading with me not to take the bait.

"No, it's not true." An audible exhalation escaped my mother's lips. "Nate never tried to convince me of anything. I like him, and I'm thinking about going out with him."

"As friends?" my mother's voice squeaked with hope and fear.

"No, Mom, not as friends."

Tears welled in my mother's eyes, and I was grateful for the numbness that was creeping towards my feet and hands, moving out from my chest. Dad's face turned purplish-red, and I wondered how much pressure that mug would take before it cracked.

"Fine. You're not welcome here anymore," Dad said.

"That's not true, that's not what we decided," Mom rushed to correct.

"What did you decide?" I asked. My tongue felt slick with sarcasm and betrayal.

"You...you can't stay here if you're in a relationship with a man. But if you want to come to church on Sundays, you can sleep in the guest room on Saturday night."

"If you're alone," Dad put in.

"I won't be going back to that church," I said. Although I hadn't fully thought out that decision, it came to my lips so naturally that I didn't bother to question it. "John made it clear that I'm a dangerous influence in the congregation, and he lied to me last night when I confided in him."

"Pastor John did what he thought was right for you, and for us," Dad said. The way he talked made it sound like I'd come down with tuberculosis and was deliberately trying to infect them.

"I'm doing what I think is right for me and for Nate," I said.

"The Bible doesn't leave any room for that kind of thought." The words exploded from his mouth one by one. In the deep pocket of my baggy jeans was a miniature copy of the NIV Bible, something precious that I always kept near me. The term "Bible" never sounded so confrontational.

"How much room does the Bible leave for lying? I thought that one was pretty clear too. In fact, there's at least one verse that says God hates liars."

"Are you saying that God hates Pastor John?" Dad looked like he was about ready to take a swing at me. Mom was crying now.

"No, I don't think God actually hates people. I'm saying that I'm not the only one who's selective about which Bible verses I take seriously."

"That's no excuse!" Dad exploded. His rage didn't touch me. If I felt anything at all, it was a sadness in the pit of my stomach.

"Okay. I'll go back to campus. Thanks for the coffee, Mom." I lifted the half-full mug in appreciation and set it on the edge of the table, as far away from them as possible. As I walked away, I prayed that my mother wouldn't try to follow me, to hug me, to tell me that they still loved me no matter what. I wouldn't be able to take it. Still, it felt weird when I packed up my duffle bag and walked out the front door and no one tried to stop me.

·•·

When the bus pulled to a stop, Nate was waiting. His faded

blue eyes were still casual and unruffled, but sympathetic. When I saw him, I wanted to cry. I'd wanted to cry for about an hour before that, but seeing him was the first time I'd considered letting it happen.

"You look like shit, man," Nate said.

"I feel even better."

"That bad, huh?" He picked up my duffle bag and slung it over his shoulder where it lay comfortably among other bags, permanent and disposable, with a Nalgene water bottle swinging around his hip.

"I can't go home." The words felt limp and tired; they failed to communicate that the world at the other end of the bus ride had just dissolved like salt in water.

"Because of me?" Nate asked, the first crease of real concern showing on his face. His worry felt comforting and friendly, just like his smile felt, and his shrugs, and his laughter. The tiny muscles in my face relaxed into a faint smile.

"No, it's not you. It's my own fault, I should have known."

Slowly, Nate shook his head. "No one can prepare you for that, man. You want to get a bite?"

Right then, something clicked. The switch was so definite it felt audible.

"Yes."

Nate paused, sensing something was different. "Yes, you want to get a bite?"

"Yes to that too, but mostly, yes let's go out together."

In the look of joy that crossed his eyes, there was a reservation, as if he already knew that we weren't going to work as a couple.

"Isaac, I'm really glad to hear you say that."

"But?" I asked, bracing myself. It would just figure that all the bridges to my past life were still in flames and Nate already found someone else.

"But, I don't think it's like a real good idea for you to start a relationship to piss off your parents."

"That's not why I'm doing it." That stinging anger was coming back, and Nate instinctively stepped back.

"No, that's not what I meant. Just that we're not going to have much of a shot if I'm all you've got, you know? It's...well it's just too much."

"Fine. Give me my bag back."

"Isaac, hang on. I don't mean like we can't...you know, ever. There's a GLBT support group on campus, why don't you come with me tomorrow? Once you're on your feet a little more, then we'll talk."

Despite the fierceness with which my head was pounding at this news, I had to admit that Nate's words had a ring of logic. What could it hurt anyway? Maybe that's where I would fit in.

"Yeah, okay."

"Cool. They've got dollar nachos at Burrito Loco tonight. I'll even buy, man."

Something about that pathetic offer made me laugh, just a little. "Isn't Burrito Loco an evil corporation that's trying to strain authentic Latin culture from the American experience?" This was a quote from Bart.

"Yeah, but I like their guac."

I shrugged. "That's good enough for me."

.•.

I stepped into one of the 3rd floor meeting rooms in the student union, eager to meet other students in need of support. As promised, Nate came with me, his long legs meandering up the stairs behind me. I felt the need to hurry, as if all the people like me might leave before I got there. My eyes fell first on a plump guy with spiked hair and a T-shirt sporting a protruding middle finger.

"I fucking hate Jesus. I wish someone had killed the guy," he said, loud enough for me to hear from the threshold.

"They did kill Jesus," I said without thinking, the defensiveness in my voice apparent to the whole room. The middle finger turned towards me, followed by the dark eyes of a girl with magenta hair and piercings in every orifice of her face.

"What, are you a personal friend of his or something?" the guy asked me. Now, I was willing to overlook drugs, sex, and alcohol, but my gut told me I was not going to shrug off that question. If I did, I would be giving up something bigger than friendship with Nate.

"In a way, I am," I said. Another, older student approached with a placating smile.

"Excuse me, we're not interested in proselytizing in this room. Please move on." He waved me towards the door.

"I'm here for the meeting." I leveled my shoulders to show that I wasn't going to be waved away.

"But you're a Bible-beater!" the spiked hair guy protested.

"I don't happen to have a Bible with me, but I'm sure I could find something if you – "

"Whoa, what's happening?" Nate asked, placing a hand on my shoulder. His touch both stopped the flow of my anger and put some strength behind me.

"Nate, is this your friend?" the waving guy asked. "Surprised" would be a very generous way to describe the look on his face.

"Yeah. This is Isaac. Is there a problem?"

"Well…" Although clearly the leader of the group, the guy was at a loss.

"What are you doing bringing a born-again in here?" the spiked

"I brought my friend in here," Nate returned.

"He can stay," the leader said, clearly uncomfortable.

"Forget it," I said, pushing past Nate to get out of the room. Without exerting much effort, Nate caught my arm and held me back.

"Hang on a sec," he said, then released me before turning back to the group. "I'm really disappointed in you guys. I brought my friend in here because he needs some help and support. I thought this was a pretty awesome group."

"Nate, he's welcome to stay," the leader protested, his face turning a flaming shade of red. Before responding, Nate looked back at me, and I shook my head.

"I've had enough rejection this week."

Nate nodded. "Chris, I expected better. You should tell him," Nate pointed at the spiked hair, "that his intolerance isn't better than anyone else's."

"Hey! Fuck you, dude!"

As if he hadn't heard this last retort, Nate turned and left the group. He laid his hand on my shoulder, partly as a display of loyalty, and I think partly to make sure I didn't run away.

"Well, that was fun," I said on the stairs.

"Man, I am so sorry. I've never seen them like that."

"You've never seen them around a Christian, I'm guessing."

"I guess not." Nate looked truly disturbed. I wondered if he depended on them like I depended on my church, if this experience was similar to my own back home. *No. They weren't rejecting him. They were rejecting me.*

The cold outside air hit my face as the heavy glass door swung open in front of me, and I felt my eyes close against tears.

"Isaac? You okay?"

My resolve cracked, and I found myself sitting on the cold

cement steps, burying my head in my arms. For a long time I couldn't speak. After a while, Nate sat next to me, and I felt his arm draped over my shoulders. He didn't speak, and I was grateful. When I felt in control of my face, I wiped my nose on my sleeve and raised my eyes very slightly. A sliver of campus greeted me; the buses coming and going on Washington Ave., framed by the mall and the edifice of Northrop Hall.

"I really have to choose, don't I?" I said at last, embarrassed by my cracking voice.

"I don't know, Isaac. It's different for everyone."

"I don't know what to do Nate. I...I really like you."

"I like you, Isaac."

"I don't want...I mean...I never expected to want..."

"It's okay, you can take all the time you want to figure it out."

I shook my head. "It's not going to change. They're not going to change, any of them."

A man in filthy jeans stopped in front of me, blocking my view of the mall. He was the dirtiest, smelliest person I'd ever seen, but his eyes were glowing with warmth. That warmth looked somehow familiar.

"Hey, I don't mean to bother you," he said, a trace of a Spanish accent in his words.

"What do you want?" I asked.

"I just felt like I should tell you that God loves you just the way you are." He smiled, and then he left.

I allowed the words to sink deep into me, the same way I did when I felt God's words well up inside me.

"Damn," Nate said, craning his neck to watch the strange man walk away.

"No joke," I said, sitting in my own stunned state.

"What do you think it means?" Nate asked.

I thought for a moment. "It means that God hasn't given up on me yet. I thought maybe he had. I haven't heard anything from him in a while."

"If you were waiting for an answer from God, that's about the coolest way it could happen, man."

"That is so strange." I shook my head. In a way, I was glad God waited until this very moment to deliver that message, and that he had chosen such an unlikely way to send it. I was grateful to get to hear those words out loud, spoken by a real person with a real smell and a real accent. Not a winged angel, not a lightning bolt, just a man.

God loves me just the way I am. Even if the whole world hated me, God loved and accepted me. That could be enough for now.

"Maybe it's not time to give up just yet."

.•.

The day was the first really beautiful day of spring, and I was scrawling in my notebook. I wanted to capture this moment in print. In the depths of summer the green leaves would go unnoticed, but after the long dragging months of gray skies and prickly dry branches, this new life was magical.

Today I was going to church for the first time in over a month. A real church, an old church, and bizarrely, a Catholic church. I wasn't going to mass, but there was a meeting in the back for the few brave souls like me who would show up at a meeting in the back room of a Catholic church. One of the girls who came, Cindy, called us "non-heteronormative," but that was a bit much for me. It was a nervous, jumpy crowd, but they seemed to understand where I was coming from. That was a miracle in itself. This was only the second time at this group, so I was still waiting for the other shoe to drop. Still, it felt good to have somewhere to go.

I was just passing the big statue of a priest on the corner, heading towards the back entrance of the church when I saw a woman on the corner. The woman was rather unremarkable, middle-aged with brownish skin and sagging shoulders. I wouldn't have noticed her if she hadn't been crying. When she looked up, her eyes looked as if she was expecting the granite priest to reach down and pat her head.

Weird. I thought. *Why doesn't she go into the church?* I wouldn't easily forget the man who took pity on me when I was crying on the steps of the student union. Even if she was weird, I should try to help her. Clearing my throat, I stepped forward.

"Excuse me, ma'am? Can I help you with anything?" I asked with a gentle smile.

Her eyes flew up to mine, full of suspicion, maybe even anger. A stream of incomprehensible words poured from her lips. Seeing that I couldn't understand her, she held her flat hands together, indicating prayer. Gesturing towards the statue she said, "Pray. Okay, I pray?"

"Oh," I said, feeling the single syllable pressed out of my lungs as I was overcome with compassion. She must feel so unwanted if she really thought that I was yelling at her for standing on the corner and praying. "Do you want to pray inside?" I asked, gesturing towards the huge church doors that were just opening for afternoon mass. Since I'd been here once before, I knew that mass would be starting soon. I'd seen the quiet congregants trickling into the sanctuary when I passed this way last week.

A sudden comprehension lit her eyes and she jumped forward a little, eager. Just as quickly, she withdrew. "I don't speak English," she said, this one phrase remarkably clear.

"It's okay," I said with an encouraging nod. "It's okay to go in." I gestured that she should move towards the church entrance. After another moment or two of hesitation, she followed my gesture. As she passed me she offered a weak smile.

"Thank you."

I kept my eyes on the woman as she climbed the wide stairs of the church. By the time she reached the dark archway, she looked just like any of the other congregants.

The Ritual of Sacred Objects

Miguel wasn't there. I stood on the windy train platform, feeling people pushing past me, but I had nowhere to go. Although my departure for the United States had been so sudden, Papí was sure his letter would reach Miguel before I was standing on this spot. After all, today was the seventh day of my journey through the wild Amazon, a narrow escape through Panama, a halting journey through the southern half of North America, and a suffocating two hours in the false bottom of a truck as I was smuggled across the U.S. border like so much coca plant. Then a series of trains and busses brought me to this very spot where my little brother should be waiting. Aunt Nanita warned me that there would be snow in Minnesota, but she did not describe the bitter cold. The winds here were brutal on my brown skin, and I pulled my shawl closer around my body.

A man in a uniform with a funny hat, a large brass button on his shirt, and a glowing yellow vest approached me, asking me something in English. Although his face looked kind and helpful, I ducked my head and mumbled an apology. I would not soon forget the two hours I had spent in a metal box, watching a tire spin just inches from my forehead. In this country, my presence was against the law. No one had to tell me to avoid men in uniforms.

The uniformed man insisted on something, and gestured toward one side of the platform. Once I stepped off the platform, I would be lost. I had no idea where I was in Minnesota, and this was where my brother was supposed to meet me. Probably he was just late, and I could wait here for him. If this uniformed man forced me down onto the street, I would never find my brother.

My last nerve was fraying as the man talked at me in English, as if comprehension would suddenly dawn on me if he kept pretending that I understood him. A fat man with white hair shouted something at me in an angry voice as he got off the train. Fumbling in one of my pockets, I found my precious piece of paper, covered on both sides with Aunt Nanita's delicate handwriting, all information I needed for my journey. Already the paper was limp with wear. On it were written all the people I should contact and the amount of money I was to spend at each stop. At the end, as an afterthought, she had written out a few English phrases phonetically.

"Eye no-t speck...speck..." the last word confused me, and I followed the letters with my index finger, slowly sounding out each one. "Aaa..nnn...gee...lissss." If my trip to America had been planned, Papí would have bought a book about English for me, and Aunt Nanita would have worked through each phrase with me until I had it perfect. As it was, I burned with envy for the children who grew up with English television in their homes.

The uniformed man said something into a black box that stuttered with static as he pushed its buttons. In a moment a brown-skinned man wearing the same uniform approached. Although his lips turned up, they had no warmth in them; these men were not friendly. My heart started to race as I realized that they were probably going to take me jail or send me back to Brazil.

The darker man started talking to me in a different language, closer to Portuguese, but still incomprehensible. I shook my head to show that I didn't understand. He kept saying "nombre, nombre" and he pointed to his shirt where a word was embroidered in glowing yellow thread. The word sounded like "nove," which means name.

"Tasía," I said slowly. "Tasía Freitas. I haven't done anything wrong," I added quickly, but they didn't understand me. The dark man shook his head and said something in English. I heard the word "Portuguese" and nodded quickly.

"Yes, yes. I speak Portuguese, not Spanish." Aunt Nanita told me this happened all the time in America. Everyone thought we spoke Spanish, and assumed we were from Mexico. The first man kept gesturing towards one side of the platform, and I shook my head. Referring back to my piece of paper, I caught sight of my brother's phone number. Papí added it in case of an emergency, and this felt like an emergency to me. I tapped the two men's shoulders so they would pay attention to me instead of talking to each other. Holding out the pinky and thumb of my right hand, I held it up to my face so it looked like a telephone. "Telephone, please," I said. Thankfully, the word for telephone in English is almost the same, and please in Portuguese is identical to the same word in Spanish. Between the two uniforms, they figured out that I wanted to make a call and directed me to a pay phone in the middle of the platform.

Armed with my little piece of paper, I picked up the receiver and began to carefully dial the numbers one by one. The pretty voice of a young woman came across the line, and I tried to explain that I'd dialed the wrong number, but soon it started ringing. A gruff, slurred man's voice began speaking English.

"Miguel? This is Tasía," I said.

"Hey, Tasía. What time is it there?" Miguel asked in badly pronounced Portuguese.

"Oh, thank God it's you. Where are you?"

"Huh? Does Dad want to talk to me?"

"No, Papí isn't here. Didn't you get his letter?"

"I moved a while ago. What's going on?"

"I'm in Minnesota. Papí got into some trouble with one of the drug lords in the favela and he had to send me away. Why didn't you tell him you moved?"

"You're in Minnesota? Seriously?" his voice jumped with excitement, and I felt relief in my chest.

"Miguel, you must listen to me. There are policemen here and I don't know what they want. You have to come get me."

"Cops?" Miguel whined into the phone. "Fuck, Tasía. You just show up in Minneapolis and you're already in trouble with cops? Do you have a visa?"

My heart pounded with fear, and my chest felt bruised from my heart pounding for seven sets of 24 hours. At least I could vent my fears on Miguel, who would understand my words even if he had no compassion.

"Don't you curse at me, Miguel. I am not in Minneapolis, I am in Minnesota, and I am not in trouble with the policemen, they are just here. I don't know what they want."

"Are you here illegally?"

"As I told you, I had to leave very quickly. There was no time for formalities."

"If you're here illegally and there are cops there, then you're in trouble. There's been a huge crackdown on immigration in the last month, didn't Papí know that?"

"You are not listening to me, Miguel. It will do no good to argue with me, I need your help."

"Where are you?" he asked grudgingly, as if I were asking him a giant favor. Forget the thousands of miles I traveled; he had to get out of bed and bring me the last few miles to his apartment.

"I don't know."

"Well I can't come get you if I don't know where you are, Tasía."

"Hang on." I gestured to the dark man in the uniform and handed him the phone. He said a few words into the phone, nodded and paused, talked a bit again, and then handed me the phone.

"Are you coming?" I asked.

"Yeah, I'm coming. I don't know where I'm going to put you though."

"Put me? I am not a doll or a chair, Miguel. I will live in your apartment with you and Celeste."

A strange choking sound came across the phone, and I held it away from my face; something must be wrong with it.

"Just shut up, I'll figure it out. Don't say anything to the cops, okay?"

"How would I talk to them, Miguel?"

"Just…just wait. I'll be there in a couple minutes."

"Fine. Hurry." I hung up the phone, praying he wouldn't fall back asleep. I smiled nervously at the two policemen.

"My brother is coming to pick me up," I said, knowing my words were useless. "One moment," I said, holding up one finger. They exchanged a few words and the whiter one left. After six aching minutes, a large man with very dark skin and bulging muscles who reeked of alcohol approached us.

"Tasía?" he asked.

"Yes?" I replied in Portuguese, praying to Guadalupe that this drunken ape was not my brother.

"Great. You'd think they would have at least sent you with a decent coat."

I opened my mouth to reply, but he was already conversing with the policeman in rapid-fire English. After Miguel smiled, gestured, and clearly lied to the policeman, the uniformed man left. Miguel grasped my arm and dragged me to one end of the platform.

"Let me go! I am your elder, Miguel!" I cried. I was more than ten years older than Miguel, and looked more like his aunt than his sister. He was the favored son, and my parents gave up their life savings to send him to America when he was boy, while I'd been left to the care of stern Aunt Nanita. Still, Miguel owed me the respect due an elder and a blood relative.

Miguel didn't loosen his grip, but stopped walking and leaned close.

"Look, I didn't ask for you to come here, and no one asked me. I know Padre thinks I live in some kind of palace, but life just isn't that way here. The very last thing I need right now is a spinster sister to support."

An icy hand reached down my throat and grasped my stomach. "Miguel...I'm your sister. My life was threatened. Papí assumed you would help me."

"You're going to be sorry he assumed that, Tasía."

Although his body was strong and threatening, his voice sounded almost sympathetic, so I stayed quiet. Clearly, something terrible had happened to Miguel and he hadn't told Papí.

If I had any choice at all, I would not allow any man who had been drinking to drive me anywhere. Since I didn't have a choice, I offered some prayers to St. Christopher who protected travelers, and clenched my growling stomach the whole way. In the last week St. Christopher and I had become good friends, and I hoped he wouldn't let me come all this way only to die in a car accident a few miles from my destination.

"What is that?" Miguel asked, pointing to the embroidered bag I was clutching. I had been clutching it for a week, terrified that someone would steal it, feeling it was my last connection to a world I understood.

"Tía Nanita gave it to me before I left."

"It doesn't have her fejioada in it, does it?" he joked.

"Please watch the road, Miguel." My voice quavered as he swerved around a median. "And no, I didn't carry this bag across two continents so you could have a nice dinner." The bag held my mother's jewels, hidden for ten years since her death and passed to me in sacred trust by Aunt Nanita. If I never had a daughter, I was instructed to give them to Miguel's daughter, Ellie. I felt secretive about them, unsure of my brother's wobbling head and erratic driving.

He pulled up to building made of crumbling, ancient bricks. Before I could ask if this was really where he lived, Miguel pushed out of the car and slammed the door behind him. Warily, I followed, clutching Nanita's bag to my chest. A faded awning covered the four crumbling steps that led to a side door. The door was thick glass with an enormous rusting lock on it, but the lock was useless since someone had shoved a rock between the door and the jamb. Although the building looked dismal, I was grateful for the rush of warm air that greeted my dripping nose as I stepped cautiously over the rock. Once we were inside, the warm air came with the stale scent of spicy meat and garbage. A heap of blankets rested in the hallway. To my horror, the heap moved when I brushed past; a mottled arm emerged from the folds along with a grumbling voice.

I had to quicken my steps to keep up with Miguel. He pushed through the halls and doors as if they were a mist concealing better worlds. When he found the door to his apartment he pushed in so quickly I almost missed it. The thin door was painted red and hung from the hinges like it was tired. One of the brass numbers was hanging upside down, so at first I thought it was some strange American symbol instead of the number 14.

Everywhere, on every square inch of floor, there were blankets, dirty mattresses, some with sleeping occupants on them, some marked out with threatening red tape. Two frightened eyes glimmered under the fat claws of an ancient dresser, two pudgy feet revealing a live child living beneath the furniture. Without a word, Miguel collapsed onto one of the mattresses in his clothes and began to snore.

The clasps and metal work of my mother's jewelry hurt where

they dug into the skin of my throat, but I couldn't loosen my grip. My feet ached, my legs ached, my whole body ached with weariness and three weeks of compounded anxiety. Through all the awful trials of traveling illegally across an entire continent, I had looked towards this moment, the possibility of a safe arrival. Now there was nothing more to look forward to; I had arrived. Yet there was no security, no safety, no certainty in this filthy, crowded room. The arches of my feet were pressed against each other in a desperate attempt not to offend someone else's space or things. There was nowhere for me to be.

A shaking began in the depths of my lungs, and I felt my chin begin to tremble. A wheedling voice in the back of my head said that I might as well cry - who would care? Before I fell into complete despair, I tried to think about what Nanita would do if she were here. That simple thought brought on a flood of righteous anger that made blood pound in my ears.

This must be an American favela, the very place of danger and insecurity from which my father had endeavored to save me. How mortifying that Miguel fell so far from the opportunities our parents sacrificed to give him. No wonder he didn't tell Papí what his life was really like; he would die of shame.

Miguel was drooling off the side of his mattress. I gave him a swift kick, the kind Nanita gave to the dogs that slept in the shade of her mango tree. My brother's shoulder slumped back lazily, and he continued snoring. After two or three more kicks, one of his eyes opened and he glared at me.

"What the fuck are you doing here?" he slurred in his bad Portuguese.

"I will ask you once again not to curse at me," I said. I heard how imperious I sounded, but I didn't care. If Nanita were here, she would have smacked sense into such a disappointing man. "I need a place to sleep, and here there is not enough room to stand."

"Go stay at the Hilton if you're so picky," Miguel muttered.

He started to turn away from me, but I kicked him again, harder this time. "Fuck, Tasía! Cut it out!"

I roused the sleeping beast, and he jumped up to a sitting position. I stood my ground. He might be stronger and meaner than I, but I stood in the strength of a hundred generations of Brazilian women who had survived worse than this. I would not allow Miguel to leave me to rot away in a tiny space in a strange land.

"I see that you didn't know I was coming, and that your...position in life is not good for helping family. But I must have a place to sleep and something to eat. It is not much for me to ask. Padre would do as much for a stranger, Nanita would do so for a stray dog. Surely you can do so much for you sister."

My brother's face became hard as I spoke. "Look, I'm sorry you're in a bad spot, Tasía. But if I couldn't pull it together for my own god damn daughter," his voice caught like a hiccup "I'm not going to do any better for you. Sorry." *Desculpe*, he said, so sorry that I must leave you with nowhere to stand. On a different day, when I had a piece of ground to put my feet on, I would have demanded to know what had happened to little Ellie, why Celeste wasn't here to pull him out of his oblivion. Today, I had to focus on my own basic needs.

"Miguel, if I die in this country it will be on your head, for you will have abandoned your own blood."

"That's not how things work here, Tasía. You want to eat? You get a job." With a dismissive flick of his wrist he flipped onto his side so his wide back faced me. I was about to kick him again, right between his stubborn shoulder blades. Before I could, he shifted slightly, then a little more. After a couple grudging shifts of his awkward body, he was lying half off the mattress, leaving a strip of the blue and white striped fabric, about four inches wide. Closing my eyes, I lowered myself onto the tiny strip of mattress, pressing my back against my brother's. I kept my eyes closed so I wouldn't see the scurrying creatures I could hear too well. Crossing my arms over my chest with my mother's jewels shoved between my breasts, I fell into a fitful sleep.

·•·

An old man stood outside a coffee shop shouting something at me in English, gesturing emphatically at the sidewalk. Since I already tried to explain that I don't understand English, I just stood there, bit my lip and tried not to cry. His bald head was shiny and red, his white apron smeared with something brown. A nice-looking girl with red hair stepped out of the store and asked the man a question, which he returned quickly. She shrugged and went back inside.

When I woke up this morning, Miguel was gone. In his place was a limp piece of green American money with a bubble-like five in one corner, and a note. The note said, "Take the #26 bus, go to the East Lake Library and ask for Julia." Papí gave me some cash before I left, but it had been transferred into ten different currencies and dispersed across Central America. That piece of paper money was my whole fortune in the world, and that short note was my one clue to this new land.

After I'd left the dank apartment I carefully examined each street sign as I passed them, marking which way I was turning so I could find my way back again, trying to keep my eye out for a bus stop at the same time. But one too many streets curved in a funny pattern, one looped around and met the same street twice, another changed its name once and then again. I was lost in the tangle of the city streets and had no hope of finding my way back to that crumbling brick building. Since there was virtually no hope of finding a Portuguese speaker by just standing on a street corner and asking passers-by, I'd continue to wander.

Somehow I'd angered this man by lingering outside his store, and when he discovered that I didn't speak English he went a little crazy. Several people walked by the scene he was making, brushing by as if they couldn't hear him shouting. There were young people on bicycles, Muslims draped in gold-embroidered fabrics, and business people in sharp suits.

Desperate to get away from the shouting, I started to back away. That seemed to anger the man even more, and he got even louder. As a last resort, I pulled out my piece of paper and tried to sound out the few English words.

"Soo-ree." I said very slowly. "Sooree, sooree," I repeated. Although the man looked totally baffled, he stopped shouting for a moment. "Eye no-t spek Aann-gee-lis." The words came easier now than they had for the policemen. The man just stared at me. "No Aanglis." I repeated. The man let out a short burst of English words. They sounded like a dog barking.

I was out of patience. He didn't want me to leave, he had no intention of trying to communicate with me, and he certainly wasn't going to help me find my way back to Miguel's room. If I had to be hopelessly lost in a strange city, I was not going to be yelled at too.

"Look, I can't understand you when you speak in English, just like you can't understand me now when I'm speaking Portuguese. Oh, you don't like it when I talk and you can't understand me? I'd imagine that's a little frustrating, sir. I'd suggest you let me go and just deal with whatever it is you're upset about so we can both stop being frustrated."

My journey to this weird place had sharpened my survival instincts to a dangerous point. Maybe that heightened sense was what drew my eye to the rumbling monster of a vehicle as it passed by. Number 26.

"Vinte-seis!" I shouted, pointing at the bus as it passed. *26, number 26*. The bald man turned to look, distracted for a moment, and I dashed past him.

His raging bald head got small behind me as I sprinted for the bus. Thankfully, after it turned a corner it lumbered to a halt. My heart was pounding so hard that my throat hurt as I climbed up the two steps to the bus. Proud of myself, I presented my limp American money to the driver.

She looked at me, her eyes dull and unreadable. Her wide jaws worked a huge piece of bright pink gum, and frizzy hair shot out all around the baseball cap she wore tight on her skull. She made no move to take my money from me, but drawled something dismissive in English. Others bus riders crowded behind me, swiping their wallets at a flat plastic oval to my right and pushing towards the two double rows of seats.

"Eye..." I began with a deep breath. "Eye no-tee spek..."

"Eh!" the bus driver grunted at me, waving her meaty hand. "Eh!" she grunted again when I didn't move. Choosing to believe this woman was kinder than she looked, I moved towards the rows of seats instead of down the stairs to the street. She was kinder than she looked, and let me ride on her bus for free that day.

The bus took off with a lurch, but didn't reach anywhere near the speeds that a bus back home would. Here the cars pushed around the bus like it was a slow-moving mule on a crowded sidewalk. The driver seemed cautious, timid even, pulling slowly back onto the street after every stop.

After the second stop I realized that I had no idea where to get off, and this bus was carrying me farther and farther from familiar territory. Summing up my courage, I turned to the person next to me and tried to sound out the name of the library.

"Eh-est Lak-eh streeeet," I said, pointing to the name on the note Miguel had given me. The slouching white teenage boy glared and turned away. Determined, I turned to my other side, where an old black woman with a soft knitted hat was reading a magazine.

"Eh-est Lake-eh streeeet," I said again, pointing to my note. She looked up from her magazine and smiled, but didn't say anything. "Biblioteca," I said, miming reading a book with my two flat palms. Recognition flashed in the woman's eyes, and she shouted something up to the driver who grunted in response. I decided that grunt was a good sign, since it meant kindness before. Sure enough, when we came to the right stop the bus driver shouted back to me, and the woman beside me nudged my ribs and pointed to the bus door.

I found myself in front of a huge glass building with a brightly colored banner twisting in the wind over the door. Although I found it strange, I was glad the building was glass; if it hadn't been, I never would have guessed that the sleek edifice was a library. As it was, I could see the stacks of books from the sidewalk. So, with my bag tucked under my arm and the piece of notebook paper in my hand, I entered the library.

The building was smaller inside than it looked from the sidewalk, the shelves of books were mostly abandoned and there didn't seem to be anyone working there. To my left a bank of computers sat, mostly unused. One older black man in a top hat sat poking at one of the keyboards. After standing there stupidly for a few moments, I saw two women chatting behind a little counter with computers inlaid in them. The sun glinted against one of their gold-colored nametags.

I approached them, glancing at the piece of paper for reference.

"Can I help you?" one of the women asked. She had a head of fuzzy blonde hair and wore glasses with thick black frames.

"Julia," I said, blindly guessing at the English pronunciation of the name my brother had given me.

"Sorry?"

"Julia?" I asked again, hoping that this painful journey wasn't in vain.

"You speak Portuguese?" the second woman said. She was tiny, brunette and asked me this question in quiet, precise Portuguese.

"Yes, I am Brazilian. Are you Julia?" I asked.

"Yes, I'm Julia. How can I help you?"

For a moment, I forgot why I made this difficult journey to the library, I was so happy to find the building and Julia inside it.

"I'm sorry. I wanted a book that will help me learn English," I said.

"Okay, well we've got the foreign language section over here," she moved from behind the counter and led me to self of bright colored books with different countries' flags on them. "Do you speak any English at all?" Julia asked.

"No. My aunt wrote down some words for me. I can say that I don't speak English, and that I'm sorry. That's pretty much it."

Julia smiled. "That's probably a good combination to start with. How long have you been in the USA?"

Her question made me nervous. Didn't the government run the libraries? Maybe they had the women who worked here keep their eye out for illegal aliens. Based on Miguel's reaction to the police in the train station, I couldn't be too careful. I could still hear the way he said "crackdown."

"Not very long," I replied.

"Well, I can give you this book which will teach you basic object names and a few phrases." The book she handed me was floppy paperback. When I opened it I could see lots of boxes with simple pictures in them, followed by huge letters. It looked like a book I used in preschool.

"It's really a very good book. Unfortunately we don't have Portuguese to English phrasebooks. You probably won't be able to find anything like that in a bookstore either. This," she handed me a printed half-sheet from a holder on one of the shelves, "is a list of English as a Second Language classes in the metro area. What is your schedule like?"

Taking the half-sheet, I tucked it into the floppy book before looking up. "Schedule?"

"Do you have a job? Children?" Julia asked. "I can tell you which classes will work best with your schedule."

"No, I don't have a job. Or children," I said haltingly.

"Do you need a job?" Julia asked, not sounding perturbed at all, her perfect Portuguese never faltering.

"I'm not sure... I have never worked outside of my home."

"Are you living with family?" Julia asked. As she spoke she was moving towards the computer bank. I followed her with a sinking feeling that it wouldn't be long before Julia knew the three or four details about my life in America.

"My brother, for the moment. I would like to live somewhere else though."

"Okay. Here we are. This is the employment area here," she pulled out an office chair on four wheels and gestured for me to sit.

"Thank you," I said.

"So you say you've never worked before?"

"No."

"All right, let's see what we have here." She started clicking around, typing on the keyboard by leaning over my shoulder.

"I know how to use a computer." I felt like a child watching her type for me.

"The employment sites are in English," she explained. "I saw a couple of spots open on some maid services this morning when I was helping someone else."

"Maid service?" I asked, trying to tamp down my pride. Nanita would have a conniption if she knew I was a maid.

"This one is really good. They hire non-English speakers and they... don't usually ask for documentation," Julia said. She shot me a little smile before going back to her clicking and typing. I felt the knot in my stomach loosen just a little.

"Thank you." This time it was sincere.

"My mother was an immigrant. She came here with nothing, no English skills, no education, no money. Now she's a professor at the University of Minnesota." Julia glowed with pride.

"That is very encouraging," I said. "Did she start as a maid?"

Julia laughed. "Don't worry, the woman who owns this company is a pretty decent human being. One second." A nearby printer shook and sputtered. After a moment it spit out a piece of paper, which Julia whipped up and handed to me.

"That's a map of where you're going and instructions on how to take the bus. Pay attention to the names and numbers of the busses, especially make sure the letters after the bus numbers match, and you'll be fine."

"Thank you?" She was being so kind, but I had no idea what she was talking about.

"For the job. Yolanda is doing interviews today. You should check in with her today, but unless there's a problem she'll probably have you start tomorrow."

"Does she speak Portuguese?" I asked stupidly. The paper hung limply in my hand.

"No. You'll have to work around that. I'm sure you can do it." Julia patted my arm. "Come back anytime, I work most weekdays."

"Okay. Thank you." I paused. I had no desire to work for a woman named Yolanda who fit the description of "a decent human being." Not to mention that Nanita and Papí might be more comfortable with Miguel's living situation than with my working as a maid. Still, it seemed clear that I would have to make my own way in this new country, and the opportunities were scarce. "Really, thank you." I said with the kindest smile I could manage. "I don't know what I would have done without you."

"You would find another way."

"One more thing," I said as she turned away.

"Yes?"

"Can I make a phone call from here?" I asked. My face was already flaming with the knowledge that I had to call Miguel and ask him how to get back to the apartment.

.•.

Yolanda was more than a decent human being. She was a square shaped woman with more determination than any five women I'd ever met. During our short interview she communicated across the language barrier by deftly using a combination of Spanish cognates and line drawings. Her questions were simple enough. Would I steal things? Would I pay for things if I broke them? Would I be polite to customers? Would I refrain from whining? After agreeing to these simple terms she handed me a green polo and told me to come back at 6am the next morning. Biting back my concerns, I nodded and left.

Miguel was shocked when I told him I'd found a job. "What are you doing? Did you find some old coot who wants you to embroider for her?"

"No. I clean houses."

He laughed. He laughed at me until spittle flew from his mouth. For a long time I stood before him, too dignified to respond.

"May I ask what you do for money in this country?" I asked after he had calmed down.

"I build houses, Tasía. I'm a skilled worker, not some nameless goon scrubbing shit from toilets."

"Is that where you go? Do you build houses until three in the morning?" Although I had lost all respect for my brother, my heart jerked at the look on his face. By implying that he went out drinking, I reminded him of his desperate need for alcohol. His right hand seemed to search for a bottle while his face screwed up in anger.

"You don't have any right to judge me, Tasía. If it weren't for me you'd be rotting in some jail for illegal immigrants."

"Yes, that's true. You have had the privilege of immigrating legally, having good papers. Just look how well you've used that advantage, Miguel."

He glared, clenching his fists. "Go to hell, Tasía."

"Papí would have a stroke if he saw how you are living here, how you have wasted everything he's given you."

"Shut up!" Miguel yelled. One of the ghostlike bodies in the room shifted and grumbled.

"You are drunk right now, aren't you? No wonder Celeste left you."

The room spun around me as something heavy slammed against my face. I stood confused, blinking away the blurriness in my eyes, holding my face. Miguel looked more shocked than I felt.

"You hit me." I said. My mouth was already starting to swell.

"I…I shouldn't have. I'm sorry." The words were mechanical. We both knew there should be some cosmic consequence for such an offense, striking a woman, his own elder sister at that. If we were home Papí would have turned him out of the house and Nanita would have called Catholic curses down on his head. There would be long conversations about what penance he would have to pay to be admitted to the family again. But here, no one would know he had done such a thing, no one besides the two of us. As much as I could say to hurt him, there was nothing I could do. He was free, unconnected, and unknown. My only defense was the strength of my arms.

"You hit me," I said again, still uncomprehending.

"Don't…don't…mention *her* again," Miguel said. Cutting a wide path so he wouldn't be within reach of me, my brother stepped towards our little mattress, reached into his dirty pillowcase, and pulled out a small bottle. Before I could even exclaim, he was sucking the amber liquid down like it was his last hope for life.

My face was starting to throb, but I couldn't decide what new fact to be baffled at first. "Miguel," I said quietly. Now he seemed more of a dangerous child than a threatening man. "Miguel, what happened? Did she divorce you?"

"I said, don't mention it!" Miguel gasped, taking a short break to speak these words before going back to drain the bottle. After all the alcohol was swallowed, he threw the bottle away and gasped for air. When he recovered, he laughed bitterly. "I was never married to Celeste. You know what else? She was black." He laughed like he laughed when I told him about my job, only now he mocked himself.

"Never married...but you had a child with her!" I cried. How could Ellie, precious Ellie that we had all adored, be a bastard child?

"You're so cloistered down there in your fantasy world. You don't understand how things are."

"I understand how real men take care of their families," I said. I was still holding my face, but I couldn't keep my angry words down.

"I warned you, okay? You've been warned," Miguel said. He bent in half, leaning his hands on his knees as if he were the one recovering from a blow. A connection sparked in my mind.

"Celeste *was* black," I said. "She isn't black anymore?"

"She died." Those words choked the air and life out of my brother. His face was red, his eyes glassy, his mouth wobbled as his lips tried to smush into some better shape. He looked like he was drowning.

"What happened to Ellie?" I whispered, unbelieving. Miguel's head dropped between his shoulders.

"I don't know," his voice gurgled.

"You don't *know*?" This was beyond me. "Mother of God, Miguel. She's your daughter!"

"No shit!" Snatching his wallet from the mattress, he pushed past me.

"Where are you going?"

"Out!" The door slammed behind him.

..•.

Although I barely slept that night, I did manage to make it back to Yolanda's office on time, dutifully wearing my green polo, and with my long hair pulled away from my face the way Nanita did hers before housework.

When I arrived, Yolanda was waiting for us in the same green polo, although hers was about five times the size of mine and barely restrained her girth. Her mouse-colored hair was pulled into a severe bun at the back of her head and her mouth was set in a pencil-thin line. When all the girls were there, she spoke to us briefly in English and then repeated herself in Spanish. Since numbers are similar in Portuguese and Spanish, I was able to catch that we would work until 6pm and have a half-hour break for lunch. From the interview, I recognized the word "whining" and got the message from the slow shake of Yolanda's regal head.

We cleaned homes all over the metro, from little houses smaller than my family's back home to palaces on the banks of glassy lakes. Yolanda packed five women into a green hatchback with a trunk full of cleaning supplies, and drove to each location with silent precision. She had a set of flashcards in the glove box with illustrations of different household rooms. First she pointed to the card that illustrated my responsibility in the next house, then she handed me the flashcards so I could study them. Behind the cards displaying rooms were cards for different cleaning liquids and tools.

The work was harder than I expected, harder than I could imagine. After the first hour all my joints screamed with pain. With envy, I watched the little teenage girls flitting about like butterflies. In my forties, I didn't have their resilience or stamina. When I faltered, Yolanda appeared at my side.

"Tired?" she asked, a word I quickly picked up. It didn't matter how I responded, with a nod, a shrug, or a tearful sob, her next words were always the same. "Hard work is good for the soul." That became the first complete sentence I could say in perfect English.

At lunch I stared off into space vacantly, pushing some of the turkey sandwich I'd purchased at the gas station into my mouth, wondering how I would ever survive another six hours. One of the young girls sat next to me on the curb. Yolanda picked the first shady spot she found after the gas station and stopped there. Two girls giggled in the car, another had wandered off to find a bench, but I plopped down on the curb, needing to get out of the stuffy car but unable to carry myself any farther.

"You're Brazilian?" the girl asked in Spanish. She was a beautiful Latina, now glowing with the delicate sweat of youth. I was pouring bitter perspiration from every fold and bend in my body. My ponytail hung limp on my back and my hands shook with fatigue.

"Yes," I answered blankly.

"Lucky," she said, pointing to me. "Yolanda is a good boss."

"Yes," I agreed, too tired to argue. At the moment I felt oppressed by Yolanda's relentless work ethic.

"Good money," the girl said, making a hand gesture to clarify that she was talking about cash. "Even with no papers."

"Huh." I didn't want to talk to anyone.

"Most bosses don't pay good money without papers. Yolanda has…good feelings?"

"Morals," I said in Portuguese. The girl shrugged; the words weren't similar enough to understand across languages.

I didn't believe her anyway. Miguel warned me when he returned at 4am that I should not try to figure out how much money I was making in Brazilian reales. "You'll quit if you do the math," he said as he laid his puffy face on the mattress. Because he was my brother, and because I loved him since his birth, I chose to believe that piece of advice was his way of apologizing for failing me so terribly, for lying to me and Papí, and for the purple bruise that already encompassed the entire left side of my face.

Yolanda's implacable determination was the only reason I survived. The woman was indefatigable, never hesitated, never rested, never compromised her commitment to perfection and hard work. She asked us to do the impossible, and none of us failed her; first because she wouldn't let us, and second because she did more work than anyone.

At 6pm sharp she delivered us back to her office and handed each of us a yellow envelope, our wages for the day. I didn't look in the envelope. Even if I hadn't believed Miguel's dismal prediction, I didn't know the value of an American dollar anyway. All I wanted to know was how many days I had to work to move into a real apartment. So I tucked the envelope into my embroidered bag, the bag that still held my mother's jewels and rested safely in a locker in Yolanda's office. She wore the key around her neck all day long and placidly handed everyone their belongings before we left.

Her massive hand patted my trembling shoulder as I left. Surprised, I turned to see what she wanted. With the smallest of smiles, she gave me a thumbs up.

"Good work," she said. "Drink," she mimed the word to me. "Water. A lot." She said the words slowly and distinctly and accompanied them with simple hand gestures. "Tomorrow come back. 6 o'clock."

I nodded, "Abrigada," I said, although I knew that my thanks would not be understood. Even so, recognition seemed to flicker in Yolanda's eyes.

· • ·

If Yolanda made me work seven days a week, I would have no way to mark time. The days blurred together in an endless stream of houses, blisters, and the aching feeling that I would never feel rested again. Because she was a decent human being, and because she knew the limits of the human body, Yolanda gave us Sundays off.

On my days off, I slept. Thankfully, Miguel was almost always gone on Sundays, which meant I could have the entire mattress. Those days were like the tic marks prisoners make on walls of their cells; they were there to mark the time, to separate one week from another.

My one purpose was to get myself and Miguel out of that horrible room. In my determination to get out of that room as soon as I could, I found myself searching the dirty sidewalk around bus stops for unused transfers, checking vending machines and pay phones for uncollected change, wedging my head under the faucet in the common bathroom to drink so I wouldn't have to buy a cup, and searching the convenience store for something cheaper than a turkey sandwich. In my third week, one of the little teenage girls showed me energy bars. For a dollar apiece, they would keep me on my feet all afternoon, a discovery that felt like a small diamond mine. I found a brand of soap at the local grocery store for less than a dollar a bar, and I used it on both my body and hair. I figured since I was eating so little, it would be acceptable for a time to forgo the expense of toothpaste and floss.

I knew that the worst insult was being called "illegal." If I had had the time or energy, I might have been angry at the people who were upset that I was living off the fat of their land. The fat of the land caused me to grip doorframes as dizziness swept over me, gave me half a dirty mattress and six hours of sleep every night, all while I was doing common household chores for Americans who wouldn't scrub their own toilets. When my limited English was discovered by a checker at the grocery store, she flatly accused me of stealing American jobs. I didn't know how to tell her that no American would work at my job.

After three months working for Yolanda and some help searching the Internet with Julia, I was ready to move out. I found a tiny apartment in a high-rise not far from where we were already living. Dirty and cramped as it was, it felt like a palace compared to this room. There weren't any children hiding under the furniture, I could keep it clean, spray for bugs, and cook my own food on the two burners of the half-stove that came with the apartment. I could cook up a huge batch of fejioda and eat it for a week. My mouth watered at the idea of black bean sauce, thickened with carne seca and served over rice. My shaking hands ached for the strength of a real meal. Life was about to change, and this time it would be better.

I was ready to leave for days before I saw Miguel. He was so drunk, I wasn't sure he would hear me. He certainly didn't see me as he slid down to the mattress in his filthy jeans, still clutching an empty bottle in his right hand.

"Miguel," I said, prodding him with my toe. He grunted.

"Miguel," I repeated a little louder.

"What? What the fuck could you possibly want, Tasía?" he demanded. I set my shoulders, raised my chin and spoke in a clear voice.

"I'm moving out, Miguel. I have saved enough money to get out of this room and I am going."

At first there was no reaction to this news. Slowly, he rolled over. "You've saved? How much is that woman paying you?"

"That is none of your business."

"Have you been stealing from me?" he demanded in a low, growling voice.

"No." The word was filled with all the resentment my body contained. "You don't have any money as far as I know, only bottles."

"Fuck off. Fine, go. What do I care?" He rolled over again.

Tears stung my eyes. I hadn't expected much, but his words still hurt. He was a drunk, dangerous, and a hideous failure, but he was still my brother and the only person in this country who might care about me. I swallowed.

"You can come with me, if you like," I said.

"I'm not paying your rent, Tasía. This place is already killing me."

"It certainly is. I can pay my own rent, and you needn't come if you'd rather stay here. You have paid for me to live here for three months, and I appreciate it. You can live with me for free."

He sat up and rubbed water out of his eyes with his dirty palm. "Are you serious?"

"Yes. You are my brother, my blood, and I will help you get out of this mess. On one condition."

He rolled his eyes. "Uh-huh." Although the bottle he had was empty, his knuckles whitened as he gripped tighter.

"You may not bring alcohol into the apartment, and you may not bring anyone else into the apartment. Unless…"

"Unless what?" he demanded.

"Unless it's Ellie. Of course, she is always welcome."

"Ha! You naïve old spinster, don't you get it? Ellie is gone. She's…" he choked. "She's just gone." Tears welled in his eyes and he turned away. Summing up the strength and compassion that Nanita has always taught me was the mark of a good woman, I knelt beside him and rubbed his shoulder. I braced myself for a violent reaction, but he didn't move.

"We'll start over, Miguel. I can't imagine what you've been through. You were so bright, so strong as a boy. You are my brother, and I love you. This apartment is an opportunity for both of us. We'll start over."

··

My knees shook as I walked down the hallway to my apartment door, but today I didn't mind. After a month of getting to sleep on my own air mattress with clean sheets and a hot shower after work, I felt like a new woman. With pride, I fingered the key that would open my very own apartment, a space that was mine and would only open for me and my brother. I knew there was leftover rice and chopped beef in the mini refrigerator that came with the apartment. Of course, my dinner would be eaten cold; a microwave was too much of a luxury, but that wouldn't bother me. Cold beef and rice was a million times better than the tiny cup of soup I had been eating on the way home for months.

The lock clicked open for my key, but the door would only open a few inches. I pushed hard, trying to get past the obstacle to my dinner and a shower. After a few good pushes, I heard a low groaning.

"Miguel! You're sleeping in front of the door," I said. I tried to say it loud enough to rouse him but not loud enough to disturb my neighbors.

"Awww, Tasía. Leave me be." He sounded like his tongue was swollen.

"Just let me in and then you can sleep wherever you want."

After a long pause, I heard shuffling on the other side of the door. When I tried it again, the door swung open for me. A huge pool of orange vomit covered half the hallway.

"Miguel!" I shouted, not caring if I woke people up this time. Gingerly, I tried to step over the mess without getting puke on my tennis shoes.

"What?" he demanded.

"You have to clean this up!" Now I was safely past the mess and stepped into the three-square-foot kitchen.

"I'll get to it, Tasí, just let me sleep first."

"It's going to stink up the apartment," I shot back. Miguel leaned against the wall and slid to the floor. His face was puffy, his skin pasty, and his hands shook like an old man's. There was so little left of the man he could be, even less than when I'd first arrived.

"I just...need to sleep."

"How did you manage to get this drunk again? Where is your money coming from?"

"Tasía, please. Not now." He held up a hand as if he could block my voice with his palm.

"If I have to wait for you to be sober to talk to you, we'll never speak again." Even though I knew I'd end up cleaning that vomit in the hallway, my stomach still rumbled happily at the prospect of dinner. I piled rice and beef onto a plastic plate, snatched one of my two forks from the drawer and started digging into the food, leaning against the counter.

"Great, Tasía. I'm a drunk, what else is new?" Miguel sat with his arms resting on his knees and his head resting on his arms.

"Seriously, where are you getting the money?" I asked. "Are you stealing?"

"No. I don't steal."

"Well, that's good." The food felt good in my stomach.

"And I haven't kept anything from you," Miguel added, lifting his head a little.

"What does that mean?" I asked. I'd never asked Miguel for money since I'd been working, and he'd never given me any.

"It means I'm not like you. I don't hide riches from my own family."

"What?"

Realization hit like a snapped cord. I jolted to the kitchen cabinet, threw the door open and plunged my hand into the hole in the bottom where I hid my embroidered bag. When my hand touched the lovingly stitched fabric I realized I'd been holding my breath. Slowly exhaling, I pulled the bag out. It was light, very light and fear roared between my ears. Before I looked, I knew what I would find. The jewels were gone. Of the twenty heirlooms I carried from Brazil, only one garnet necklace remained.

The earth spun beneath me as I sat there, holding the last remnant of my mother's wealth. All the tension dropped away and tears clouded my vision. Even in the midst of my despair, I checked for the yellow envelopes I stored in the bag. To my surprise, they were still there and full of five-dollar bills. I should have been glad, but I couldn't muster the strength to care. After a long, long time of silent, airless anguish I issued my first whining plea.

"Why would you do that?"

Miguel shifted uncomfortably, looking away from me. "They were as much mine as they were yours," he mumbled.

"They were not! Those were madre's, they were for me and for my daughter! Those jewels were the riches of the women in our family, just the women! How selfish can you be? You stupid men, you get everything: all the wealth, all the respect, all the power, all the advantages. I had this *one thing* and you stole it! For God's sake, Miguel! Those were for Ellie!"

Suddenly he was on his feet, towering over me with all the power and rage he could muster.

"I told you...not to talk about them!" he sputtered.

"Someone has to care what happened to your poor abandoned daughter, Miguel! I guess it will be me, since you seem to have no intention of being man enough to care for one little girl."

My words dripped with pain. I let it go, God forgive me, and let him sit in his denial. I even provided him a clean place to live for free, let him eat my food and sleep on my floor. In return, he betrayed me down to my core, and I had no will to protect him any longer.

"Watch your step, girl!" Miguel roared.

I leapt to my feet and shoved his chest as hard as I could, which knocked him back against the kitchen counter. "Don't you boss me around! You're not Papí. You haven't earned the respect to be master of a household. You're nothing but a drunk, a vagrant, a beggar. You wouldn't be welcome in our father's home if he knew what you'd become. You're not even master of this apartment. This is mine, do you hear me? *Mine*."

Reeling against the counter, my brother blinked at me like I had just sprouted a new head. Maybe I had; a head that wasn't putting up with any more of this shit. While he was still stunned, I moved in for the kill.

"Get out of my house. You aren't welcome. I've helped as much as I can, but you are beyond hope. Don't even think about coming back here again. If you can forget your own daughter, you can forget me too. Just get out!"

I expected him to fight. My nose was just inches from his by the time I made my final demand. I knew he would hit me again and declare that as the man he had every right to live here, even if I was paying the rent. That all the money I made was really his anyway. Waiting for his response, I bristled up, prepared for a battle. He didn't hit me. He dropped his head, stuffed his wallet in his back pocket and shuffled to the door.

His shoulders were still wide and powerful and his frame filled the small hallway, but his spirit was small and withered. For a moment, I regretted my harsh words, realizing that he felt every ounce of his shame.

"Hey," he called from the doorway, his voice thick. "Sorry about the puke."

••

Even after Miguel left, I found myself waking in the night, shaking with anger and grief at the loss of those precious pieces of my mother. After cleaning up that last mess of vomit I was able to clean the apartment knowing that it would stay clean unless I personally made a mess. It was a relief to know what I would find when I came home at night.

Then Sunday rolled around. Now that I had a bed all to myself, a hot shower every night, good food in my stomach, and no roaches to worry about, I no longer needed the entire day to catch up on sleep. I enjoyed waking up at 5:30, looking at the clock, remembering it was Sunday, and rolling over to enjoy as many hours of slumber as I desired. After a month or so, I would wake up two or three hours later with the rest of the day at my disposal.

First, I cooked. This week I made lentils, chopping a whole onion and stewing it in with the beans. I took a roll of carne seca out and carefully carved three or four slices into the pot, just enough to flavor the stew. When I was done cooking, it was noon.

The dishes sat in the sink, so I washed them, meting out the tiniest drops of dish soap I could manage. There were only the two pots, so the chore didn't take long.

Of all the challenges I'd encountered in America, what to do with my extra time wasn't one of them. I would have studied the books on English that Julia had helped me find, but of course they'd been returned to the library long ago. If I wanted a book I could study over and over again, I'd have to buy it. As much as I wanted to learn English, the expense of a new book was more than I was willing to part with, especially now that my hidden fortune was gone.

Still, maybe I could borrow that book again. Having something to work on during these Sundays afternoons would be pleasant. Perhaps it would fill up the day, and help distract from the aching sense that I was now completely alone in this huge, impersonal country. Even if they didn't have the book, it would be so good to talk to Julia. With Miguel gone, I had no opportunity to speak my native tongue.

Although I knew it was nearly two miles to the library, I decided to walk. I didn't want to waste good money on a frivolous bus trip, and it was a lovely spring day. My view of the Cities was entirely composed of the busses and the homes I cleaned. Until this moment, I'd never had the chance to simply look around.

By now I could read most of the signs, and I was familiar with the street names. Although I would have to walk along the bus route to keep from getting lost, I understood how the street numbers became tangled around downtown and the University campus, but straightened into a more comprehensible pattern as they moved south. The streets were crowded with people taking advantage of the gentle weather. Students on bicycles and young men in tight T-shirts and ripped jeans, girls wearing the first of their summer dresses and skirts. A parade of mothers pushing bright strollers passed by, not noticing me as they jostled and chatted along. Groups of three or four Muslim women passed by, draped in their beautifully colored fabrics, their dark faces looking me over suspiciously as they passed.

I knew now that these were immigrants from Somalia and Ethiopia, refugees from the civil wars that raged in that part of the world. One of the women who worked with me kept her head always wrapped in a hijab. Neither of us spoke much English, but she had managed to tell me a bit of her story. Like me, she was smuggled out of the country when her family was threatened. Her journey was even more terrifying than mine. She pantomimed covering her eyes and running across a road full of dead bodies while shots rang out around her. Once, while we were eating lunch together, a lanky teenage boy threw a rock at her. She trembled as he stalked passed her shouting something about Jesus. While tears edged her eyes, I took her into my arms and patted her head like a child.

As I walked past these Muslim women, I wished I could tell them that I sympathized with them, that they didn't need to be afraid of me. Instead, I lowered my head and walked on. Cold comfort it would be anyway, knowing that a penniless Brazilian maid was on your side.

By the time I reached the library, I was tired and damp. I decided I could spare a dollar and seventy-five cents to take the bus home. The air conditioning in the library felt good, and I sat in one of their soft chairs. These chairs were a luxury for me. Since the only furniture in my apartment was an air mattress and a blue plastic crate, sitting in a chair was a special event.

A pinched-looking woman approached me with a frown.

"Can I help you?" she asked.

I knew that phrase very well. I also knew its secret meaning. That phrase really meant, "You don't belong here."

"Julia here?" I asked, pointing to the floor where I wanted Julia to be.

"No, not today." The woman almost hissed. I wondered why she was so upset. This was a public place, wasn't it? Julia said anyone was allowed to come to the library and read, even if they didn't have good papers or any money.

"Sorry," I said. "No help, okay?"

She said something very quickly that I didn't quite catch, something about reading and people. I made out the word "dirty," because I knew that word very well.

I shook my head. "Too fast, not understand."

She spoke again, too quickly. Although she clearly didn't want me here, I knew I had a right to sit quietly in this chair.

"I quiet, not trouble," I said. The woman made a skeptical sound and left me alone.

I felt tears sting my eyes. I knew I was right to make Miguel leave, but he was the only person in the country who knew me. The people I knew here, I barely knew. They were my boss, my coworkers, my librarian, not my friends.

If only because I was sure that a crying dirty immigrant would be even less welcome than a happy dirty immigrant, I left the comfort of the library. The bus was pulling away as I stepped onto the sidewalk, and I realized I didn't want to return to the apartment yet. This was precious time. After today I wouldn't have time to do anything but eat, sleep, and work for another week.

I wondered if Papí would let me come home if I told him how miserable I was. Of course, that would mean risking my life, and possibly bringing the wrath of the USA government down on my family for sneaking me into their country. The decision to come here and live with Miguel was made so quickly, none of us considered the permanence of the arrangement. No one asked Miguel what he thought.

I walked around the neighborhood near the library. Cute little houses lined the streets, surrounded by giant trees in full bloom. Four children of various races clambered around one bicycle, everyone trying to get a turn at once. I turned one corner and then another, trusting in the numbered streets. One block this way, one block that way, straying farther from the busy street where the bus stopped. A Catholic statue stood on one corner. Although I couldn't read the sign, I knew that it was St. Albert, one of Papí's favorites, holding a fat frog to his side. Although the carving was not in the same style as the depiction of saints back home, there was something familiar about him, and I lingered.

St. Albert was not my favorite saint, and I didn't know if the old scientist would have anything for a tired old woman, but still I searched his face hoping he would touch me with some enlightenment. Closing my eyes, I let my tears run down my face, glad to be in the presence of something familiar.

An English voice interrupted me, and my eyes flew open angrily. "Can't I even pray here on the street? Why do they put a saint here on the corner if they don't want people to pray?" The words were out of my mouth in a slew of liquid Portuguese before I realized that the young man standing before me had a gentle smile and kind eyes. He was not like the bald man screaming at me, an angry teenager with a rock, or even a sour-faced librarian. This was only a young person, dressed in black and badly in need of a haircut, watching a woman weep on the corner.

Pressing my open palms together to mime prayer, I gestured toward the saint. "Pray," I said. A word I had picked up from

Yolanda. "Okay, I pray?"

"Oh," the young man said, his eyes filling with compassion. Though he couldn't say two words together that I would understand, there was no mistaking that look. He said something in English, very gentle now, and gestured to the front of the church.

Following his pointing finger, I saw a few people trickling into the church. I knew what I would find inside: the scent of long burning candles glowing in their red glasses, perhaps a lingering haze of incense, the long robe of the padre in front of the altar. Inside, I ached for something familiar and welcoming. Yet I hesitated. If I was hated for my foreign skin in the holy church, I wouldn't be able to take it.

"I don't speak English," I said, enunciating each word so the young man would understand. The young man nodded, and smiled.

"Okay," he said, gesturing towards the church again. He put "okay" in a sentence that I didn't understand, but I was sure he meant that I was okay. He meant I was welcome here, even if I was a poor Latina who scrubbed toilets and didn't speak English. With a full heart, I ducked my head and followed where the young man pointed, joining the other parishioners as they climbed the cement steps to the open doors of the church.

The design of the church space was the same pattern as my little chapel back in Brazil. The archways displayed more depictions of saints. Back home saints were carved out of wood, painted to look realistic, and dressed in real clothes. These were all carved out of a sandy white stone and all their eyes were lowered. They had the narrow jaws and aquiline noses of rich Europeans. Their positions and props told who they were.

With a gratified sigh, I found one of Saint Sebastian, the patron saint of Rio de Janeiro. His stone body was pierced with four arrows and he hung limp from his stone tree. Back home, he was alive and defiant, his chest bristling with arrows like a porcupine. Still, he was our saint, and I murmured a prayer to him in

Portuguese, knowing that he would hear and understand me.

After saying a few words to St. Sebastian, I settled into a pew. For the moment, I was happy just to know that I could stay and wouldn't be a bother to anyone. My folded hands were bony and trembling, the cuticles of my nails eroded with the chemicals and hard labor. For the first time in months, I felt the tension ease from my shoulders and neck.

Although my family rarely went to mass more than once a month, Nanita still felt superior to the Three Holiday Catholics, who came only for Easter, Christmas, and Ash Wednesday. With a lift of her chin, she said that four months worth of confession should last an hour at least. At the time, I'd felt a blush of shame at her hypocrisy. Now I felt that shame turn inward as I realized I'd be in America for close to six months without setting foot in a church.

Preoccupied with my own thoughts, I hadn't realized that mass was about to begin. A few souls began drifting into the church, whispering short prayers to their preferred saint, just as I had, before taking their seats, crossing themselves as they did so. Although none of these people spoke my language, they shared this ritual with me. If I didn't open my mouth, they would never know that I didn't belong in this country. I did belong in this church.

The priest stepped solemnly down the aisle, swinging a censor of sweet incense. When he reached the altar, he faced the crucifix, extended his hands and began praying loudly. Although I could not understand each word, I knew the meaning of his prayers and my heart warmed with the knowledge. As the service continued, I found I could predict each step, each move of the priest's arm, each call to prayer.

Something shifted in my chest, as if my organs were rearranging themselves into their natural order. Sitting here was like finding the combination for a lock; I could feel each gear shifting, each tumbler finding its place. By the time we were called up for communion, I could feel that my face was warm with sweet emotion.

When it was my turn, I knelt before the priest and opened my mouth to receive the host. Just as I knew he would, he laid his hand on my head and blessed me. I wept there at the altar, feeling the love of my savior wash over me as I never had before.

When the priest saw my tears of gratitude, he smiled and touched my chin with affection, the way my Papí would, and spoke a few extra words over me in English. I had no reply, and I didn't need one.

·•·

After that first experience at St. Albert's, I went there every Sunday, and sometimes to the late mass on weeknights. Even when I was worn down to my bones it was worth the trip. The relief of getting my own apartment was nothing compared to the salve those days at mass were to my soul. I began to wonder how I survived so long without the weekly refreshment of hearing familiar words spoken in blessing over my head.

After a few weeks, I started going early so I could pray and light a candle for my lost family before mass. My prayers ranged around the globe, touching Papí and Aunt Nanita, of course, but lingering on my brother and niece. Although my anger could still flame up over heirlooms Miguel threw away, I began to regret kicking him out. Without someone to stabilize him, I worried he wouldn't last long.

And of course, poor Ellie. I hoped St. Anthony would take special care of that lost little girl. I had no idea how to find her. When I'd asked Julia, she'd held up her hands helplessly. Without Miguel, there was no way to prove that I was Ellie's aunt, and she could be anywhere by now. My heart wrenched whenever I thought of her, feeling somehow responsible for losing her, frightened that she was being shuffled from house to house, when I was here and more than willing to care for her.

That Friday was a particularly brutal workday. We had two big mansions in a row with a plethora of knick-knacks which all had to be dusted and carefully replaced. Like the leader she was, Yolanda led the charge with the knick-knacks, but set me to the infinity of marble floors which all had to swept, buffed, swept again, and washed. Sun poured in the side of the house that was almost entirely glass, making me feel like a bug under a microscope. By the time I was halfway done, my arms were limp as steamed spinach. Still, I worked on, like I did every day.

My skin jumped when I felt something warm on my shoulder. It was Yolanda's hand, getting my attention.

"Bad work?" I asked in my broken English.

"No. Good work. Very good. Stronger now," she pinched the fleshy part of my upper arm to show me where she saw strength. "And here," she added, thumping me on my chest. "Strong heart." A rare smile touched her lips, and mine.

That night on the way to mass I wished there was a way I could thank the priest or even the kind young man who invited me in. The benefits of their work were visible even to the tireless Yolanda. If Aunt Nanita were there, she would tell me that my devotion would be thanks enough for a man of the cloth, but I longed to express my gratitude.

When I entered the church it was almost empty. Sunlight slanted through the stained glass windows, and the colored light only landed on one or two heads before kissing the floors. As usual, I walked up to the candles and lit two; one for Miguel and one for Ellie. Placing my hands together the way Aunt Nanita had taught me, I began to pray. Papí used to tell me to keep my prayers short, since others might want a chance to kneel before the altar. I thought he just didn't want to wait around for longer prayers. Today there was no impatient Papí, and no one waiting behind me.

Taking out the precious beads Aunt Nanita gave me, I began counting off my rosary, murmuring the familiar words in Portuguese, comforted that Holy Mary would understand every word. I prayed for Aunt Nanita, for Papí, for Miguel and for Ellie, crossed myself and stood.

My head swam and my eyes were suddenly crowded with black splotches. Putting a hand down to brace myself, I felt my body begin to fall. Luckily, I caught myself on the hard side of the pew, but not before running into something soft and warm. After shaking the splotches away from my eyes, I saw that I'd run into a brown little girl with huge black eyes. She was curled up on the pew, hugging her knees to her chest. After a moment of hesitation, she smiled.

"I'm so sorry, please excuse me. I guess I worked a little too hard today," I said. Even though she wouldn't understand me, I hoped she would grasp that I was apologizing.

"That's okay. I hope you can sleep for a long time," she replied easily. A reply rose to my lips, but I bit it back in my surprise. She had spoken to me in perfectly formed Portuguese.

"I didn't mean that you look ugly or anything," the little girl explained. "Mommy used to say that she would feel like a million bucks if she could get enough sleep. I just wanted you to feel like a million bucks, that's all."

"You speak Portuguese," I said dumbly. "You speak it perfectly." I tried to size up how old the little girl was.

The little girl shrugged as if everyone spoke perfect Portuguese. "My Daddy was from Brazil when he was real little, and Mrs. Krantz speaks Portuguese too, but she has a bad accent. Mrs. Krantz says that it's super important to know about both sides of my family, even if Daddy is a no-good drunk."

Tears welled up in my eyes as hope twisted in my chest. Concern wrinkled across her pretty little face as tears dropped from my eyelashes.

"Mrs. Krantz said he was a no-good drunk, not me. I think he's just very sad because Mommy...well, she died."

A gasping sob escaped my throat. All these months, praying and worrying, and there she was, sitting behind me as I prayed for her.

"You're Ellie, aren't you?"

The Prayers of Frightened Children

Mommy got hit by a car. The man who was driving the car was a bad man who was being stupid. That's what Mrs. Krantz said, and then she said some other things in Yiddish, like Daddy sometimes says things in Portuguese when he's mad. I can understand Daddy, because he's been talking to me in Portuguese ever since I was a tiny baby. I don't understand Yiddish yet.

Mommy went into the hospital and she didn't come out again. I saw Daddy while they were trying to fix Mommy, and he was so sad. Mrs. Krantz says there's no excuse for him, but I think he just didn't want me to see him so sad. I wish he hadn't gone, because I already knew that.

So many people came to talk to Mrs. Krantz. A man with a brown striped tie and sad blue eyes came and talked to her first. He talked to me too. He told me that Mommy wasn't going to come out of that scary room. I wished I had Paddy with me; I missed his soft fur, and I wanted someone to hug. Mrs. Krantz is a nice lady, but she's not a good hugger.

After the man with the sad eyes left there was a lady in a silky shirt, but she didn't talk to me. I wanted to touch her silky shirt, but that would be rude. She had a clipboard and a big brown folder. She seemed tired and a little angry. I heard her say "Ellie is the responsibility of the State." When she said that, Mrs. Krantz' held me even tighter. Mrs. Krantz gets mad really fast, but this time her voice was slow and calm like Mrs. Ellison, my teacher.

"I have known this child since her birth, and I will take care of her. I will answer all the questions you like, and I will fill out any forms you need, but I will not let her become lost in the foster system." That's what Mrs. Krantz said to the lady with the silky shirt. I didn't know what a foster system was, but I knew that Mrs. Krantz thought it would be a very bad to get lost in it.

Mrs. Krantz sat in that scratchy chair for almost forever, and she would talk very slow to all the people. I knew she was scared, because I was sitting on her lap and she was holding me so tight it hurt my arms. I didn't whine though. Mommy says that whining hurts grown ups' ears. The sun went down and then came up again and we were still in that scratchy chair. A nurse brought me some crackers. Mrs. Krantz's voice was starting to sound crackly.

I guess I fell asleep for a little bit, but when I woke up there were red marks on my arms where Mrs. Krantz held me. Now there was an old lady with grey hair and a big sweater who was talking to Mrs. Krantz.

"Can we go home, now? I'm tired and hungry," I said. When Mrs. Krantz turned towards me, I could see that she was crying.

"Just a little longer, Ellie, then we'll go home." She smiled, so I knew that she had happy tears.

"You understand that this is a temporary arrangement, right? We'll have to do a full inspection of your home and you might have to make some changes before we can approve you as a permanent option."

"It is no problem. I am a landlady, I have a man who works for me fixing my apartments. I will fix anything you need, and if it is not good enough we will move."

The woman with the sweater looked nicer than the woman with the silky shirt, even though I liked the silky shirt better.

"I can see that you care very much for this little girl. She is lucky to have you, given the situation."

"Yes. It is my honor to care for her."

The woman in the sweater patted Mrs. Krantz on the knee. "We'll get you home in about an hour. More paperwork, of course."

An hour seemed like a long time to me, but it went by super quick, because now I knew that I would get to go home with Mrs. Krantz. Her house smelled funny, but it was next door to mine so I knew that I could get Paddy from my shelf.

Since Mrs. Krantz was our landlady she already had a key to our house and everything. She told me I could bring anything I wanted over, and I could get more stuff later too. I grabbed Paddy right away, and my Strawberry Shortcake pajamas. At first I was going to take my pillow, but I decided to grab Mommy's pillow instead, because it smelled like her. I also took my school backpack and an outfit for the next day. My arms were getting kind of full by then, so I was glad that Mrs. Krantz was already putting my toothbrush and paste in a little plastic bag, and my banana soap with the koala toy inside. Mommy said that if I was careful to wash every day, I could get the toy out in two weeks. I was really close to getting that toy, and I hoped Mrs. Krantz would let me keep it.

Mrs. Krantz made me a special dinner from a green box she got out of the freezer. She told me that it was kosher Salisbury steak. I wanted a grilled cheese sandwich instead, but the steak was yummy. I especially liked the sauce. Mrs. Krantz let me have two scoops of ice cream since I ate all of my dinner. She only had vanilla, and didn't even have chocolate syrup. Mommy and I always had chocolate syrup, even if the ice cream is already chocolate. I asked if we could go to my house and get the chocolate syrup, but Mrs. Krantz said that she was too tired. Vanilla ice cream is still pretty yummy.

Mrs. Krantz didn't eat very much of her dinner. I think it wasn't as yummy as mine; it had olives in it. It was only seven-thirty when we finished dinner, but Mrs. Krantz said that it was bedtime. I don't usually go to bed until eight o'clock, and I think Mrs. Krantz was sleepier than me. I asked her if I could read a book until eight o'clock since it wasn't really my bedtime yet. Mrs. Krantz doesn't have any books for kids, but Mrs. Ellison let me take a book home from school and I had it in my backpack. I was super smart to bring my backpack.

Mrs. Krantz's bed smelled really funny, like soup, and it was kind of dusty too. It made me sneeze. I was also really smart for bringing Mommy's pillow. It made me feel better since this was the first time I had to sleep in a room all alone. Mrs. Krantz showed me that I could turn the lights on and off just by clapping, so I didn't have to get up. That was fun, so I clapped a bunch until my head hurt. Mrs. Krantz tucked me in, but she didn't do it like Mommy does.

"Can we go back to the hospital tomorrow?" I asked.

"No, Ellie. Why would you want to go back there?" She looked super tired, the way Mommy looks when she has to work a double shift and doesn't get home until morning.

"Mommy's stuck at the hospital. She'll be lonely if we don't go visit her."

Once we were playing water balloons at school, and one of the older kids showed me how to poke one with a needle. The water slowly leaked out of the tiny hole, and I could barely feel it getting smaller in my hand. Mrs. Krantz's face made me think of that balloon.

"Oh Ellie. Celeste…Mommy, she's…not stuck at the hospital." Mrs. Krantz was crying again, but these weren't happy tears.

"That's what the man with the brown tie said. He said she wasn't coming home from the hospital because she was in a bad accident." I was sad that I wouldn't get to sleep next to Mommy anymore, but I had her pillow with me. I would have to go see her, like Daddy came to see me. Maybe I would be sad like Daddy was sometimes, but I wouldn't drink all the yucky stuff he did, so maybe Mommy would come home again.

"Ellie, *ketzele*." Mrs. Krantz was crying a lot now. Her voice got all stuck in her throat.

"It's okay, Mrs. Krantz." I patted her knee like the nice lady in the sweater.

"No, Ellie. It is not okay right now. We can't go see your Mommy. She...she died because of the bad accident. We can't see her anymore."

I thought for a minute. Mrs. Ellison said it's better to think before you talk. It was hard to remember.

"Is she dead like Snow White?"

"What?"

"Well, Snow White died because she bit into that bad apple, after the witch tricked her. All the dwarves were sad because they thought she would never talk to them again or anything, but when the prince came and kissed her she woke up. Is Mommy dead like Snow White?"

"No, *ketzele*. Mommy is dead like your school hamster."

I sucked air through my teeth, because my lips wouldn't open. My school hamster died because we didn't feed him for too long. He got all cold and stiff and didn't move anymore. Mrs. Ellison buried him under a tree.

"But...but Mommy can't be dead like a hamster, she's a person! Mrs. Ellison...Mrs. Ellison said people are different from animals."

"I know, Ellie, but humans and animals both die eventually."

"When they're old!" I shouted. "Mommy wasn't old! Mommy was young, younger than *you*!"

I knew it was wrong to hit, but I hit Mrs. Krantz. I hit her on her big saggy boobs. She didn't spank me or even put me in a time-out. Instead she hugged me. She hugged me so tight I could hear her heart thumping while she cried and cried.

．•．

The school bus stopped two blocks away from my house, and Mrs. Krantz's house. I lived with Mrs. Krantz since Mrs. Ellison was using raindrops on our calendar for April. Now there were flowers for May, but it was still rainy outside. Mommy used to meet me at the school bus, but Mrs. Krantz's hips were old and creaky. I knew how to get home by myself anyway. Mrs. Ellison said that I'm very mature for my age. I was in charge of making sure Swishy the fish got fed every school day. So I guess I could walk home from the bus.

Even though I knew Mommy died, I wished so hard that Mommy would be waiting at the bus stop, and I thought maybe my wish would come true. Of course she wasn't. She got buried on a big hill. My chest hurt, and I started to cry while I walked to Mrs. Krantz's house. Cold air makes tears sting my face, but it felt kind of good.

Mrs. Ellison told me that I should be extra good to show Mrs. Krantz I was very grateful. Mrs. Krantz usually cried when I was sad, so I tried to be happy for her before I opened the door. It was nice and warm inside, even if it did smell funny.

"Mrs. Krantz, I'm home! Mrs. Ellison put me in charge of feeding Swishy the fish today, because I am very mature for my age." I put my backpack by the door and took my boots off before I walked onto the carpet. In my house we had linoleum, and Mommy didn't care about mud. Mrs. Krantz had carpets with little white flowers on them, so she wants me to be careful with my shoes. She wears slippers all the time, but she said it was okay if I just wear socks.

"Mrs. Krantz?" I called down the hallway. Usually she was in the kitchen getting a snack ready for me by the time I came home from school.

"In here, *ketzele*," Mrs. Krantz said. Her voice sounded scratchy. She was in the living room, sitting in her special rocking chair in front of the tv. There was a show with people in bright clothes yelling at each other, but there was no sound coming out of the television.

"Did you lose the remote?" I asked. Once Mommy said I couldn't watch cartoons until we found the remote. It took four days.

"The remote? Oh no, Ellie, I was just taking a little nap." Mrs. Krantz didn't get up, so I thought she might still be sleepy.

"I don't have to take naps anymore. Now I have enough energy for the whole day, and I don't even get cranky."

"That's right. Sometimes old people need naps to keep from getting cranky at night," Mrs. Krantz said. She looked very tired, and her hands were shaky.

"Do you need medicine or something?" I asked.

"No, *ketzele*, I'm fine. Could you make yourself something to eat? There are granola bars in the cabinet if you'd like them. They're chocolate chip."

"Hooray!" I dashed into the kitchen. Mommy didn't like me to eat sugar after school, but Mrs. Krantz didn't mind so much. Chocolate was an extra special treat. I got the box out and took one.

When I came back into the living room, Mrs. Krantz was asleep again. I had some spelling words to memorize, so I took my backpack to the table and started working on them. Mrs. Krantz was very tired, so I stayed quiet. After spelling I worked on adding and subtracting. Math was hard for me, but Mommy was good at it and she would help me. Maybe Mrs. Krantz would help me too, but I wasn't sure how good she was at math. I marked the problems I couldn't figure out and did the rest.

Around five o'clock Mrs. Krantz woke up in a rush. Her breath sounded like dead leaves crunching, but after a few minutes she sounded better. Then she got up and smiled at me.

"You are such a good girl, Ellie. Do you need help with your homework?"

"I need some help with some of the math problems."

"Hm, I will look at them in a moment. Dinner first, I think." She moved towards the kitchen very, very slowly.

"Are you feeling sick?" I asked, following her into the kitchen.

"No, *ketzele*. Just old."

"Do you need to see a doctor?" I asked. One time Mommy had a real bad cough and sounded like Mrs. Krantz. The doctor gave her some red medicine and she felt a lot better.

"I wish there was a doctor who could make me young like you again, but I think I will just have to struggle on until God takes me home." She smiled, leaning over to see what dinners we had in the freezer. My mouth got dry and my face got hot. My chest hurt again, but this time I wasn't sad.

"God will have to wait until I grow up!" I shouted.

"Ellie! What do you mean?"

"My mom already died, and my dad left me in the hospital. God will just have to wait until I can take care of myself. He doesn't need you *and* Mommy anyway. That's just selfish!"

"Oh, Ellie." Mrs. Krantz was sad again, and she opened her arms to hug me.

"No!" I pushed her away, and she made a sound like my push really hurt her. I wasn't even sorry. "You can't leave! You can't just hug me and say it's going to be okay, you have to stay here! I don't...I don't...I don't have anyone else!" I had new tears, these ones were hot and stung my eyes.

"I'm not going anywhere, Ellie."

"But you just *said* — "

"I'm sorry, *ketzele*, I wasn't thinking. I'm just tired. My mother lived until she was a hundred and two, and I'm only seventy-nine. You've got plenty of time to grow up before I go anywhere, Ellie." She smiled, but it wasn't a good friendly smile.

I bumped my big toe against the doorjamb. I felt guilty for yelling at Mrs. Krantz. It wasn't a very grateful thing to do. Still, if I ever got to talk to God, I was going to give him a piece of my mind. That's what Mommy said she did when Daddy came to visit, because he needed to shape up. Shaping up meant being around more often, and not doing stupid things that meant we couldn't be a family together. Shaping up meant he should take better care of me. God had some shaping up to do too.

·•·

Mrs. Ellison was using bright yellow suns for June now. Once I'd been sent home from school early because I hit a kid who called Mommy a name. I wouldn't say I was sorry, so Mrs. Ellison had to send me home. Mrs. Ellison looked more sad than angry when the vice-principal came to get me. Mrs. Krantz never said anything about it, but for a couple of days she would mutter under her breath in Yiddish.

For a week or two, I wanted to be a bad kid. I didn't do my homework, and I didn't line up the first time I was told. Once I tricked the hall monitor so I could go sit on the swings during the math part of the day.

It was starting to rain, and the sand was flat. The whole world smelled like wet concrete, and that made it okay to cry. I missed Mommy. I missed her smell. Her pillow just smelled like me now. Mommy would spank me for cutting class. Mrs. Krantz was too sad and too tired to punish me for anything.

Today I had to get Mrs. Krantz to sign a written warning from school. I stuffed it down into the bottom of my backpack while Mrs. Ellison was watching me, glaring at her so she would know I wasn't going to give it to Mrs. Krantz and she couldn't make me. Mrs. Ellison frowned and put her hands on my shoulders.

"Listen, Ellie. I will still love you no matter how angry you are or how bad you act, you hear me?" She had sad eyes, and I knew she wanted a hug. I was tired of grown ups who needed hugs, tired of being happy so they wouldn't be so sad. If Mrs. Krantz could be too tired to make dinner, I could be too tired to give hugs. And if Daddy could just walk away and leave, I could too.

I tried to stay mad all the way home on the bus. I didn't want to feel bad for making Mrs. Ellison sad, or for being a bad kid. When it was time for my stop, I didn't look at the corner, because I didn't want to hope that Mommy would be there anymore. On the walk to Mrs. Krantz' house, I screwed up my face into a tight knot so I couldn't even want to cry.

When I got home, the door was hanging open. Mrs. Krantz's cane was lying down in the hall.

"Mrs. Krantz?"

A yellow striped cat stood in the middle of the living room, its tail standing up and twitching back and forth. Mrs. Krantz didn't have a cat. The cat glared at me with its green eyes like I didn't belong here. Then I saw Mrs. Krantz's rumpled grey socks. They always slid down around her ankles and she complained that her shins got too cold. But what were they doing on the floor in the living room? Mrs. Krantz didn't leave laundry sitting around.

As I moved around the sofa, I saw that the sock was still on Mrs. Krantz's foot, her foot was attached to her leg and her whole long body, crumpled on the floor. Her mouth hung open, and I could see her red tongue. Her white arm with all its loose skin was stretched above her head.

I wanted to touch her, wanted to see if she was cold like my school hamster. But I was afraid. What if she was hurt really badly, and not dead? Would she be mad at me for letting her get hurt? Would she still be able to take care of me? What if she was really dead? Would I get lost in the foster system?

I remembered a song we sang in school, about what to do in an accident. *Stay calm, stay cool! You know what to do.* I took a deep breath and tried to think cool thoughts. I thought about ice cubes and penguins. I looked for the phone to call 911. That's what you were supposed to do in an accident. Then the police or firefighters would come and take care of things. I dialed 911 and waited for an answer.

"Emergency operations, what can I do for you?" a bored voice asked.

"Mrs. Krantz had an accident. She's lying on the floor."

"What is your name?"

"I'm Ellie. You need to send the policemen right away. I think she's hurt really bad."

"Is she breathing?"

"I don't know. Her mouth is open."

"Can you go see if she's breathing?" The operator seemed mad at me, but I didn't want to check Mrs. Krantz' breath. If she really was…dead, I didn't want to touch her cold skin. I wanted her to be sleeping in her chair, waiting for me to come home. So I just got mad right back at that operator.

"I don't know how, and it's not my job. That's a grown up job."

"How long has she been lying on the floor?"

"I don't know. I just got home from school."

"What's your address, Ellie?"

"I'm not at my house, I'm at Mrs. Krantz's house."

"Is it on 20th Avenue South?"

"I think so. That's the street my house is on, and it's really close."

"All right, I've sent out some paramedics, and they'll be there in a few minutes. Just stay put and they'll take care of you."

"Are they going to put me in the foster system?"

"I don't know anything about that." The operator hung up.

Maybe a really good girl would have waited to see if the paramedics would put her in the foster system. I didn't know exactly what a paramedic was anyway, and I didn't wait and see. I'd had enough of that.

I remembered Mrs. Ellison saying she would love me no matter what. That's what I needed. I needed a grown up, a young one, who loved me and would help me know what to do. This was grown up stuff, like the tv shows Mommy watched after I went to bed.

I went outside again, but I shooed the cat out with me. I was afraid it would hurt Mrs. Krantz before the paramedics came. I didn't know how to get back to school, but I thought I would follow where the bus went. I walked the two blocks to where the bus dropped me off. I looked both ways before crossing the big street and ran as fast as I could. A car still honked as it zoomed by.

I did my best to follow where the bus went, but the bus makes lots of turns. Other kids knew how to take city busses, but Mommy said they weren't safe for little kids. Of course, Mommy also didn't let me walk far by myself, and it was a long way to the school.

I wondered if Mrs. Ellison would be angry that I hadn't gotten Mrs. Krantz to sign my warning, especially after I was so mean. Maybe she would feel sorry for me because Mrs. Krantz had fallen down.

I ran into a big wooden fence that wouldn't let me go any farther. The bus used a special bridge to get across the really big road, the one with no crosswalks. But I couldn't use the special bridge because there wasn't any sidewalk. I knew better than to step off the sidewalk unless it was in a marked crosswalk. Mrs. Ellison taught us that, and I wanted her to be proud of me when I found her.

So I followed the big wooden fence and I found a bridge just for people. I went up the stairs and started walking across the bridge. The bridge was a sidewalk hanging in the air, with a cage to keep people from falling off. I knew the cage was probably strong, but I was still scared. Cars zoomed under me, honking their horns, making a bad stink in the air. When I got to the highest part, I got too scared to walk. I got on my hands and knees and crawled. I made it all the way across, but my knees were scraped from the sidewalk and they stung. Mrs. Ellison would fix them up with her first aid kit; I just had to find her.

I kept walking. I found a park that was in a wedge between two streets and I decided to stay there for a minute. A park was a safe place, and other kids were there, so I sat on one of the swings. I had a little bit of leftover scared-ness from the bridge, and I needed a rest. I pumped my legs hard and made the swing go high.

After I got tired of the swing I felt a different kind of scared. I'd never been to this park before. I would remember its funny shape. I didn't know where I was, or where school was. I couldn't remember exactly how to get home either. It would be dark really soon. My chest hurt.

Another kid wanted a turn on the swing, and his mom asked if I would get off.

"You've been on there a long time, little girl," she said. She was fake-nice, like the principal when he came to visit our classroom. "Where's your mother?"

"Mommy was in a car accident, and she died in the hospital," I said. I jumped off the swing and landed with a big thump, spraying sand on the little boy who wanted the swing.

"Who's here watching you?" she asked. Her voice sounded squeaky and scared.

"No one. I'm trying to find my teacher, Mrs. Ellison. I go to Longfellow Elementary School, do you know where that is?"

"Are you on a field trip? Did you get lost?" the lady asked.

Now she sounded mean. I didn't like her.

"I'm not lost, and I'm never going to be lost. You leave me alone, your son can't even pump the swing." I said, pointing to the little boy swinging his fat legs. I walked away from her fast. That was just the kind of person who would put a little girl like me in the foster system.

I had to cross another big street, but then everything got quieter. The sun was going down, and I was glad it was summer. If it was wintertime I would be frozen already. Still, I knew it was really bad to be walking alone after dark. Mommy told me there are bad people in the city who will hurt little girls. Whenever we went to the grocery store after dark I would hold Mommy's hand so tight while we walked inside. I didn't want a bad person to jump out and grab me.

When I got to the next big street it was really dark. The streetlights turned on as I came to a big intersection. All the cars had their lights on too, which just made the scary corners darker. I knew I was in trouble. If I did find Mrs. Ellison she would be really mad. Even though I really liked Mrs. Ellison, she might not understand that I'd meant to walk right to the school. Getting lost was an accident.

Someone touched my shoulder and I jumped back.

"Hey, little girl." A big man with a gold tooth smiled at me. His breath smelled bad. "Where's your mommy?"

My lip trembled, but I didn't want to cry in front of the man. He was dirty and scary. "She's in the store!" I shouted. "She'll be out any minute!"

The man backed away and waved, still smiling. I knew it was wrong to lie, and I knew it was wrong to be out by myself. It was probably wrong to leave Mrs. Krantz alone when she was hurt. I didn't like being a bad girl; I wanted to be good again. All the grown ups liked me when I was a good girl. Now there were bad people who wanted to hurt bad little girls and I was scared.

There was a bus stop nearby and I went into the little booth because there was a light in there. I was scared of bad people, so I hid under the bus stop bench. Maybe no one would notice a bad little girl under a bench. Curled up in a ball, I started to cry. I cried quietly, because I didn't want the bad people to find me, but I cried for a long time. I wondered if I would ever be found, and where I would go if Mrs. Krantz really was dead like my school hamster.

Since there weren't any grown ups around, I decided to talk to God. He was supposed to be really big, so maybe he had big ears too and could hear me talking super quiet.

"God, I don't know if you're listening, but if you are I need some help. I need some help right now. I'm lost and it's dark and there are bad people around. I don't want to be lost in the foster system, and I don't want to be lost on this street either. Send someone to find me, God. I want to be found."

My arms and legs ached. A car drove by the bus stop and its bright light flashed in my eyes. A couple people walked into the bus stop, and I squeezed my eyes shut and hoped I was invisible. I thought of clear things like plastic wrap and glasses of water. The cement floor felt dirty.

A woman poked her face under the bench. "Hello, I'm Sister Angela. Are you lost?" She was a tall black lady in jeans and a big yellow t-shirt. Her hands and face were smooth chocolate brown like Mommy's. She didn't look like a bad person. Slowly, I nodded.

"It's not safe for you to be out here by yourself. Would you like to come into the church while we call your parents?" She held out her long, smooth hand and I took it. I thought angels would be white, all dressed in white, with big halos and wings and long blonde hair. But this was the angel God sent for me, and she looked like Mommy. I couldn't stop staring at her. She took my hand and walked towards a big white building with a cross on top.

"What's your name?" she asked.

"Ellie," I answered in a very little voice. I couldn't believe I was talking to a real angel. She was holding my hand tight so I was safe.

"Do you know your phone number?"

I gulped. "Yes." I was afraid to tell her that no one would answer my phone, because no one lived in my house anymore. I looked up into her deep black eyes. She wouldn't let me get lost again; she found me.

"My mommy died. Daddy didn't live with us."

"Oh, you poor thing!" Sister Angela cried. "We'll figure it out, don't you worry."

"Mrs. Krantz fell down," I said quieter. I hoped the angel wouldn't be mad at me because I left Mrs. Krantz alone.

"Who is Mrs. Krantz?"

"The lady who was taking care of me. She fell down, and I think she might be dead too. I called 911."

"That was the right thing to do." She smiled. She didn't ask me why I wasn't with Mrs. Krantz, or why I was walking by myself. We got to the church and she led me inside the big main doors, past a bunch of statues of people. Some statues looked sad, and some looked proud, and some looked like my angel. They looked like people who would help a lost little girl.

We came to the front of the church where there was a big slanted table full of candles in red holders. Some candles were flickering gold and red light, and some were dark.

"Sit here, sweetie. I'm going to make a few calls and find out how to take care of you. Don't wander off, okay? I don't want you to be lost again."

"I don't want to be lost again either," I agreed.

"That's a good girl." She patted my shoulder before she left.

I curled up in a little ball, since God heard me when I was in a ball before. "Thank you, God. She's perfect."

It was a long time before Sister Angela came back, but I sat still

because I wanted to be a good girl again. Some people came and
went, but they were all very quiet and they didn't bother me. They
knelt at the edge of the benches before they sat down. Some of them
knelt in front of the flickering candles and lit some new ones. I
wondered if they blew out all the candles at night. Mommy said it's
very important to keep an eye on candles while they're burning. I
liked the candles, and since there weren't any grown ups watching
them, I kept my eye on them so they didn't catch anything on fire.

A woman came and prayed in front of the candles for a long
time. She held her hands together flat like pictures of people
praying, and she prayed out loud. Most people are super quiet when
they're praying; they know God has big ears too. This lady wanted
to make extra-sure God heard her. When she stood up she bumped
right into me. She looked super tired, like how Mrs. Krantz looked
sometimes, or like Mommy after a long shift.

"I'm so sorry, please excuse me. I guess I worked a little too
hard today," she said.

"That's okay. I hope you can sleep for a long time," I said,
giving her my friendliest smile. I was an extra good girl now.

The woman stared at me for a long time, and I wondered if I
said something bad.

"I didn't mean that you look ugly. Mommy used to say she
would feel like a million bucks if she could get enough sleep. I just
want you to feel like a million bucks."

"You speak Portuguese," the woman said. "You speak it
perfectly."

I shrugged. I was just talking Portuguese because she was. "My
Daddy was from Brazil when he's was real little. Mrs. Krantz speaks
Portuguese too, but she has a funny accent. Mrs. Krantz says that it's
very important to know about both sides of my family, even if
Daddy is a no-good drunk."

The woman started to cry, but I didn't know why. I hadn't said
anything super sad.

"Mrs. Krantz said he was a no-good drunk, not me. I think he's just very sad because Mommy...well, she died."

A big sob came out of the woman's throat. "You're Ellie, aren't you?"

"Hey, you know my name! Did God tell you what my name is? I asked him to send someone to find me, but Sister Angela already did. Maybe God sent you too just in case."

The woman hugged me so tight, tighter than Mrs. Krantz had held me.

"God did send me, Ellie. God sent me all the way from Brazil for you. I'm your aunt, I'm Tasía. I have been praying and praying that you would be found. Your Daddy told me that you were lost and it made me so sad. I lit candles for you every night."

"Those candles are for me?"

"Yes, they are. Where have you been all this time?"

"I was living with Mrs. Krantz, because she came with me to the hospital and she didn't want me to get lost in the foster system. She fell down, and she might be dead. I was too scared to check."

"My poor niece. You needed family so badly, and I didn't know where you were."

She seemed sad, but I thought this was a time to be happy. "I'm glad you found me today, even though Sister Angela found me first. We have to find out if Mrs. Krantz is okay."

"We will, Ellie. We'll see if Mrs. Krantz is all right. You won't be alone anymore, not if I can help it."

She still had her arm around me, and I snuggled into her side. This lady was a really good hugger.

"Are you really my aunt?" I'd never had any family except Mommy and Daddy. And Mrs. Krantz, she was good family too.

"Yes, Ellie. I am your daddy's sister. If Mrs. Krantz can't take care of you, you can come live with me."

"Really?" I couldn't believe it. This was even better than an angel. My aunt was a grown up. She wasn't quite as young as Mommy or Mrs. Ellison, but she was young enough and strong. God wouldn't want to take her home for a long, long time.

"Yes, really. You are my blood and I will love you and take care of you no matter what."

I smiled. "That's just what I wanted."

.•.

Mrs. Krantz wasn't dead, but she was hurt real bad. So bad that she had to stay in her bed all the time and a nurse came every day. Even the nice lady with the big sweaters didn't think that I should live with her. My Aunt Tasía didn't think that the lady with the big sweaters would like her, since she wasn't quite American yet, but that didn't matter. I didn't think it would anyway; Brazilian is just as good as American. Mrs. Krantz still is in charge of me *officially*, but Aunt Tasía takes care of me most of the time.

She lives in my old house now, and I live there most of the time too. I like her more every day. She gives really good hugs and makes yummy snacks. She talks in Portuguese all the time. I love how she talks; she makes all the words more pretty than my Daddy ever did, and she doesn't sound funny like when Mrs. Krantz talks Portuguese. I'm helping Aunt Tasía learn English, which is easy because she is super smart.

Today when the bus stopped, Aunt Tasía was waiting for me with her pretty smile and bright clothes. She was the most beautiful lady, except for Mommy. Since Mrs. Krantz let us live in my old house, Aunt Tasía got off work early on school days and always waited at the bus stop. Everything was better since my angel helped me find Aunt Tasía.

"Hello, Ellie. How was school today?" Aunt Tasía asked.

"Good."

"What did you do?"

"We played dodge ball during gym."

"Oh? Do you like that game?"

"No. I like it better when we play red rover."

"Oh." Aunt Tasía didn't know dodge ball or red rover, so I had to explain. I explain a lot of stuff to Aunt Tasía, but that's okay. Grown ups explain stuff to me all the time, and I like to have a turn.

When we got home there were warm cheese rolls waiting on the table, and some special juice Aunt Tasía found at a Brazilian bakery. It was from a kind of fruit we don't have in America, and it was the yummiest juice ever. I love the cheese rolls too, and I ate two of them.

"Not all at once, Ellie. Finish chewing first."

I tried to slow down, because I wanted to be a good girl for my Aunt Tasía. She'd come all the way from Brazil to take care of me. She told me how long it took her to get here, and all the kinds of things she rode on. Trucks, bicycles, trains, busses, even a donkey!

"We have to go out shopping today," Aunt Tasía said. She didn't look excited.

"What kind of shopping?" Since she was distracted I popped another roll in my mouth and tried to chew it up before she noticed.

"I asked you to slow down, Ellie." Aunt Tasía had a scary way of talking when I did something wrong.

"Sorry."

Aunt Tasía sighed. "Target."

Aunt Tasía did not like Target. All the signs were hard for her to read and it was easy for her to get lost. Sometimes people were rude to her when she was lost. Aunt Tasía worked very hard during the day, so she did not like to get lost in a big store at night.

"It's okay, Tía." Aunt Tasía liked it when I called her Tía. That's what she called her favorite aunt. She smiled. "I'll be a super-good helper," I told her.

"I know, Ellie. This time I have made a complete list so we'll be able to find just what we need. I even put a piece of candy on the list, and you pick it out in the aisle while we're waiting. We won't buy anything that's not on the list, okay?"

"Okay, Tía." A piece of candy was a good prize.

When we got to the store, I kept my eyes on my power puff tennis shoes. If I didn't look around I wouldn't see things that I wanted, and that would help me be a good helper for Aunt Tasía.

"What's next on the list?" I asked. Aunt Tasía's face looked like Lonnie Adler's when he had to do really hard math.

"You wanted some cereal," she said. Slowly, she sounded out "cereal" in English. It sounded funny, but I didn't laugh.

"That's close by, right over there by the granola bars and other breakfast stuff," I said, pointing.

"Okay, Ellie. You pick out your favorite kind of cereal, nothing too sugary, and I'll get some batteries from across the aisle, there." She pointed.

"Okay, Tía." Picking my own cereal was a special treat, especially after living with Mrs. Krantz. Mrs. Krantz only had raisin bran, and she got kinda mad if I just picked the raisins out.

They had Honey Nut Cherios, but I liked Frosted Mini-Wheats too. Aunt Tasía didn't always let me pick the cereal, so I wanted to make a good decision. I held both boxes and squeezed my eyes shut, thinking about how they taste.

I heard someone sniffling so I opened my eyes. A nice looking man was trying to pick between two different kinds of granola bars, but he must have had a harder time picking than me, because he was crying some.

"It's hard to pick sometimes," I said. I didn't want him to feel bad. Mrs. Ellison says that everything is difficult for someone.

"What?" The man looked at me and then at his granola bars. He threw both boxes into his cart and wiped his eyes quick with his sleeve.

"You look sad," I told him. "It's okay to cry if you're sad."

"Yeah. I know." The man smiled a tiny weeny smile. "Usually I tell other people that it's okay to cry."

"So it's okay for you too." I waited, because I thought he might leave, but he didn't. "Why are you sad?"

"I'm okay."

"People don't cry when they are okay; they only cry when they're sad," I said. The man shrugged. He looked like he might need to cry a little more.

"My wife is going to leave me." His voice was so super sad, I thought I might want to cry too.

"You seem like a very nice man." I hoped that would make him feel better.

"I am nice, but I'm not a very good husband. I'm too tired."

That man was not talking to me, really. I bet he was talking to God. Maybe he needed help.

"I know! I'll pray for you. I once prayed that God would help me when I was really scared and he sent an angel to help me."

Now the man looked at me for real. "I don't believe in angels."

"Well, they probably will help you anyway." I patted the man's arm and held his hand. Aunt Tasía always held my hand while we prayed, and I liked that a lot. I squeezed my eyes shut and tried to think of a really good prayer.

"Dear God, this man is very sad because his wife doesn't want to live with him anymore, and he loves her very much. Please come help him to be a good husband so she will stay with him a long, long time. Give him lots of energy so he is not tired anymore."

When I opened my eyes the man still looked pretty sad. "Don't worry," I told him. "The angel will come."

"Ellie! What are you doing bothering that man?" Aunt Tasía said, rushing to jerk me back. I think she thought the man was bad guy, but I knew he was nice.

"I was just helping him because he's very sad," I explained.

"Sorry," Aunt Tasía said in English. "Sorry to bother."

The man waved his hand and shrugged before walking out of the aisle. I guess he didn't need any more granola bars.

"You should say, 'sorry to bother *you*.'"

"You should not talk to strangers in the store. It isn't safe."

"It was okay, Tía. He was sad, so I prayed for him."

Aunt Tasía looked at me like I was worth a million bucks and gave me one of her very best hugs.

An Infusion of Sunlight

The last patient of the day was always the hardest. Today it was particularly difficult to focus since my mind was preoccupied with getting home to see my new wife, my Alice. It was only Tuesday, but I already longed for the weekend. I struggled to concentrate on the obstinate teenager on my couch, oscillating between the impossible task of keeping my eyelids from drooping and the crushing guilt of giving this girl less than my full effort. She sat across from me with her arms folded, glaring from the soft loveseat she was sitting on without relaxing a single muscle. I felt sorry for her. She didn't want to be here, and she had the bad luck to end up with me for her therapist.

In college I had every intention of taking my hard-earned psychiatric skills onto the streets, to the tragically undiagnosed masses we read about in our classes. After graduation, a mortgage and a penchant for expensive wilderness sports pinned me to a more respectable clientele. That was a decade ago, and I was still making feeble attempts to counsel the spoiled kids of suburbanites who didn't have the common sense to talk to their kids themselves. I felt pity for these kids, but I had no idea how to help them. The skills I'd learned in college were never honed to a sharp point of expertise, and none of the classes I'd taken bore any relation to this field. The angry girl across from me had a legitimate reason to be peeved.

"You know my mom paid over a hundred dollars for me to be

here, and you're just sitting there." Terrance was her name. I had it written on the pad in front of me.

"You refused to answer my questions, Terrance." This was true; I just hadn't made the appropriate follow-up effort.

"So you just give up? Not much of a doctor, are you?"

Nope. "If you're concerned that you're not getting enough out of our sessions, you could be a little more cooperative."

"Whatever."

She seemed to grow even more taut as she glanced at the clock. I followed her gaze and found that we had half our session left. I thought about laying my head down on Alice's stomach, listening to her heartbeat. Somehow, somehow I had to get there from here. Then I could finally rest without this horrible guilt. Guilt, right, I should be paying attention to Terrance.

"Do you know why your parents wanted you to come see me?" I asked. She rolled her eyes.

"Isn't it written on one of the forms or something?"

"I didn't ask you if *I* knew why you're here, I asked if *you* know."

The girl leveled me with glare. "Yes."

The word came very distinctly. She caught me in a mistake no first-year psychology student with any self-respect would make. I asked a close-ended question.

"Can you tell me about it?" I asked, as if being ridiculously obtuse would somehow correct my earlier mistake.

"No thanks."

The last dregs of motivation were seeping out my pores. I hoped Terrance couldn't see the hopelessness in my eyes. I looked at my notes, but the page was nearly blank. I had written Terrance's name, her age, and then "possible drug use?" Basically what I'd gotten out of talking briefly with the parents, and not much detail on that.

I told myself that it was really only fifteen more minutes, nothing compared to the seven hours and forty-five minutes I'd already worked. With one final effort, I gathered my last bits of energy.

"Look, Terrance."

"I like Terri," she cut into my sentence like she'd been dying to talk to me all along.

"Terri, then. Even if your parents are paying for this session, you're only going to get out of it what you put into it. If you don't want to talk to me, we can just sit here. But if you would like to tell me what's been bothering you lately, then I might be able to help."

Terrance had black eyes, and they wavered as she looked me over. I knew what she was seeing; a guy who couldn't understand her development as a woman, who was so much older than her that there was no chance I could relate to her. When I was her age, cell phones didn't even exist. Despite all that, ten years of experience told me that she was considering it, thinking about opening up to me.

"Nothing." She tightened the fold of her arms and looked away.

"Okay." I said that like it was her choice after all, so she had no one to blame but herself. I knew better. I was the professional, the grown up, and it was my job to draw her out. Feeling my failure like molasses in my joints, I checked the clock again.

"Looks like our time's about up."

"You don't have to be so cheerful about it," Terrance mumbled.

As she left, something caught my eye. Low on her neck there was a small purple spot. A bruise. If anyone else saw it, they would assume it was a hickey, and maybe it was. To my eye, it looked too finger-shaped. Of course that wasn't conclusive. Still, I'd have to send a line over to my contact at the Department of Human

Services so she could check it out, which was just another way of admitting that I wasn't skilled enough to find out what was going on.

After Terrance left, I started working on my paperwork. As I let my pen glide along the familiar check boxes and signature lines, I felt my eyes drooping again. When I woke up the clock had ticked off a half an hour. I rubbed my eyes and checked to see what else I had left to do. Quickly finishing up the last form, I grabbed my briefcase and headed for the door. Alice would wonder what had taken me so long. We hadn't been married long enough for me to admit that I'd fallen asleep at my desk.

By the time I was on the freeway, rush hour traffic had died down. Someone honked at me as I pulled around a sharp turn, and I sunk down into my seat to avoid their angry gaze. As I came closer to home the traffic thinned out, and my driving took less and less thought. Although I was still mentally exhausted, I enjoyed having the space to let my mind wander to thoughts of Alice, anticipating seeing her in mere moments. My dazzling bride.

Unlike my reluctant career, Alice relentlessly pursued a job in the corporate world ever since she graduated from Brown. I was shocked when she offered to move to Minneapolis after our marriage; I knew I'd never land a job that paid as much as I was making now. I couldn't interview with any conviction. But Alice was sure she would find a new job and work her way up. "Income increases quickest when you switch companies," she'd said. It was impossible to argue with Alice.

When I pulled into the garage, she was already bursting through the door. I'd barely pulled to a complete stop before she was jerking the car door open.

"I'm so glad you're home! I've been so bored. Why are you home so late? You told me that you got off at five-thirty sharp so I ordered pizza at five. It's a little cold now. I ordered it too early, but I just couldn't wait for the day to end. I job searched all day long and

I can't find anything. Everyone told me the Minneapolis job market was booming, but there is seriously nothing. It's probably because Target has a hiring freeze in corporate right now, and they seem to set the tone for everything around here. I called Honeywell, 3M, Pillsbury, everyone. Crazy huh? Oh, do you need help?" she asked, reaching for my briefcase. I found myself snatching it away from her. Her strong blue eyes widened in surprise.

"Sorry," I mumbled. "I keep confidential stuff in here."

"I wasn't going to read the stuff, I just wanted to help."

"Of course. Just slow down a little." I smiled at her. She gave me a quick look before moving back to the kitchen.

"You don't mind that I ordered pizza, do you?"

"No."

"I got the supreme kind that you like, I'll just pick the onions off. And you'll have to take a breath mint before you kiss me." Alice winked from the door, but I still wasn't ready to get out of the car.

"Uh-huh." I was looking for my water bottle. Had I left it at the office?

"Are you coming? It's already getting cold. Oh, do you want to order a movie tonight? I was thinking that new Bond movie looks mildly interesting. Good for a weeknight, don't you think?"

"I…" I still couldn't find my water bottle, and I had a distinct memory of carrying it out of my office with me.

"Are you having trouble?" Alice asked, looking irritated.

"I can't find my water bottle. Oh, there it is." My fingers brushed the smooth surface as I felt under the passenger-side seat.

"Come on," Alice said, gesturing for me to hurry up. I grabbed the water bottle and tried to quickly get out of the car. The cap clicked off and poured water all over my pants.

"Oh great." I brushed the excess moisture off with the palm of my hand, shaking my briefcase so none of the papers inside would be damaged.

"It's just a little water." Alice leaned against the doorjamb, looking sultry. Or maybe she was just bored. "Consider it a good excuse to take your pants off," she said, raising an eyebrow. That suggestion should have broken me out of my seriousness, but it just reminded me how weary I felt.

"I'll do that." I double-checked to make sure I had my car keys in hand before locking the car door and slamming it shut.

"You're slow," Alice said with a smile as I approached the door.

"I'm meticulous," I corrected, avoiding her gaze but brushing her soft hand as I passed. I didn't want her to know how that comment pricked me.

"Do you want a beer with your pizza?" Alice moved into the kitchen with the sharp efficiency for which she was known and feared.

I imagined all the energy still pounding in her veins after a whole day in the house. If only there was a way to even out our energy levels so that she wouldn't feel cooped up and I could a have pleasant conversation. All day I'd pictured being with Alice, but we weren't talking in those pictures, we were just existing together.

"One piece or two? Do you like olives? I can't remember," Alice asked as she loaded a paper plate for me.

"What question do you want me to answer first?" I asked, hoping I sounded amused. It didn't come off that way.

"Hm?" Alice's quick glance looked like fair warning that I was on dangerous ground.

"I think we're up to nine in the last two minutes."

"Really." She gave her attention to removing thin strands of white onion from her pizza. Clearly she was annoyed, and I couldn't blame her. I just wasn't sure I could fix it either. If it was just quiet for a moment, I could gather my thoughts.

"Thanks for ordering the pizza." I took the plate she left for me. The air in the kitchen felt awkward.

"No sweat," she said around a mouthful of the pizza. "Okay if I start the movie?" she asked, moving towards the den.

"I don't – " I held a hand out to stop her. She turned on me with a very scary look, as if to say that I'd already pushed my luck this evening. I looked at my shoes.

"I hate it when you hang your head like that, Peter. It makes me feel like a mean mommy."

"Sorry," I mumbled.

"Did you want to say something?" she asked crisply.

"I don't usually take food into the den. But it's fine, I'm sure you'll be careful," I added quickly. That didn't come out right either.

"Uh-huh." Alice was just looking at me, piercing me with those sharp eyes that summed up all of my insecurities. My palms started to sweat.

"What?" I asked finally.

"I'm just waiting. It seems that you have a very specific idea of what this evening should look like, so I'm waiting for you to tell me what it is so I can stop bothering you." That speech was hard and mean, but her voice quivered ever so slightly on the last part.

"I...I don't really. I'm sorry."

"I'd like to eat dinner with you and watch a movie if that sounds like fun to you. Is there a problem with that?" she asked. I felt like I was at a job interview that wasn't going well.

"Not really."

"Peter, please stop looking at your shoes." Her voice softened, enough so I knew that she knew she was making me uncomfortable. I couldn't imagine how I was making her feel. If only to please her, I raised my eyes to hers.

"I don't usually watch movies on week nights, and I don't usually eat in the den. I don't usually talk to anyone when I get home, actually." She opened her mouth to speak, but I held up my hand to let her know I wasn't finished. "But things are different because you're here, and I'm really glad that you're here." I smiled. Fake and tired as it was, I knew I needed to reassure her. After all, this was my house and my town and my furniture. My routine. She uprooted her whole life for me, and I could adjust some for her.

"So, is it okay if I eat in the den?" Alice asked.

"Of course. This is your house too. Do whatever you'd like."

"Whatever...I'd like?" she asked, raising an eyebrow. Alice's body was sleek and firm, a perfect sculpted result of her philosophy that exercise enhances the mind. Even the way she was standing with her hip against the wall, one hand on her slim waist and the other holding a paper plate on the flat of her palm, seemed a picture of domestic allure. Yet, the idea of connecting with her on that deep level made my eyes drop again. I could barely sum up the strength to eat pizza next to her.

When I looked up she was near tears. Alice almost never cried, but her blue eyes would darken and her cheeks would warm from fresh pink to blushing red, and that's how I knew she was hurting.

"I...I'm sorry. I'm just not...not very good at this," I fumbled. Recovering herself, Alice pushed off the wall so she was standing solidly on both feet. She squared her shoulders and leveled her chin. I imagined that this is how Alice would look in the final round of a tricky business negotiation.

"It's fine. I'm going to eat in here and watch a movie. You do whatever makes you comfortable." She brushed into the den and flipped the television on.

Slowly, I followed her, lugging my plate of pizza. When I sat down next to her, she ignored me. I tried to touch her hand, but her skin was cold under my fingertips, her expression non-responsive. So we let the movie play.

• •

After a few weeks, Alice gave up on me. She loved me, but I'd always known she didn't need me. She was so fiercely independent, so brilliant and motivated, I was never going to be more than a comfort for her. Now I'd failed at that too. Undaunted, Alice started setting up a life for herself that didn't require my comfort or my presence.

When I woke up in the morning she'd be gone, the absence of her running shoes the only sign of where she was. I'd shower, eat my oatmeal, read the newspaper, all the while watching the back door for her. If I'd seen her return, she would be bathed in sweat, her eyes and body glowing with vitality, still moving to the beat of the music in her headphones. But I never got to see her return. The clock would run down to the last minute I could make it to work on time, and I'd have to go.

All day long I'd resolve over and over again that I would be there, really be there when I came home to Alice. It took a herculean effort to keep my mind on my patients, I'd become so focused on being a better husband. Ironically, it was that very effort that wrung the life out of me. When I got home, I could barely answer yes and no questions.

At first Alice would try to get me talking, but she knew a lost cause when she saw one. Now when I came home she'd be pulling away on the rowing machine in the basement, sending e-mails in the home office, or painting the guest bathroom. Half the time she'd already eaten dinner, and occasionally there were leftovers for me. The rest of the time she said she wasn't hungry and that I should go ahead with dinner. I tried to make sure I left something for her, but sometimes I forgot. Either way, she didn't say anything.

We'd been married just over a month, and it felt like we weren't going to make it. I knew it had been sheer, shattering luck that Alice agreed to marry me in the first place, and now I was ruining everything. What was more crushing than that was my complete inability to do anything differently. The harder I tried, the more exhausted I felt, and the worse things became.

On Saturday I laid in bed for an hour after I'd woken up. Alice was long gone, had probably run, showered, and engaged in some project by now. It was after ten. When I did get up a delicious smell greeted me halfway down the stairs. Pancakes.

I was still in my robe and slippers, but Alice was showered and dressed, her hair pulled away from her face and her hands busily preparing a giant breakfast. Her laptop sat open on the kitchen counter and she wiped her hand on a towel before she fingered the touchpad.

"What's all this?" I asked. Alice looked up and smiled. She was devastatingly beautiful; I couldn't believe I was waking up with this woman in my house.

"I thought I'd make a nice breakfast. I found this full meal schedule thing on a website and it looked like fun. While I was at the store I picked up some of that gross energy juice you like so much. I'll be drinking my fresh-squeezed goodness," she said, holding up half a glass of orange juice. "Yours is in the fridge."

"Wow. This is incredible." I gave her the warmest smile I could muster, but she'd already turned away from me.

"I was going to try eggs benedict, but I thought hollandaise sauce was too ambitious for my first fancy breakfast. There's bacon though. I bought two pounds just in case I ruined the first one, but I think we can put one of them in the freezer. This looks okay, doesn't it?" she held up a perfectly crisp piece of bacon for me to examine.

"It's great." I paused, not sure if she wanted something from me. Should I help? She didn't look like she needed help. In fact, she looked like she would have more fun with her fancy breakfast if I wasn't staring at her. "Where's the newspaper?"

"On the porch, I'd imagine. Would you like to go for a walk or something later? The weather is really beautiful and who knows how many days like this there are left. I thought maybe we could go out to the lake; I got stuff for a picnic." She still wasn't looking at me. Instead she was zeroed in on the pancakes, timing them on her wristwatch.

"I'm not sure. It sounds like fun though." I went to the front door to get the paper. Retrieving it from the porch, I came back inside and set it on the counter. The rubber band around it had gotten twisted, so I started working on it with my fingers. Sounds of things sizzling and steaming floated across the counter, signs that I didn't live alone anymore. I liked that.

"Are you going to get dressed?" Alice asked, sounding irritated. I looked up at her in surprise.

"Yes. I'm just trying to get this – "

She leaned across the counter and deftly cut the rubber band with the kitchen scissors. It snapped against my fingers.

"Oh."

"Why don't you go get showered and dressed while I finish up breakfast, then we can eat together and decide what to do today?" she suggested with a half smile. Those blue eyes glittered, her shoulders bent like she was about to lift something heavy, her hand still extended towards me.

This was an olive branch, her offer to try again. I knew this, which was why it was weird to hear myself saying, "I usually read the paper first in the morning."

Alice said nothing, just went back to her cooking. Maybe I was being sensitive, but it seemed like there was less sizzling and steaming and more slamming and banging in the kitchen now.

"I'll go get dressed," I offered, sliding the paper off the counter with a sad flapping sound.

"Whatever you want," she replied without turning.

After that, I did go back upstairs and get in the shower, leaving the limp paper on a corner of the bed as I passed by. The hot water felt good on my shoulders and neck, and I lingered.

Really, what Alice was doing made perfect sense. It was the weekend, and the last few had been eaten up getting the yard ready for the winter and finishing up replacing the vents under the eaves of the house. Perceptive as she was, she knew I was tired and she had very logically hoped that on a day free of work and home projects, I might be more willing to engage with her. She'd done everything she needed to do to make that happen. She even bought my energy juice.

I swirled white soapsuds over my arms and chest. The thing was, I'd just woken up. Even if the day was free, I still wanted some time to settle in, to wake up, and read my newspaper. I enjoyed eating breakfast in my pajamas on the weekends. If she could just let me do that stuff, maybe then we could have a nice day together and we could stop doing this awkward, halting dance. I had distinct memories of really enjoying Alice's company, and I think she had enjoyed mine too. We were smart people, surely we could figure out how to do that again.

After my shower I carefully picked out weather appropriate clothes, pulling out a light sweater in case we did decide to do something outside. I shaved, slapped on some aftershave, and combed my hair. Picking up the pair of shoes I had deemed the most versatile, I walked back downstairs in my socks.

There was no more sizzling and steaming, or banging and slamming for that matter. All the food and dishes had vanished, the laptop had been put away, and Alice was just wiping the last corner of the counter.

"What happened?" I asked. When Alice looked up at me, her eyes were hard, her cheeks flushed a deeper shade of pink.

"You were up there for an hour and a half, Peter."

A glance at the microwave clock told me it was nearly noon.

"Oh." I paused, unsure of what she wanted me to do. I hadn't told her how long I'd be upstairs, I hadn't even thought about it. "Is there still food?"

"Look, Peter." Alice snapped the dishtowel around the handle of the fridge door. This is how Alice would begin a meeting where she was firing someone.

"I'm going camping," I blurted before she could continue. Whatever I was going for, it succeeded in making her pause. "I think it would be good for me, and you by extension. I'm so tired lately. I just need to get away for a couple days."

The constant energy pulsing through Alice's veins seemed to slow for a moment, and the sleek muscle of her arms and legs lost some of their tension. The glowing skin of her face suddenly went slack.

"You're leaving. Aren't you?"

"No," I said. I approached her, and she let me. I took her hand. "I love you. This is all my fault, and I want to make it right."

Her hand was cold and limp in mine, and though I was close to her, her eyes seemed to withdraw. That was self-protection, and it broke my heart. My wife should not have to protect herself from me. If only she knew all the tender feelings I had for her. How could she, when all I asked her to do was go away?

"You do what you have to." She sniffed, trying to pass if off as catty, but I was too close for that. I touched her face.

"You are so fantastic, Alice." I moved in to kiss her, but she pushed off the counter and walked away from me.

"No, Peter. You've hardly glanced at me for weeks, so if you think that you're going to walk down here at noon on a Saturday after I offered to make you a fabulous breakfast, tell me you're running away to the woods, and then I'm going to have sex with you, that is just not going to happen."

"That's not what I – "

"I don't care what you meant. Go camping, go fishing, go do your manly things. Why did you even ask me to marry you if you weren't willing to change anything for me?" she demanded.

"Because you're incredible, and I couldn't help myself," I confessed. Finally, the right words came to my lips at the right time. I smiled, but she didn't.

"You know," she said, sounding like she was gearing up for something big. A long pause followed, and she seemed to deflate. "You're lucky that you're so cute."

I nodded. "I know."

She looked away and shifted her weight. "Are you really going camping?"

Slowly, I nodded again.

"And you don't want me to come with you."

This was not a question, but I shook my head to confirm that I wanted to go alone. She folded her lips into her mouth and let them slide out again, making them red and wet. Tempting.

"I'm not going to sit here waiting for you to figure out if you want to be married. I'm not a decoration."

"I know." And I did.

· • ·

Although I had most of the equipment I needed for a camping trip, I still had to shop for food and other supplies. So I had plenty of time to kick myself for this idiocy. In theory, this would work. I'd get away from the stress of my life for a few days, go fishing, soak in the long silence of solitary camping, and return refreshed and ready to commit to my marriage. But in theory, Alice would still be patiently waiting for me. If she couldn't wait an hour and a half while I showered, why would she sit around for four days while I rejuvenated? Even if she did, how long would a refreshing camping trip last? A week? Two? What then?

My mind started racing, seeming to punctuate each item I threw into the cart. A jar of peanut butter. *She's going to leave me.* A jar of strawberry jam. *If I think my life is meaningless now, how is going to be after I lose my wife?* A bag of tortillas. *I knew I'd never be able to make this work.* Four packages of ramen noodles. *I can't do anything the way I mean to.* By the time I got to the all-important granola and breakfast cereal aisle the rational thoughts had run themselves out. All I could think of was how much I loved Alice, and how I was throwing her away. As I held two boxes of granola bars up for inspection, I felt warm tears in my eyes.

"It's hard to pick sometimes," a friendly little voice said.

"What?" I asked, quickly wiping my eyes. The voice belonged to a little girl with big black eyes. She smiled at me.

"You look sad. It's okay to cry if you're sad."

This was just perfect. I was being counseled by a six-year-old in the breakfast cereal aisle at Super Target. It didn't get any lower than this. The fact that she was giving me really good advice only aggravated my feeling of stupidity.

"Yeah, I know. Usually I tell other people it's okay to cry."

"So it's okay for you, too." She paused, her chubby face full of adult concern. "Why are you sad?"

"I'm okay."

"People don't cry when they're okay; they only cry when they're sad."

I shrugged. "My wife is going to leave me." The words came out before I could think about them, and I realized they came because they were the only answer to an honest question. I was sad because Alice was going to leave me.

"You seem like a very nice man." The little girl perked up her eyebrows, like this compliment would fix all my problems.

"I am nice," I said. If I weren't nice, I would have told this little do-gooder to mind her own business. "But I'm not a very good husband. I'm too tired." So simple, so direct. Why couldn't I talk to Alice like this? That soft, suffocating feeling of overwhelming inadequacy threatened to smother me right here in front of Captain Crunch.

"I know! I'll pray for you. I once prayed that God would help me when I was really scared and he sent an angel to help me."

I shook my head. "I don't believe in angels."

"Well, they probably will help you anyway." The little girl said this like I was being just a little bit silly. She patted my arm and grasped my hand. Her little fingers gripped mine. She squeezed her eyes shut.

"Dear God, this man is very sad because his wife doesn't want to live with him anymore, and he loves her very much. Please come help him to be a good husband so she will stay with him a long, long time. Give him lots of energy so he is not tired anymore."

When she was finished she looked up at me with expectation written all over her, like I was supposed to be fixed. I tried to smile.

"Don't worry. The angel will come." She was so sure. I didn't believe her, but I'd rather be her than me.

An older woman appeared in the aisle and shouted softly at the little girl in a foreign language I couldn't place. The girl responded in the same tongue, easily, seeming undaunted.

"Sorry," the woman said in a strong accent. "So sorry to bother." She took the little girl by the hand and dragged her away, chastising her all the way. Maybe it would have been nice to tell the woman that the little girl was okay, and maybe she would have understood me if I'd tried, but I didn't try. I was still too tired.

·•·

The last pound of my hammer slammed against the last stake and the last strap of my pop-up tent snapped. The four square feet of indoors I had spent the last hour constructing shivered and wilted to the ground. It wasn't supposed to take an hour to set up a pop-up tent, but the wind whipping across the water complicated the operation. I neglected to buy a new tent on my way out of town, opting for the ancient metal poles and musty green canvass of my father's backpacking tent. Now dusk was threatening, so I had to get the tent up in a hurry, or continue with flashlight between my teeth.

My body was already tired from the hike here and the canoe I had carried on my back. My fingers were raw, and now I would have to start all over again, with no hope of eating before dark. I hadn't even gathered wood for a campfire yet, assuming I had plenty of time.

I turned towards the lake, which looked like an angry ocean. My intention was to curse it, but the winds smacked me in the face and sucked all the motivation out of my body. I took a deep breath and turned back towards the useless tent. Removing the Leatherman tool from my belt loop, I flicked the knife out and took it to the tent. If the angry cutting of tarp and canvass had been merely for revenge I would have enjoyed it a lot more. In a few minutes I separated the base of the tent from the walls and rain fly. Taking a pea cord from my pack I tied it between two trees, looping the familiar knots around the rough bark, giving each side a good tug to make sure it was secure. The cord was pulled taut about two or three feet above the ground. I spread the base of the tent between the trees on the ground, then threw the body over the cord. The wind resistance sucked, but if it rained it would keep me dry, mostly.

Retrieving my pack from the original tent site, I extracted my food bag and tied another cord around it. I was preparing to throw the tail of that cord over a high branch to keep my food away from critters and bears when a particularly vicious gust of wind blew one side of my makeshift tent back over the cord. The whole green mass floated away like dry leaf. It settled down a few yards away, rippling at the edges to remind me that it obeyed the wind.

I dragged my hammer up from the ground and began pulling

up the stakes I had painstakingly driven into the earth. After all four had been retrieved I snatched the rebellious tent and threw it back over the taught rope. Holding the stake over a corner of the tent, I drove it through the canvass and into the dirt with far more force than necessary. When I had the tent securely nailed to the earth, I went back to protecting my food.

Throwing the tail of the rope over the highest tree-branch I could, I pulled the tail end until the packet hung high above the ground. Then I tied the tail off to the trunk to hold it in place. As I was finishing off that knot, a monumental bolt of lightning lit up the whole lake and surrounding forest. The sheer breadth of the incandescent blue light amazed and terrified me. Five seconds later a giant clap of thunder shook the earth. In the split second that I paused, rain began pouring down. Gallons upon gallons of water dumped down from the sky, catching in the trees and landing in sloppy bucket-loads on the ground.

No hope of finding firewood now. I wasn't hungry anyway. Trying to be grateful that I had nailed down my tent before the rain started, I crawled in the tiny dry space, kicking my boots off before dragging my feet in.

I checked my jacket pockets for something to eat and found a packet of ramen noodles. After moving my sleeping bag aside so it wouldn't get crumbs on it, I broke the packet against my knee and opened it along one edge. I fished out the flavor pouch, ripped it open and sprinkled it over the dry noodles.

The rain seemed to increase its intensity as I contemplated my sad dinner. I might as well have set up camp under a waterfall. In ten or twenty minutes the canvass would start to leak. My best bet was to try and be asleep before that happened. The dry, cold noodles crunched between my teeth, a mockery of the warm meal they should have been.

I wondered why I came. Had I really left Alice alone so I could be stressed out by wind and rain and obstinate camping equipment? I would take pizza ordered from that same stupid pizzeria for the fifth night in a row over raw ramen noodles any day of the week. What magical catalyst had I expected to find in pine trees, lakes, and fish?

A drop fell on my head. I chucked the remaining noodles into my mouth and pulled out my sleeping bag. My stiff jeans were exchanged for my sweatpants, my white cotton socks for wool ones. I pulled on a stocking cap to keep my body temperature up. The rustle of down-stuffed nylon was familiar and a little comforting, despite the damp already creeping in.

I closed my eyes and thought of Alice. Alice scanning over a financial report. Alice in her sports bra and shorts with a sheen of sweat on her arms and shoulders. Alice chatting with total strangers like they were old friends. Alice conforming to my shape when I embraced her as she slept. Alice's shoulders slumping over the stove as she put her hopes into perfectly browned pancakes.

As dreams started to play on the edge of my consciousness, there was something else. Something that wasn't Alice, that was bigger and calmer than Alice. Something that blocked out everything else and filled me with a peace that muted the noise within. I dismissed it as a dream, the effect of too much silence. Yet there was something there, something real and alive on this side of silence. Despite the cold, the wet, and the loneliness, I fell asleep with a smile.

·•·

As unpleasant as it is to fall asleep in the rain, it is far worse to wake up in it. I was wet down to my wool socks. The green canvass tent sagged with rainwater. Every piece of clothing was wet, my sleeping bag was wet, the tent was wet, my hair was wet, my feet were wet. My clothes grated against my soaked skin.

When I crept out of the tent, the torrential downpour had eased to a steady drizzle. I guessed a lot of my food was ruined, but I was too tired to check just yet. I took out my mini propane tank and started heating water in my blue metal mug. There wasn't enough propane to last the week, but I could spare a little for a hot breakfast this morning.

I held my hands towards the tiny blue flame. There wasn't any real warmth that reached my hands, but it made me feel like I was doing something. I could be rushing around wildly trying to cover everything to keep it dry, but everything was already wet and wasn't going to get any wetter.

Fog covered the tops of the trees. The lake looked gray and gauzy with a thick cover of mist. For the first time during my trip, I felt the comfort of silence. This was what I had wanted after all, wasn't it? Although I still missed Alice, this was one moment I wouldn't have been able to share with her; her presence would change it.

That thought made me sad. Here I was, miserable, wet, cold, exhausted, frustrated, and thinking I was glad Alice wasn't here because she would ruin my quiet. Yet it was true; this morning would not have been peaceful and sleepy if Alice had been with me. She would have been up hours ago, hanging tarps or wringing water out of something. She would have gone on a run or for a dip in the lake already, despite the rain, and would be talking a mile a minute about how invigorated she felt. That's why I loved her. I was just as caught as I was at home, except now I was wet.

I sighed. This trip was a mistake. The real problem was that talking to people, even my beloved Alice, made me tired. I remembered that I usually needed some recovery time even after a vacation. Why was I so constantly exhausted?

The water started to boil and I went to get my food pack down from the tree. The drizzle weakened to a thick mist, which made it easier to look up and catch my bag. The pack was drenched, and hit my hands with a sloppy sound. As I feared, my bag of oatmeal was swollen and mushy, my teabags wet and sitting in their own half-brewed juices, and a bag of tortillas had become a goopy paste. My peanut butter seemed to have survived the night, and the other packets of ramen noodles were still dry inside.

I took a handful of the oatmeal mush and crumbled it into the boiling water. Oatmeal was pretty forgiving, and maybe I could add some peanut butter to give it some more substance. As I crouched over my little metal cup, bits of soggy grain clinging to my hand, the sun touched my face.

Pure light poured down from a sky, crisp and gold. Warmth far too intense for the early morning wrapped around me, touching all the creases of my face and hands. The golden light made the lake glow with warmth and color. Steam was rising from the lake, its daily offering to the skies. The whole landscape responded, the flowers opening and turning their faces towards the sky, the leaves glowing their saturated green, the very branches of the trees creaked and stretched towards this ultimate source.

Unbidden, my own arms were reaching, stretching towards the sky. I saw a magnificent energy that existed somewhere in the universe, a being so massive it would stun the life out of a mere man like me. For some reason, today, this morning, that being offered a small touch to the surface of earth. Everything, absolutely everything around me was soaking in the energy, absorbing the force of that gentlest contact. My hands began to shake with the magnitude, which worked down my arms and shoulders, vibrating through my whole existence.

I had no idea how long I stood there with my hands stretching towards the sky. Just before I thought the force of this encounter would rip my physical self apart, the energy dimmed ever so slightly. That being withdrew, just enough so I remembered to breathe.

Marathons seemed like they would be a paltry effort; I was so sure I could rocket off the ground and soar across fields and mountains. My hands were shaking with inconceivable energy. Still the same hands I had known my whole life, still with bits of oatmeal on them, but different now because they were full. Full of life, full of vitality, full of everything I had ever wanted and thought I'd never have.

When I looked back at the sky, it had turned clear blue. Although it was just a morning sky, I could tell that the being was still out there, still close. The sense of nearness was not identified by any of the five senses I could name. It was an inner knowing; the same part of me that knew Alice was waiting for me at home.

I longed for Alice. Not just to look at her, not to simply absorb her presence, but to really communicate and interact with her. At my core, I realized that this was what I had been longing for. I'd been wasting my time with Alice because I couldn't engage with her. My wife, my Alice, had been waiting for me to rise to her vigor. A true, joyous smile spread across my face, and an eager jump in my chest prompted me to start moving.

·•·

All the way home I decided to call Alice, then decided it'd be better to speak to her in person. Then I'd realize that she might have left already, and I'd panic and pick up my phone again. Of course, a pleading phone call wouldn't convince Alice to do anything, so I put it back down again. It's amazing I didn't run myself off the road. My heart leapt and fluttered and performed all kinds of new acrobatics. Despite my nerves, I couldn't keep a goofy smile off my lips.

As I pulled into the garage, only one light was on. A gold glow trembled in a guest room window. Alice would never leave a light on, so she was still here. My smile grew another size. I moved through the dim rooms and hallways and up the shadowy stairs to the lighted room.

Alice was sitting in an armchair, her back straight, clutching crumpled Kleenexes in her fists. I'd never seen my Alice cry, but her red-rimmed eyes and pale face spoke of tears. My whole core softened with compassion for her. My own journey was difficult enough, but I'd left her here alone to wonder how her life might shift or fade. As I moved toward her, my heart was untouched by my familiar crushing guilt. I was free to love and comfort her without that heaviness holding me back.

I embraced her, caring for her first, letting my excitement wait. She clung to me like she'd been clinging to her tissues. To my surprise, she wept on my shoulder. I felt her narrow chest heaving against me, and I held her tighter. When she pulled away, I looked deep into her blue eyes, brushing tears from her cheek with my thumb.

"I thought I would be crying today. I thought you'd be gone."

Alice sniffled and nodded. "I meant to. My sister Laura and I had it all planned out."

"I'm so glad you're here." I touched her cheek again, squeezed her arm. She felt cold. "I'm so sorry I left you alone like that. But this trip was really great for me. Something happened out there, it changed me. I feel so different, so full. I want to be there for you, now. It won't be like before."

"You do look different." Alice agreed, although her tone was dubious. I didn't expect her to believe me, I only hoped she'd stay long enough to see for herself. She cleared her throat, straightened her shoulders, drawing into herself and reclaiming her composure.

"There's a reason I stayed. I wasn't planning on it."

"What is it?" I asked, feeling something wonderful coming. Maybe she had a transcendent experience too. If the incredible energy could find me in the middle of the woods, maybe it could find Alice in the suburbs.

"I'm pregnant."

I smiled so hard my face hurt. "That's fanstastic!"

Anger covered her eyes, and she looked through it like dark glasses. "No, it's not fantastic. I don't want to be pregnant."

"What do you mean? We both want kids."

"I didn't mean that I don't want to be pregnant ever, I just don't want to be pregnant right now. I'm on birth control, how did this happen?"

I shrugged. "It's not 100%. Maybe you took one of the pills late or — "

"So this is my fault?" she demanded.

"That's not what I meant. I'm just saying that it happens. We'll be okay. We'll be great."

Alice was not buying it. "Peter, I haven't found a job yet. What do you think my chances are of finding one that's going to give me maternity leave in less than a year?"

"Is that what you're worried about? I make enough for us to have a baby, and I have a lot in savings. Both of our cars are paid off. We're in a good position financially."

"You don't get it, do you? I hate being stuck in the house all day. I hate waiting for you to come home. I hate feeling like I don't accomplish anything, ever. The last thing I want is to be tied down to this life for twenty years. You won't be able to work any less. You'll probably work more so we can get baby piano lessons or an ergonomic high chair."

That did sound like something I would do, but I brushed that thought aside. We didn't have to submit to our natural tendencies. We could choose.

"We can make those decisions as they come up, but I'm not going to settle for any lifestyle that makes you miserable. You're still important, and you'll always be important, even when we have a baby."

A small smile touched her lips. "Is that shrink talk?"

"No. That's husband talk." I smiled.

"That's good to hear." She touched my hair gently.

"There's something else," I said, plunging ahead. There were good reasons to wait for a better time, but I was tired of that.

"Oh, really?" She raised an eyebrow.

"I want to do some volunteer work. With homeless people."

She crossed her arms. "Isn't that taking it a bit far?"

I shook my head. "I've wanted to work with the homeless since college, I just never got around to it. For once I want to do what I've always meant to do."

She looked away, thinking.

"I don't know, Peter. I feel like...you say you feel different, and you look different, but I was hoping you'd be different enough to be here, really be here with me. Shouldn't you see if that works out before you take on a whole new project?"

I mulled over her words. "That makes sense."

"But?"

"But, I really think this is something I'm supposed to do. If I've taken on too much, I can give up other things."

"Like what?" She sounded angry, like she might be expendable too.

"Like hiking. Or canoeing. Or re-landscaping the back yard."

She laughed, just a little. "Wow, this is serious stuff, huh?"

"It's great stuff. Really great stuff."

•.•

"Fan out, stay with a partner, give people space," Hank said, flicking his hand in three or four directions. I clung to my plastic shopping bags, turning my knuckles white. In the bags were sandwiches I personally prepared for this outing, along with fruit and hygiene products. I was with a team of ten or fifteen other people, mostly teenagers, here to serve the homeless in our city. Here I was, living my dream. I wasn't exhausted, but I was terrified.

"You gonna give those out, or you keepin' 'em for yuhself?" a lanky man asked me, holding out a bony hand but not moving from where he was reclining against a cinder block wall.

"You can have one," I said, trying to smile. Moving towards him, I held out one of the plastic bags.

"You got tracts or some shit in here? 'Cause you can just take that straight back, huh?" The long fingers went digging through the bag, searching for some contaminating item.

"I-I don't think so. What's a tract?"

Cackling laughter began from a cardboard box nearby. A woman's face that looked older than time emerged with a toothless smile. "He ain't been here no more, got us somethin' fresh here."

"Hush your mouth, ya old bitch!" the lanky man shouted back at her. She hissed at him like an agitated cat.

"A tract is a little book like thing that tell us poor folks all 'bout Jesus or Mohammed or some other dead dude who got the answers to everythin'. I already knows Jesus, don't need no fuckin' book to tell me." The man unwrapped the sandwich and dug into it. "Ain't half bad, thank ya."

"You're welcome. There aren't any tracts in there," I added lamely. "Do...do you want one?" I pointed this question towards the woman in the box.

"You say the sandwich is okay?" the woman asked. The man was already done with the sandwich and was munching on an apple.

"Yeah, it's pretty good. Got mustard though."

"Ugh! I don't want nothing with mustard. Evil stuff, mustard. Don't you know nothing? Mustard is damn poison."

I swallowed and tried to smile. "Sorry. Someone else might have one without mustard." I paused. "Or you can take the bag and give the sandwich to someone else, if you like. There's some other food in here, fruit and – "

"You think I want to poison someone? You think I'm a murderer?" the woman was getting louder. I could dismiss her as crazy, but really, she just said it was poison. I just assumed she wouldn't think it was poison for other people.

"No, no. I'm sorry."

"She's just fuckin' with ya, man. Give her the bag," the man said. I didn't believe him, but the woman took the bag from me. I even saw her taking the plastic wrapping off the sandwich as I walked away.

"How is it going?" Hank asked me.

"It's interesting, that's for sure."

"Feel free to step back and just observe some if you want. We're not used to having someone with your qualifications here. I'll hand out your bags for you," he offered.

"No, thank you. I need the excuse to talk to them for right now."

"Oh, they'll be happy to talk to you. Probably more than you'd like."

"Just the same." I held onto my bags, because without the bags I was just a guy trying to talk to complete strangers. Still, I took some of Hank's advice and hung back from the crowd.

As I did with my regular clients, I tried to separate myself just far enough to see the dynamics at play. I saw the wild attention-grabber, a tall white man in a skirt, doing sloppy pirouettes and singing "The Star-Spangled Banner." The rationalist, sitting and arguing with a hapless volunteer about how aliens had infiltrated the government for decades and were poised to take over the world. From my detached viewpoint, I could see where there were drugs being traded, and a young girl peering from behind a huge man like a mouse behind a cat's tail.

My eye caught a shapeless form peering out from a greasy blanket, only the glittering eyes showing. Whoever it was, they were wearing a crumpled knitted hat and I could hear a stream of muttered chanting coming from the blanket. Later, I would conclude that this was the image I'd seen when I thought of someone who really needed my help. For now, I knew that I had to approach the muttering heap of dirty blanket.

"My name's Margot," the mound said. The eyes were glassy and darting and the muttering was distant and robotic. This introduction wasn't meant for me, but I plunged ahead.

"My name's Peter, it's nice to meet you." I paused, a habit of two-way conversations, but there was no reply. "Do you want some food?"

"I want Cheryl."

Until now the voice sounded like a machine whirring on its last battery, but these words came out plaintively human, pleading. Whoever this Cheryl was, she had already cut through the worst of this woman's disease.

"Who's Cheryl? Is she a friend of yours?"

"You sound different." The robotic voice was back, with a hint of suspicion added now.

"We've never met before, so you wouldn't recognize my voice. I'd like to get to know you though. Cheryl isn't here right now, but I can help you find her if you want." Provided Cheryl was a real person, I was very willing to reunite her with Margot. If I couldn't do anything else for Margot, which was a real possibility, connecting her with someone who cared would help.

"Cheryl's not selfish, she doesn't want to keep all the warm for herself."

This sounded defensive. It was possible that mine wasn't the only voice Margot was responding to. "Do you know where she works?"

"At the shelter, at Caring Hands. Cheryl has caring hands, but her words are the most pretty. She says please all the time."

I'd heard of Caring Hands, it was a homeless shelter nearby. There couldn't be many Cheryl's working there.

"It's nice when people say please." I shifted the heavy plastic bags. Even if I couldn't find Cheryl, I could at least give Margot a meal. "Here, take this food. There's some toothpaste and stuff in there too. I'll try to find Cheryl and come back to find you, okay?"

"No, I can't feel my hands."

I could still only see her eyes, only the murky green pools that were Margot's connection with the outside world. The blanket she held around herself was pulled taught around knobby hand-shapes near her chin. Nothing but a blanket to keep her warm in this Minnesota chilly weather, and it was only November. Without thinking, I slid off the red knitted mittens my mother gave me for Christmas and tossed them to Margot.

"Here, take my mittens." They landed silently, resting half on the colorless blanket, half on the dirty sidewalk.

"These mittens are for babies, not trash."

For a moment my voice stuck. Maybe some people really would call this collection of blankets and dull eyes trash, but I knew there was a person in there; a person with cold hands.

"Please wear them, they'll keep your hands warm. I'll come back, I'll try to find Cheryl at Caring Hands, okay?"

The blankets shifted, and the knotted hand shapes melted into the lower half. Two, claw-like fingers emerged from a fold near the ground, drawing the mittens under the protective blanket.

"Babies can't trick me, 'cause they aren't smart."

"I'm not trying to trick you."

She tried to get the mittens on under the blanket without revealing any body parts. In her eyes I saw the same look Terrance had once. A slow uncertainty as she considered trusting me.

"Well," she said after a long pause. Her red nose appeared over the blanket. "I like your shiny shoes."

A True Silence

"You know that they're going to make you leave, they're going to throw you out in the cold."

"They seem nice here."

"They're not nice here, they're cruel. They've got you used to being warm all the time, they wore your skin down until it's thin and now they're going to throw you into the cold, and you'll die because you don't have your thick skin."

I pinched my arm to check the thickness of my skin, but I didn't feel anything, so I pinched it harder.

"You can't tell like that. You know that they're just waiting until you're thin enough to die, and then they'll kick you out. You don't want to go out in the cold, do you?"

I shook my head violently. Once I had to stay outside the whole winter. Two of my toes were missing from that year. In the morning, I pressed the empty space where they should be, trying to teach that skin that it was all alone now. Still, it itched for those toes to keep it company.

My wool blanket wrapped around my shoulders. I liked the feel of its tightness, although it worried me sometimes. Just when they started to say...

"You know that blanket isn't going to make you safe. It makes you a mark, it says to people that you're crazy, that you're trash, that you're worthless, that you don't deserve anything."

"I'm not trash."

"Yes, you are trash. You're garbage and nobody wants you around. That's why they're going to throw you out into the cold to die, because you're garbage."

"Cheryl says – "

"Cheryl's a fucking liar! Cheryl brought you here to get all thin and weak."

I pinched my skin again, hoping it wasn't as thin as they said. I sunk down lower in the couch in the common room, tightening the wool blanket around me. If I stayed inside this blanket, I would always be warm. My blood pumped warm all around my skin and it seeped out through my pores, but the wool blanket caught that warmth and put it back. I liked that feeling, knowing I wouldn't lose any more of that warmth. I could store it up, in case they really did throw me out.

My blanket was moving, shifting around like the wing of a bat, all silky and tight, but flapping and flapping to get away from me.

"I want my blanket!"

"They're taking your blanket away because they want you to get thin and die."

"I want my blanket!" I clung to the edges of the wool with my hands, but my hands were crooked and couldn't be straightened, so the fabric slunk away from me.

"It starts with the blanket. Next they'll take your clothes, then they'll make you sleep on the floor, and then they'll put you outside."

"I want my blanket!" But they were pulling it away, pulling it away and making it cold, making me lose my warmth. I struck out, snatching it back to me, looping it under my chin, feeling the warmth against my face, pressing against my eyelids. Now the hands pulled harder, pulling that warmth away from me. Didn't they understand that this was the only way to survive?

"They don't care! They want you to die."

"No! No! No! I don't want to die, I don't want to be cold again, don't make me cold again!"

"It's no use to argue with them. They want you to die; they don't care if you're scared. If you want to keep that blanket, you have to fight for it!"

My crooked hands couldn't hold on to the slippery blanket. Hundreds of hands reached out, some grabbing my blanket, some pushing me away, always pushing. Something ripped and the whole air filled up with tiny pieces of blanket. All the warmth I had saved up was spilling out in the air. So much precious warmth. Stretching my neck as long as I could, I opened my mouth and screamed, screamed to get that warmth back. Then I was pushed down on the ground, my old cheek pressed against the cold tile. I wailed, I wailed, I wailed because I was cold and I didn't want to be cold anymore.

I saw Cheryl's face and another woman too. Those young, pretty women, those women with houses and dogs and husbands and locks on their doors. They didn't know, didn't care what it was like when it was cold outside and there was nowhere to go. Their eyebrows bent down, wondering what to do with me, but I wanted to do something with myself. I wanted to bury myself in that wool blanket, and why couldn't I?

"…erratic behavior…disruptive to other residents…" they were talking about me, but I couldn't hear them because my ear was pressed against that cold floor.

"See? I told you they don't care about you. They're just leaving you on the floor like trash, because that's what you are. Why should they care about you? You're just trash, trash that wants a blanket. They won't give it back to you. Next they'll take your shirt."

"Let me talk to her, please." That was Cheryl. She always said please.

They put me on a hard chair, but they didn't give me my blanket back and I was still cold. My shirt was thin, and the shirt underneath it was very old and felt wet. Wet meant cold, if it wasn't in a shower. Even that wet could get cold if there wasn't a blanket or a towel. They wouldn't ever get me in that shower again if they didn't give my blanket back.

"Hah! As if they're going to give you a choice. Don't you remember they forced you into the shower? When they stripped off all your clothes and made you stand under the water? It wasn't even hot water!"

"It wasn't so cold."

"It got cold very fast, don't you remember? Are you too stupid to remember something like cold water? No wonder you're always in trouble, you can't even remember how to stay out of trouble."

"Margot. Margot, can you hear me? Will you listen to me, please?" Cheryl always said please.

"They took my blanket, and I'm cold."

"Margot, they were worried you were going to suffocate in that blanket. You were holding it over your face. Doesn't that make your lungs hurt?"

"She's trying make pain for you, pain in your lungs. Your lungs didn't hurt, did they? Pain is nothing, numbness is scary. That's what happened to your toes, they got too numb and then they died."

"Margot, are you listening to me?"

"I was cold."

"Is it cold in here?" Cheryl asked.

I sighed. She wasn't going to understand, because she was all clean and had thick skin and never had to spend the whole cold season outside.

"I have to save up the warm, or it will get away. I need it for when it gets cold again, when they make me leave."

"Margot, that blanket was filthy, and old. We can get you something better to keep warm in."

"They took my blanket away! They hid it in the room with all the warm because they are greedy little bitches and they don't want to share with nobody!"

"Not with garbage anyway. Who would want to share with garbage?"

I shut my mouth because I didn't want Cheryl to know that I was garbage. Cheryl still said please instead of saying "goddamnit, Margot!"

"Margot, you are making it hard for the other people. They get scared, too, especially when you scream like that. You have to leave the shelter. I know you're afraid of the cold, and it is going to get cold soon. You can go to the hospital where it's warm and they'll help you so you can come back and stay here."

"No! No! Don't send me there, don't send me away, don't lock me up! Don't send me there! I'll be good I'll be good I'll be good I'll be good!"

"They'll send you there again and you'll never come out, you'll disappear in that hell hole and you know it. You're just putting off the inevitable, just waiting for Cheryl to agree with them. They'll send you away, they'll lock you up with no blankets and no pillows and just that thin white sheet to wear. It'd be better to lose all your toes and fingers too before dying alone in a room with no windows. That's all a coffin is anyway."

"They probably kept her under wraps at that hospital."

"Ryan, that attitude isn't helpful. Things are bad enough as it is."

"I don't want to be wrapped! Cheryl, please! Please don't let them wrap me up, that's what they do to dead bodies, they wrap them up and don't let them loose. I don't want to be in a coffin, it's too dark in there and there are no blankets in a coffin. Please, please, don't send me there." I cried and cried, and I used Cheryl's word because that's what made her a good person.

"Margot, if you don't go to the hospital you're going to have to go back to the street. I don't want you get cold again."

"Like hell she doesn't, she's been waiting for this moment ever since your stinky ass showed up in this place. Waiting for you to go so she can spray her chemicals and make your gross smell disappear."

"Cheryl's not like that, she not red like the others."

"Who are you talking to? No one here wants you to be on the street again."

"Some of them do and some of them don't, and some of them tried to fit me in boxes and some of them were afraid to touch me with their packing tape, but all of them are red except you. You have blue eyes instead."

"That didn't make you sound crazy at all, you old coot. No chance they're going to let you stay now, no chance at all. You can freeze to death on the street with all the little pieces being eaten off of you one at a time, or you can go die in a room with no air in the hospital. Take your pick."

"I don't want to go to the hospital. I'd rather be cold than get wrapped. At least when I'm cold I can walk and talk and find little pockets of things and people. When I'm wrapped I'm dead already, only the scientists with the tongs can see me and I can see them."

"Oh, Margot." Cheryl was crying. Her nice please words were coming out her eyes because she was so good she couldn't keep it inside.

"It's okay, Cheryl. I still have eight toes left."

· • ·

"Bitch! You miserable fucking bitch! Trash! Garbage! Get out of my house!"

Breath caught in my throat, where it got stuck.

"You don't belong here, you don't belong anywhere, bitch!"

My crooked hands searched for somewhere to be, but there were only walls and air.

"You're filth, you're never going to be anything, get out! Get out!"

I cried, because the words hurt my insides.

"You can't stay here, bitch! No one wants you, you can't stay here."

Sometimes the words weren't real and the people were like water that goes away when it gets hot. On the streets the words all blended together, because there were no rooms to hold them in, no walls or doors or handles or brooms to sweep up the mess. I never liked brooms anyway.

"This is my spot, it eats up my voice and feeds it back to me like a baby bird." I talked with my eyes closed because then other words wouldn't get in the middle and mess up my thoughts.

"Fuck that, you don't have a claim here just 'cause you're messed up in the head."

"Get out of here, you don't want to get your ass beat. Better to leave without getting your nose broken or losing blood here. This spot is nice, but it's not worth it. Everyone wants in on this spot."

"I don't want to share this place. I'd rather sleep alone."

"Like there's a thug on the planet that would bang your flabby snatch. Get outta here before I give you something to remember me by."

"Stay low, then you won't be seen. Think about the earth and the sky and the ocean and maybe you'll be like them too so no one will notice that you're weird and made out of trash."

"I'm not trash."

"Oh yeah? What do you call scum that clumps up on the street when it's cold and miserable? You call that gold? Jewels? Sorry, but there's just no other way to look at the situation. Better own up and deal with your shitty self. There's no reason to sit around pretending you're a real person with a name."

"My name's Margot."

"Do you want some food?"

"Do you want to get even fatter and more disgusting?"

"You know she does want just that, wants to turn into a pile of goo that will stick to the pavement so everyone who walks by will be disgusted forever and ever. This city will never be clean again because she's such a stinking mess."

The words hurt my guts. Where all the tubing of my body came together, that's where the words hurt.

"I want Cheryl."

"Who's Cheryl?" That wasn't a real voice, it was a baby voice. If I squinted, I could see the baby's shoes, which were shiny like glass.

"You sound different."

"We've never met before. Cheryl isn't here right now, but I can help you find her if you want."

"Cheryl isn't lost, Cheryl is waiting in that warm room where they kicked you out, soaking up all the hot air that comes out the vents. You want Cheryl? That just proves how stupid you are. Don't you know that Cheryl always wanted you to freeze?"

"Cheryl's not selfish. She doesn't want all the warm to herself."

"Then why did she make you leave, huh? You think she wanted to share all that clean shiny space with you? With you?"

"Do you know where she works?" That baby voice again. It was new.

"At the shelter, at Caring Hands. Cheryl has caring hands, but her words are the most pretty. She says please all the time."

"It's nice when people say please. Here, take this food. There's some toothpaste and stuff in there too. I'll try to find Cheryl and come back to find you, okay?"

"Food is plastic when it comes from babies, it's just going to hurt your teeth and make your insides hard and slippery. But go ahead and eat it, it isn't the dumbest thing you've ever done. It won't matter, because you're going to die in this cold. Can you even feel your hands?"

"No, I can't feel my hands." I looked at my crooked hands. They were crooked, but they were mine and I wanted to keep them. The pinky fingers were the bluest. They would go first.

"Here, take my mittens."

The mittens were red and soft, because they came from a baby and some grandmama somewhere was knitting things to keep babies warm. Things that were red and soft because babies need to see color, and because they don't know that hard things will make them strong. But my skin was gray and full of holes and it wasn't right to put something so pretty and real on it.

"These mittens are for babies, not for trash."

"Please wear them, they'll keep your hands warm. I'll come back. I'll try to find Cheryl at Caring Hands, okay?"

"Cheryl wants to wrap you, do you really want to go back there? Won't she tell this baby to trick you so you'll go to the hospital? Or they'll take you in a van, the vans with no windows. Can't you remember the vans?"

"Babies can't trick me, 'cause they aren't smart."

"I'm not trying to trick you."

"If he's not even trying to trick you, what is he trying to do? Babies want stuff all the time. They're not smart but they can't even see other people. What makes you think this one cares about some piece of trash sitting on the side of the road? Just because it doesn't want its mittens anymore doesn't mean that it's up to something good."

"Well. I like those shiny shoes."

· • ·

My mother was arguing with a friend. Well, not a real friend, like Cheryl. Arguing with the lady who lived across the street, the one with no teeth, the one who told the men who came around that she was "just a friend of the mother's." We never knew what that meant, but Cheryl said that real friends say please and are kind. That woman never says please.

She has angry red hair, and she says things that even my mother wouldn't say. She has a gun, a thick black thing with a smushed nose so it always looks like it's sniffing for something, searching for something bloody to eat up. But I'm not afraid of the gun, because it is little and smushed even if it is heavy.

I'm afraid of my mother with the broom in her hand because it's not just a broom anymore. The flat wooden end has broken off so now it's sharp and scary and it has a spiked face that's squinting at the whole world. I'm afraid because the broom can see right into your soul with the sharp end, and my soul is sick and mucky and I don't want anyone to see it, especially not the broom.

So I stay quiet, I listen to them yell at each other.

"You get off my land!"

"I own this little piece of grass, you bitch!"

"Like hell you do. This here is my porch and that there is the street, and that's the only place you belong."

"Ha! I wasn't the one selling my pussy for ten-buck blow when I was fifteen."

"You wouldn't know; it's not like you can remember back that far you dried-up dyke."

"I'd rather be a dyke than a slut whose vag could swallow a watermelon after all the brats it's pushed out."

I didn't like their talk because it's ugly. I covered my ears.

"You're just like them. Trash, they're trash. You can't be any different because that's all there is in your world. Trash and more trash. Can't get away from where you're from, people can smell it on you."

The words came from inside. When I covered my ears they bounced between my palms. They hurt my head.

"Margot? Do you remember me?" That baby was back with his slow words. I wanted to tell him not to talk so loud in front of my mother, not while she was holding that sharp broom. But I was afraid to talk, so I tried to tell him with my eyes.

"What is that lily-white pansy doing in this part of town?" the friend asked.

"I don't know." Mother looked suspicious. "Margot, you didn't let that man touch you in a bad place did you? You let that one man touch you a bad place, do you remember? She can't remember anything I tell her, and she'll let anyone doing anything to her. Did that man touch you?"

Hot water bubbled up inside of me, but I didn't like that kind of warm. It was too hot; it burned me.

"He did not! He did not!" I shouted. They were too ugly to talk to a baby with soft baby hands. He wasn't trash like them, he was like Cheryl. He would probably say please any second now.

"How have you been feeling, Margot?"

"I not cold," I told him. I didn't want him to give me anything, not while my mother was here. But I wanted to cry because I was so cold. My fingers were stiff all the time and my heart could barely beat.

"Am I talking too loud?" he asked. He smiled like he already knew he wasn't talking too loud, just barely whispering.

"No."

"Why are you covering your ears?"

"Because she doesn't want to hear the truth, but it's going to come out sooner or later. If you don't shape up you're going to get pregnant, and I won't have any bastard brats in my house, I'll tell you that."

"I don't like the broom!" I told her.

"I don't see a broom."

I looked back at the baby, then at my mother again.

"Oh yeah, go ahead and tell him that I have a broom but he can't see me. That's going to go over really well. If you end up in the hospital again, I won't be able to help you get out. There's only so much I can do, and you have to take responsibility for your own actions."

"You have different shoes."

He looked at his feet. "I guess I do. You have a good memory." He smiled. I blinked. Even my mother couldn't think of anything to say.

"Oh."

"I would like you to do me a favor today, okay?" he said.

"Not okay to do a favor," I shook my head. "Favors are for princesses, not for garbage, not for trash. I don't smell good, and I'll get you dirty. Ask a princess, ask Cheryl. She's made of gold."

He was confused. I could tell because his eyebrows slanted down to get a better look at me. Two thin brown caterpillars. They needed more leaves.

"Margot, you are not trash."

I realized my mistake, my big, big mistake. I'd told him that I was trash, now he knew. I couldn't breathe again, and my lungs hurt. I gasped, but my mother just shook her head.

"You'll only get what you deserve. I can't do anything about it. They're going to stuff you in a can and leave you to die, just because you're too stupid to live."

I strained every molecule of every muscle toward my lungs so I could push the stuck air back out again.

"I'm not too stupid to live! You're too stupid to live! You're not really alive, are you? No! You're just hanging around because you were such a crappy person you had to come back and be more crappy now!"

My mother was in a rage, her face was purple and her knuckles white. I hit the floor and looked for somewhere to hide. My chest was collapsing because she was going to find me with that sharp broom.

"What's going on?" the man asked.

"Watch out for the broom!" I shouted. I squashed my body to the ground as flat as I could. I was not very flat.

He stood very still, and he turned into a granite pillar. My mother's broom would smash against him if she hit him with it, and the tiny sharp face wouldn't be able to see into the rock. His soul was hidden.

"I don't see a broom. Margot, I would like you to take some pills for me. If you take these pills, then you can go back to the shelter. Cheryl will help you remember when to take them and how many."

"You don't have pills, you're just a baby," I said. Only the yucky men on streets and in old houses had pills, but they wanted all your clothes if you wanted one of those pills. Then it was too cold, and to stay warm it took lots of pills or lots of clothes. I only had my two shirts, my pants, my socks, and my wool blanket. I wouldn't give anyone the soft red mittens, not for all the pills in the world.

"Actually, I'm a doctor, Margot. I think you have a sickness that these pills will help. The shelter agreed that you can stay as long as you want if you take these pills when Cheryl tells you to."

"He's lying. No shelter would agree to take you in forever.

They'll kick you out as soon as it gets cold. Any day now, the wind is coming."

"It's already cold!" I hissed at my mother. "Do you promise?" I asked the baby.

"I promise. I've spoken with the director, and as long as you are med compliant you can stay. But I think these will make you feel better."

"Will they make me warm?" I asked eagerly.

"If you stay in the shelter you'll be warm, and if you take the pills you can stay in the shelter."

"He's so tricky, so smooth and sure of himself. He's probably not a doctor at all. He's probably a lawyer."

"You're not a lawyer, are you?" I asked.

The man laughed. "No. I'm a doctor. Lawyers can't give people medicine."

That was true.

"It's poison! Are you stupid? You don't just take anything someone gives you. A pill can be anything, it could be cyanide or puke or shit."

"Please? Would you please take these pills for me?" the baby said.

"Cheryl says please," I said.

"Cheryl cares about you. I care about you, too. I want you to feel better."

"Cheryl gives me the pills?" I asked.

"Yes, Cheryl will give you the pills."

"And I get to stay inside?"

"Yes, you can stay inside as long as you take the pills."

"It's poison, you idiot! You're just going to swallow poison down and let it rot away your insides because he said please? Please is just a word, it's nothing, it's not going to keep you safe and warm, and it's not going to make you normal like other people. You were born garbage and you'll die garbage."

"Then I want to die in the shelter, not here in the cold. Even garbage wants someplace warm to rot away into dirt."

"Margot," the baby said in a sad, silky voice. "Margot, you are not garbage."

·•·

At first it was okay. Kind of nice, a glowing flame deep in my belly. At first I thought, maybe those pills really were going to work; they were going to make me warm from the inside. Then it started to hurt, sometime in the nighttime, when Cheryl wasn't there.

They complained, but they always complain. No singing, no talking, no walking, no nothing during the nighttime. They asked, "are you okay?" but they meant "stop making noise!" So I stuffed the scratchy sheets in my mouth and held the pillow over my face. I liked how the soft cotton felt against my eyelids. But they didn't like that either.

"It hurts, it's starting to hurt," I told them.

"They don't care." He was getting loud, so loud that even when he wasn't shouting it jangled the little bones in my ears.

"What kind of hurt?"

"The kind they don't care about."

I covered my ears, but it didn't help.

"The fire, the fire hurts inside. It's too loud, it's much too loud, it's hurting my bones. Can you make the bones stop hurting?"

"She does feel warm, maybe she's feverish."

Icy cold, wet, rough, touched my forehead. "Ah! No! No! Not the cold, don't make me go in the cold. It's okay, it's okay, the fire is okay, don't put it out! I don't want to be cold!"

"Oh for pete's sake."

"I told you they didn't care. They've been waiting for an excuse to throw you out and you just handed it to them."

"Too loud! It's too loud, it hurts my bones."

"What is she talking about?"

"Who knows what she's talking about?"

"Because you're trash, and they don't know what to do with you, and they're hoping you just keep on being trash so they can get rid of you. That's why they gave you those pills, to push you until they felt good about leaving you to die alone."

"Please, please, not so loud," I whispered. Even my own voice was too loud. The flames were licking up my ribcage, they burned all my bones and stung my skin. They were eating me, eating up from the inside out. Those pills were worms, worms with fire in them and they were eating me up like old meat.

"He tricked me, he tricked me," I wailed.

"I told you it was poison! Poison worms that are eating you up. You'll be full of holes before morning."

"Something's wrong. That doctor left his number, didn't he? Give him a call."

"He tricked me! He said they would make it better. My bones hurt! It's burning, it's burning!"

"Quit your whining!" My mother shrieked. Her voice broke my ears and cut my brains into little pieces.

"Mama, please, it's too loud."

"You're always complaining. When I was a kid if I complained like you did they'd beat me until I was black and blue. There wasn't any whining in my house then and I won't have whining in my house now."

"Please!" The voices were sharp like glass under bridges, like the ends of frayed metal cords. They stuck in my skin and caught on fire because the worms were still eating me up.

It was torture, I was being tortured by these worms and sharp things and the screaming inside. Now everyone was screaming and everyone was screaming at once and I couldn't make out any words just the screaming, just the shrieking terrible noise of it all while I was burning alive with sharp things that wriggled into my skin and ate out my eyes and munched on my tongue so I couldn't even scream anymore.

"This can't be right!" someone shouted, and I was glad because I could hear their words over the screaming. I reached a hand out to touch a person who must be kind because they were not screaming or burning me. I felt a long soft baby hand, a hand that was not burning up with flames or full of sharp things and I knew the baby face man was here.

"I'm so sorry," he said with a thick voice like syrup that got left out in the snow. I liked his hand but it did not stop the screaming, did not stop the burning, didn't make the sharp things stop wriggling and burning and cutting. I wanted to tell him to take the pills back out, but they were eating up my tongue and working into my throat, and I couldn't talk because all my tubes and pipes were full of the burning worms.

"Margot, I'm so sorry." The worms must have left a little piece of eyes, because I could see that baby face one more time. That baby face was crying, the caterpillar eyebrows scrunched up. "I didn't know this would happen, I'm so sorry you're hurting."

I saw the flash of a needle, and I was scared of needles, but I couldn't feel the poke because there were already so many sharp things, and a needle was still; it didn't wriggle, and it wasn't on fire and I hoped that it was poison they were putting into the needle so that I could die and stop the burning and the screaming and the shrieking and wriggling and cutting.

A deep black hole yawned wide and came after me and I think I screamed but I couldn't hear the sound of my own voice anymore. I wasn't so scared because I was hoping the blackness would put out the fire and kill the worms. Soon everything was quiet and black and cold. I would die this way, alone and freezing to death, but now I knew that was better than burning forever.

Light poked into my eyes, but I thought I was dead. The baby face was looking at me out of the light, that white blindness that made his face fuzzy and round.

"How are you feeling?" The words came separate, low and booming. As they floated through the air they warped so they didn't fit together in a row. My mind slowly chewed on the light, but it was tough and rubbery. He shouldn't have been dead.

I tried to talk, but my mouth was shoved full of cotton. "Uhn…Ahg…" strange sounds came out, but no words. I had cotton instead of a tongue, and when I tried to move the cotton, it remembered the worms that had eaten it. I ached.

That slow voice started talking again, but I was too tired to put his words together. The pieces didn't fit anyway. When I closed my eyes and felt a heavy blanket pushing on my arms, my legs, my middle and my chest, the words started to keep their shape better.

"…reaction to medication…not usually…consistent with…" Doctor talk.

"Look around you, moron! You're in the fucking hospital! I told you! I told you! Who would want you anyway, you filth? You pathetic excuse for a human!" My mother's voice was high and screeching like a cartoon mouse, but so loud! So piercing, and I was still healing from the sharp things.

When I opened my eyes, I saw the bright light again, not so strong this time. The baby face man was still there, and he wore a white coat. A tall coat rack stood next to my bed, but it didn't have coats on it. Just big wet bags, goopy and dripping through tubes.

"You tricked me! You tricked me! You said! You said I could

stay in the shelter! Where's Cheryl? What did you do with Cheryl? You didn't say please, you tricked me!" I tried to get up but my arms and legs wouldn't move. They wouldn't move because thick black cords were wrapped all around them and the bed, holding me down so I was stiff like death. But I wasn't dead!

"You wrapped me! You wrapped me!" I wailed. "I don't want to die here! I don't want to die wrapped up! Where is Cheryl? What did you do to Cheryl? Did you wrap her too? Did you put her in the room with no windows and bury her in the ground? Where's Cheryl? Dig her up, dig her up before she's gone all the way. You...tricked...me!"

"Margot, Margot, please." He patted me with his baby hands, but I growled at him like a dog.

"That's Cheryl's word!" I raged. "You killed her to get her word! You tricked me! You *wrapped* me!"

Mother was shrieking again, so loud and high now that there were no words anymore. More booming words layered on top of the shrieks, burying them but not deep enough so the whole mess of shrieking and booms heaved and breathed like a monster about to be born.

"Don't burn me, don't burn me again!" I begged. I should never beg, it never works, and the flames were already starting on my toes. This time there was no wriggling because they killed my whole body with the wrapping and I just had to lie there and burn.

"I'm not a martyr! I'm not a martyr!" I shrieked, and it sounded like my mother. The baby face man said something very fast and more hands touched me, but they were all made of hot tar. I wailed and begged and screamed and it didn't make any difference. The black yawn came again and everything stopped dead.

·•·

When I woke, I was alone. For a long time I waited, bracing myself for the screaming to start, waiting for the flames to burst. As

I waited, I looked around. The room had a window, and I could see bricks and ivy outside. I liked the ivy, the bright green color, how it clung to the wall but never felt desperate or scared. The coat rack still loomed with its clear goopy bags. The light was bright and white from the ceiling. Above the door was a clock with a black frame and three black hands but no numbers. I watched the hands travel around and around, always returning to the tippy top of the plain white circle with the black frame.

It was silent; the whole room was silent. This bothered me, and I searched my mind for the last time I'd felt this kind of silence, this emptiness of sound. The clock hands went around, and around again. My head hurt from thinking, but I could not remember one moment of my life when it was quiet and I was alone. Not even a moment in childhood, an achy loneliness in my teens, or a tragic abandonment under a bridge. There was always something, always someone, always some instruction or statement or question or warning. Now there was nothing.

"Where are you, Mama?" I asked. She must be hidden in a closet or crouching beneath the bed, waiting to pounce. Sometimes she did that. Still, where was everyone else? My ears felt hollow, like caves with bats in them. Only there were no bats, nothing.

Panic worked its way into my chest. What if I'd gone deaf? Almost as soon as the panic started, it was smoothed down with a nice warm feeling. The peace of silence washed over me, and I felt really clean for the first time. No one told me I was garbage and no one called me a bitch. There was no reason to be afraid, nothing scary to jump out of the closet, and no plot against me. After all, I was just one old woman sitting quietly in this bed.

I felt my breath, the clean air drawing deep into my soft lungs and then pushing back out into the atmosphere.

The door to my room opened, and the man with the soft baby face came in, still wearing his white coat.

"Margot, you're awake. Are you in pain? You look…better."

"I am better. Thank you, Peter."

He stared at me for a moment, then a big smile spread all across his face. He looked like a freshly frosted cake.

"You know my name," he said.

"Yes, I do. Could you untie me, please?" I pointed my chin toward the black straps that held me.

"Of course! I'm sorry about the restraints, but you were getting so erratic. They…well, I was afraid you would hurt yourself." He removed the black straps. "I'm so sorry this happened, Margot. I've never seen anyone react to that medication like that before. It's in the literature, but it's so rare. I weaned you off of the meds as quickly as I could. You're on a very low dose now." He paused, looking deep into my eyes, trying to read the stars in them. "You seem much calmer."

I felt better without the straps, free to fold my hands in my lap. After a moment I held my hands out, stretching my fingers, examining each one. They were all perfectly straight.

"Calmer. I like being calmer." A smile felt funny on my face, but it was good.

"I like it, too." He looked over a clipboard, and he read bright blinking numbers on the machines. "Hm." He didn't know why breathing was suddenly so nice. I thought for a moment.

"I think it's the silence. It's hard to feel better when it's so loud."

Peter blinked hard four times.

"Doesn't that make sense?" I asked.

"Yes, it makes sense." He nodded.

With so much time and space to think, I felt pretty smart. I thought about all the shouting that I'd heard, how it came from everywhere and nowhere, and how objects and bodies melded together so I couldn't see exactly what was going on. I looked at the doorframe's strong, straight line, and the perfect roundness of the clock.

"There must be something on the other side of the silence." I thought about it some more, since my thoughts lined up so neatly like little children, each holding onto a knot in a rope as they trotted along. "You didn't know that I needed it nice and quiet, but someone did. Maybe some people don't need it quiet; maybe some people need other things. But it was too loud for me, too messy. Now it's quiet, and everything is tidy. I like it here."

Peter still looked confused, and I thought he was going to argue. Then he remembered that he had seen the other side of silence too. He must have, he was such a good person. He tried so hard to help me even when I could only see his baby face.

.•.

Slowly, I picked up each piece of trash from the South common room. In one day I could make it to all four of the common rooms. West, East, North, and South common rooms. I could travel around the compass, picking up trash and making things nice. If I didn't pick up the trash myself, Eunice or Trevor would call the trash names. They would say "damn trash" or sometimes even "fucking garbage." They say that because they don't understand that it isn't the trash's fault it's dirty and smells sometimes. It was people - people who used things up and didn't put the leftovers away. I picked up each cup and plastic bag and placed them in the garbage cans so no one would yell.

I couldn't pick up trash at the shelter every day. Now I had a job where I got to make things clean and shiny. Cheryl helped me get a job at the Holiday Inn where there are hundreds of rooms all exactly the same. The job is easy for me, because it feels like cleaning the same room over and over again. When I start, it's like a puzzle, finding what's out of place. First the easy things, like the sheets, the wastebaskets, the little soaps in the bathroom. Then it gets harder, putting the shine back on the counters, making the folds of the comforter just so, replacing the box of tissue. Some people clean faster than me, but my boss said my rooms are the best. Perfect, she said, they are always perfect.

Today I made the common rooms perfect.

"Hey, Margot. Thanks for helping out," Chris, the shelter director said, patting me on the back. Chris still thought I was a little girl, or a trained puppy. But Peter showed me how to treat Chris's petting just like the trash. No need to yell about it; just put it in the can where it belongs. Every time someone spoke to me now I would stop and think, "are those words I want to keep?" If I don't want to keep them, I put them right into the can. Kind things and smiles I could keep with me though, and hold them close.

"You're welcome," I mumbled. Chris didn't like it that I mumbled, but my voice was still weak and needed time to get stronger. Just like my eyes liked to point down instead of straight, so I knew most people by their shoes.

"Do you know if Peter's here today?" Chris asked.

"No, I don't think so."

Peter usually came to see me first, before he talked to other people. Peter was a very good man and came to the shelter to help people get out of bad trouble in their heads. But he liked to talk to me because we were friends. Sometimes I helped him think about talking to hard people, because I used to be one of those hard people.

"Hm. His wife is here looking for him."

"A-alice?" I asked.

"Oh, you know her?"

Peter talked about Alice all the time, how beautiful and smart she was. When the months were still blank and white, they had a baby. Thomas. Peter called the baby Thomas, but that seemed like too big a name for a tiny person. I called him Tom.

"Not...not really," I had a plastic cup in my hand, and there were tiny dried drops of something bright pink crawling up the inside. Punch, maybe.

"She seems kind of upset," Chris said. "I'd talk to her, but I've got staff meeting in ten and I have a couple Power Point slides to brush up." Chris stopped talking, because he remembered that I wasn't normal. He smiled his fake smile again. I took that smile, and I put it in the can with the cup and the dried punch.

"Alice can talk to me," I said. I didn't want to talk to Alice. Peter never said anything bad about Alice, but I knew that he was a little bit afraid of her. I liked Peter a lot, and he was a good friend, but I was a little bit afraid of him sometimes. He had answers to everything in the whole world. But Chris was not a good person to talk to, and he was too busy for Alice anyway.

"Great, she's in reception." Chris was gone, because Chris was very busy all the time. His world turned faster than everyone else's; that's why his smiles were never real.

I went to reception, where I had to talk to Regina. Regina lived in the little box of the reception desk, because that's where she belonged. Some people like to be in boxes, but it makes me nervous.

When I got to the right door and pushed through it, I saw Alice there with her little baby. I didn't have to talk to Regina. Alice was so pretty today, but Alice was pretty every day. Her hair was light all around her face, and she was so skinny and strong. She looked like pictures of angels.

Her baby was crying in his stroller, big crying that was loud inside the ears like gunshots or cars with bad engines. Alice was crying a little bit too, probably because her ears hurt.

"H-hi, Alice."

"Oh. Hi, Margot." Alice tried to push the tears out of her eyes with the palms of her hands, but she needed a tissue. Palms just push stuff around. "Peter isn't here today?"

"He usually talks to me first. He hasn't talked to me today."

"Right." Alice looked at her shoes. She had white shoes for exercising in, and they had a pretty green line around the toes. I liked those shoes.

"Can I hold the baby?" I asked. The whole baby looked like a red bruise, and his face was mostly screaming mouth.

"He's kind of upset right now," Alice said. Tom did look upset, but so did Alice. So I just shrugged. "Sure," Alice said finally.

When I picked the baby up he bent his back so his tummy pointed up like the top of a hill. It made him hard to hold.

"I know it looks awful, but he really is okay. I've fed him and changed him and he's even had a nap recently. I rocked him, we went for a walk, I tried to get him to play with something."

I shrugged again, tucking the wriggling little body in the big crook of my arm. I could feel his tiny muscles struggling, but he couldn't get out 'cause my arms are fat and strong.

"Maybe Peter can talk to him. I used to scream a lot too." I wondered if the baby had mean voices in his head. But he wouldn't mind if his mother was around. Alice wasn't like my mom; she was beautiful and nice. She really wanted him to be happy.

"Well, I was hoping Peter would take him for a while. The house is such a disaster ever since the baby was born and I thought if I could just get a couple hours I might...I don't know. I guess I got his schedule wrong."

The baby screamed and barked and twisted in the crook of my arm. I'd seen people look like that before, their heads rolling around on their necks because there was nowhere left to look. None of those people had food in their tummies and a soft place to sleep, though.

"I don't know about this baby," I said, handing Tom back to Alice. She took him and let him thrash and scream on her lap.

"Me neither," she murmured. Chris wouldn't like her talking quiet like that.

"But I do know about dirty houses. I clean things all the time.

That's my job."

Alice smiled, but it was a weak smile. For a moment, the baby stopped crying and the silence was big and thick. Alice tried to get a pacifier in the baby's mouth, but it didn't look good to him, I guess.

"I bet you're really good at it," Alice said.

"I am. I make all the rooms perfect." I let my eyes rest Alice's lap, where the baby was. Her deep blue eyes were too pretty for me, but she had pretty knees too. "I'll make your house perfect, too."

"What was that?" Alice asked. The baby had her eyes and some of her ears too, but he wasn't crying anymore.

"I'll clean up your house. Then there won't be trash and mess around. The windows will let in all the sunlight in and all the dishes will be ready for food." This was a good plan; it would make Alice less tired. Peter would be happy if Alice felt better.

"Oh, that's okay. Nice of you, though." Alice was paying attention to the baby, but I knew my plan was good.

"If your house is perfect, you won't be so sad." I looked right at Alice's blue eyes, sharp like the sapphire in my mother's ring. Alice didn't know that I knew she was sad. She thought I wasn't so smart, not smart enough to see she needed help, too.

"I can clean up my own mess, Margot." She was mean, but I knew that was fake meanness so that I wouldn't tell her that she was sad again.

"Peter came and helped me. I didn't lose anymore of my toes because of him. Peter is my good friend, and I want to make him happy too."

Alice laughed, and it made sadness tickle all my ribs. "Peter doesn't care about the mess."

I shrugged again. "Peter loves you more than the sky. If you feel better, he'll be happy, too."

"Oh," Alice cried, like I'd stuck her with a thumbtack. Then she looked like she might cry again, exactly like I'd stuck her with a thumbtack.

"It's okay, Alice. The things will all get better."

The Hand of Service

Thomas started crying, and I rolled over to see if my husband heard him. Peter was snoring, but that didn't bother me. He couldn't feed Thomas anyway, since we'd decided on breastfeeding for the first six months. I walked down to the baby's room and clicked on the Winnie-the-Pooh lamp. The light bulb was a very low wattage, to avoid jarring the baby awake.

"Hey, Tommy. You couldn't hold out for twenty more minutes and let Mommy get two hours of sleep in a row, huh?" Thomas calmed when he heard my voice. Lifting him out of the crib, I unbuttoned my pajama top and sat in the ergonomic rocking chair Peter had brought home during the last month of my pregnancy. Thomas latched onto my nipple, and I felt the steady pull that was draining my breast.

I told myself this was the most important job I'd ever have. That was my mantra since the baby was born. When I was working as a corporate executive, I'd developed a daily mantra to keep me focused on the main goal of the company. In the last three weeks I'd discovered that strategy worked better in my corner office than it did in a custard-colored nursery.

Thomas was nearly as exhausted as me, and after a few minutes he yawned and dozed in my arms. Daily e-mails warned that holding a new baby while it slept was damaging to their sleep cycle and perpetuated their dependence on Mommy to soothe them to sleep. Mostly I tried to make sure that Thomas slept on his own, but times like these it was just so much easier to doze off in that comfortable chair, knowing he would just latch back on if he woke up hungry.

"Alice...Alice..."

Before I opened my eyes, I could feel drool dripping down my cheek. I jumped and wiped my face, instinctively cradling the baby in one arm. "What?"

"I'm going to leave for work. I thought you might want to go to bed."

"What time is it?" Everything was still fuzzy, even the looming face of my husband, smiling patiently.

"It's seven-thirty. How long have you been in here?"

The part of me who used to be an intimidating, powerful, sexy woman was really insulted that Peter didn't notice my absence from our bed.

"Forever," I said flatly.

"You know, you should really look into some postpartum depression treatments. They might make you feel better."

He's trying to help, he's trying to help, he's trying to help. This was a mantra I was developing on the spot. I tried to smile.

"I'm not up for a diagnosis yet." With some effort, I stood up and deposited the baby back in his crib. He fussed a little, but settled down once I'd placed his pacifier in his mouth. Putting my index finger to my lips, I pushed Peter out the door and carefully closed it behind us.

"It's nothing to be ashamed of," Peter said, touching the side of my face.

"I'm fine. Just a little antsy. I haven't left the house in..." I tried to remember what day of the week it was, tried to count backwards to the abortive trip to the grocery store sometime last week. Or the week before that. "I can't remember the last time I left the house."

"You can do anything you like. You've got a car."

My mind slowly turned over the events of the last few days, trying to find a break long enough to leave the house. I was trapped in an endless cycle of feeding, burping, changing, and soothing. When Thomas finally dozed off, I usually did, too. On the rare occasions when I wandered downstairs with the vague idea of cleaning something, I was so overwhelmed by the mess that I'd retreat to my room and sulk. The idea of getting Thomas packed up into his carrier and out the door was so intimidating, I couldn't even think ahead to what we might do. So I glared at my husband. I was too tired to yell.

"Let's talk about this later. I'm exhausted right now and I'm not going to express myself effectively." This was corporate talk, and I could tell Peter was disappointed.

"Okay. We'll talk when I get home."

I nodded, holding back a smart comment about how Peter could make a discussion sound like a threat. Peter already had his briefcase in hand. Moments after a brief kiss I heard the front door close behind him.

Collapsing into bed, I intended to sleep until Thomas woke up again. Unfortunately, the twenty years I spent conditioning my body to wake sharply with the first buzz of the alarm was not easily dismissed. Never mind that I'd only slept four hours, mostly in twenty-minute increments.

If I went downstairs I would see that the entire living room was a wreck of baby clothes and various baby tools I hadn't figured out how to use yet. The kitchen was stacked with dishes I'd been too overwhelmed to do, and the trash was full of Styrofoam boxes, evidence of Peter's coping mechanism for my lack of domestic skills. He never complained. If he came home from work and didn't find me cooking, he just picked up the phone and asked if I felt like

Chinese or pizza.

Because of Peter's tendency to find a diagnosis for any discontent, I'd searched the Internet to find out if I really did have postpartum depression. I didn't. My unhappiness couldn't be cured with a nice little hundred-milligram pill. Instead, I turned to more ancient methods. Reaching for the cordless phone, I called my sister Laura in Pittsburg.

"Hello!" she called, cheerful as ever.

"Hey Laura. It's Alice."

"Yeah, I know. It's seven-thirty. Did Peter just leave for work?"

"What does that mean?" I mumbled, slouching under the covers.

"Nothing, just that you've called at seven-thirty three times this week. I don't know what you want, exactly."

"Some sisterly commiseration? Sympathy?"

"How's that working out for you?" she asked, sounding amused.

"Not great."

"Well, you do sound a bit disheveled this morning. Rough night?"

"Is my voice disheveled? I didn't know that could happen."

"It's a side effect of not leaving the house for *over a month*."

"It's really hard with the baby and everything. There are very short windows of time between feeding and napping."

"I'm sure it is hard with a baby, especially when that baby wasn't part of your life plan."

"Please let's don't do this again." I could hear myself whining.

"I don't know what else to tell you. Your situation is a result of your life choices."

I sighed. "You act like I decided to shoot heroine or something."

"Nope, I act like you left your dream job for a man and forgot how to use a condom."

I wanted to be mad at her, but I would have said the same thing if our roles were reversed. In fact, I would use more sarcasm. So I just sighed.

"Got any cheerful thoughts for me?"

"It's sunny today?" she said hopefully

"It's sunny in Pittsburgh, Laura. It's raining in Minneapolis."

"Oh. Sorry."

I could hear the morning news playing in the background of my sister's phone. Right now she was cooking an egg and making toast before settling down to her desk for the day.

"Why do I even call you?" I asked.

"Geeze, you are grumpy today."

"Your assessment of all the stupid things I've done in the last two years is bound to improve that situation." I was too tired to be really angry.

"You have to laugh at your mistakes, Alice. Otherwise they're just unsightly."

"I agree with you there." I paused.

"But?"

"But I can't see them as mistakes. I love Peter, and even though I wasn't planning on getting pregnant this early, now that Thomas is here I feel kind of…bad about referring to him as a mistake."

"It never stopped Mom."

"Yeah, I think I'm going to avoid using 'mom did it' as an excuse for the kind of parent I am."

Laura laughed. "That sounds like a plan. I should say, just so I don't lose my title as the most awesome aunt ever, I don't think Thomas is a mistake. And Peter's all right, so we'll let him stay too."

"I'm so relieved."

"Your mistake, my friend, was trading a life you loved for one you're not so sure about."

My smile faded and I squeezed my eyes shut against the light. "Not much I can do about it now."

"Sure you can! You're still a crazy intelligent, qualified, and talented woman. Hit the pavement and find a new job already. Minneapolis is a booming little city, there has to be a place for you somewhere."

"The economy is bad right now. No one is hiring."

"Alice, really. When has a little thing like a lagging economy held you back? Do you think there's a sudden glut in the market for executives who can boost a company's profits by a double-digit percentage?"

As I took a deep breath, I felt my shoulders start to relax a little. "I knew there was a reason I called you."

"As much as I love giving you this pep talk, stop calling me. Start calling employment agencies."

"Can't I wait until I've got my figure back and I've figured out how to wash my hair every day?" I mock-whined.

"Nope. Self-pity doesn't burn calories, you have to get a life before you'll feel better."

Rolling over, I pulled my covers over my head. "It's not that simple, Laura. Thomas is barely a month old, and I'm still breastfeeding. Not to mention that the only reason we'd need my income is to pay for daycare."

"There's more to work than money, Alice. No one knows that more than you."

"I'm not sure how I feel about turning my newborn over to a stranger just because I can't – "

"Be content as a full-time diaper changer? That doesn't make you a bad person, Alice."

"There must be a way to figure this out, that's all I'm saying. I want to raise my own child, I just have to find a better way to do it."

"You aren't made to be a mommy, Alice. You're a powerful and intelligent woman, there are bigger and more important things you can do. Not everyone has what you have, and I think it will be a terrible waste of talent if you become content sacrificing your life for someone else's."

"When did Scary Laura grab the phone?"

"I'm serious, Alice. There's more to you than making babies."

"I got it. Don't you have to start work soon?"

"I do, actually. Sorry to leave you, consider it a kick in the pants. At least get out of the house, okay? Even full-time mommies leave their homes occasionally."

"You're right. Maybe we'll go to the park or something today."

"Not exactly what I had in mind. Better than nothing, I guess. Except…"

"What? Will I betray the feminist cause by taking my baby to a park?"

A carefree bubble of laughter floated across the line, my sister flaunting her happy, simple life. "No, silly. Isn't it raining there today?"

· • ·

After another week of hibernating and a few more conversations with my sister, I knew if I didn't do something I was going to lose my mind. So one morning, bolstered by three hours of sleep, I shook the dust off my life.

I tried anyway. Thomas woke promptly at 5:30 needing to be fed. Determined, I took him downstairs with me so I would at least be closer to the work I needed to do when he was done. My proactive self grew impatient as Thomas dozed while he nursed, and I tried to remove my nipple from his mouth, hoping he would just go down for a nap so I could get started. Of course, as soon as he felt his breakfast leaving, he'd wake up and started guzzling again.

My acute sense of time passing made me a great executive. I could clock cubicle conversations with the beating of my heart, and I'd always cut them off after five minutes. That sense was becoming a huge liability as I felt forty-five minutes tick by while Thomas ate.

When he was finally done, I wiped his mouth and cleaned his chin with the burp blanket. Shifting him so he was lying vertically, I patted his back, trying to get him to burp so I could move on. I jiggled, patted, patted harder, rubbed, then patted some more. His grey eyes stared at me as his tiny eyebrow ridges lowered, demanding to know why I was harassing him like this. By the time he worked the gas bubbles out of his stomach his diaper needed to be changed. While he was eating he was ready to slip into a blissful sleep, after a rough burping and cold air on his wet bottom he was wide awake.

Somewhere in the living room, in the mass of baby items that crowded the floor and stacked the tables, most of them still in the box, there was a brand new, ergonomic infant car seat where I could safely set my child so I could use my hands. Peter turned all the attention he usually spent on canoe paddles and Leatherman tools onto baby stuff during my pregnancy, purchasing every item guaranteed to boost, prop, primp, or probe an infant. Finally I found the car seat, buried under a collection of onesies in various pastel colors.

Thomas protested as I tucked his head into the little fleece frame that would keep his neck from getting torqued, but I ignored it, hoping he'd settle. He did not settle. He let out a pitiful wail, reaching out his tiny hands towards the empty air. For a while, I pretended like I was going to let him cry while I straightened up. When I realized I was just watching him cry, I picked him up. Tucking his body into the crook of my left arm, I used my right to gather the onesies I'd displaced. I set the whole mess of pastel fabric at the bottom of the stairs since they belonged in the nursery. Contented to be near me, Thomas drifted to sleep while I did my straightening one-handed. I snuck upstairs and laid him in his crib, tucking his blanket around his body. At first he whined, thrashing his arms, but when I tucked his pacifier into his lips he sank back to sleep. It felt like a miracle.

Resisting the urge take advantage of Thomas's nap and sleep myself, I settled down at the desktop. Although I knew my sister gave me her best advice, I wasn't ready to give up on being a mommy yet. Laura didn't realize that the very determination and structured thinking that made me a dynamite executive made me stubborn enough to search out a compromise-free lifestyle. I could find a way to stay with my child and stay sane.

With that resolution, I began searching for activities for moms in the area. Without much effort, I pinpointed a mom's group that met at a nearby coffee shop. Picking up the phone, I dialed the contact number and listened to the droning ring.

"Hello?" The word sounded like a response to a demanding question.

"Hello, my name is Alice Anders. I'm calling about the mom's group."

"Oh, are you a new mom?" she asked eagerly. "Angie, put that down!" A long stream of whining followed, like a siren.

"Yes, I have a one-month-old. His name is Thomas."

"Wow, and you're already looking for a mom's group? You're certainly on top of things."

My heart warmed. Maybe this was my answer.

"Thanks. When is your next meeting?"

"We're getting together this afternoon at 3pm, why don't you stop by and see how you like it? The girls will be happy to meet you."

"Great, I'll be there. And it's okay if I bring Thomas?"

"Who's Thomas?"

"My son, the newborn."

She laughed. "It wouldn't be much of a mom's club if we couldn't bring our kids!"

Despite how friendly the woman sounded, I couldn't bring myself to go to the coffee shop without at least a shower. This was the first time I'd dared to shower while Peter was away; I was so worried that Thomas would need me. My fears came alive as I heard him start screaming while I was rubbing suds into my itchy scalp.

For a moment, I considered running to him wet and covered in soap. Pausing, I did a reality check. *He's fine. He's in his crib with a pacifier, a blanket, and a padded bumper.* Still, I rushed through the rest of my shower as if I were in the army, not pausing to consider shaving a few weeks of stubble off my legs before rushing out in a towel to see if my baby was still alive.

Thomas's little face was scrunched into an expression of abject abandonment, his skin was purplish with rage, and his lips trembled around his pink gums.

"It's okay, baby. Mommy just had to shower, I'm here now."

He continued to scream and fuss, making occasional little gurgling sounds when he tried to cry and breathe at the same time. None of my rocking, cooing, bouncing, walking, or any other form of pacifying made a dent in his angst. After five straight minutes of constant screaming, I had the strange thought that he could sense my guilt for leaving him alone and was punishing me for it.

Although I was frustrated and exhausted in my first weeks months of motherhood, this was the first time I was feeling my hand tense under that little downy head. Websites about postpartum depression had described women having thoughts of harming their babies. Still, the sudden mental image of flinging the little screaming bundle across the room shocked and frightened me. Carefully, I set him back down in his crib and placed his pacifier in his mouth in tightly controlled motion. Of course he spit the rubber nipple out and wailed with a renewed sense of maltreatment. I spoke calmly over the screaming.

"Thomas, I need a break. I will be back in five minutes. You will be okay."

I walked out of the room, shutting the door behind me. Even while I felt a blush of shame on my face, I turned the baby-monitor off and stretched myself out on my bed to cry. The mom's club would probably kick me out if they knew I was abandoning my baby at this very moment. And why? Because I wanted a shower.

Rage washed over me. What was so horrible about what I'd done? I wanted to bathe myself, was that so selfish? What if I did want to go back to work? What if a nanny was dealing with this moment, would that mean that I wasn't worthy of the title "mother"? When was that a title I wanted?

After another feeding, burping, and changing routine, which took just over an hour, I set Thomas back in his carrier. He didn't like it any better the second time, but I let him cry while I quickly packed the diaper bag with everything he could possibly need in the next two hours: burp blankets, diaper change kit, extra wipes, an extra onesie, plastic bags for dirty diapers, a fleece blanket, and a few other things just for good measure. I cooed and talked in a low, soothing voice while I packed up, hoping Thomas would know that I was nearby and he was safe. Apparently, my presence wasn't reassuring.

At twenty minutes after three, I headed out to the coffee shop. On a different day I might have walked since it was only ten or twelve blocks. Today, I packed Thomas, still fussing, into my new baby car seat and strapped him into the backseat of my Prius. The ride calmed him, and he was awake but quiet when I pulled up to the coffee shop.

I'd seen the coffee shop before, but I'd never stopped. The place with the strongest espresso was on the other side of town. This shop had a very different appeal, featuring a huge kids' area full of toys, painted on three sides with an ocean mural. Kids from infancy to age six ran screaming through the room, chasing each other and trying to wrest toys from each other.

"Brianna, you share with your brother!" one of the women sitting near the kids' room said, pointing at a curly haired little girl who responded by smirking and running away with the toy. Her mother shrugged and turned back to the circle of women she was sitting with. As I approached the group, I caught sight of the sign that read, "All unattended children will be given an espresso shot and a puppy."

Clutching Thomas's carrier close to my side, I stepped up to the circle of women.

"Is this the mom's group?" I asked.

"Oh hi! You must be...Allison?" a tall, brunette woman in a stained T-shirt greeted me, holding out her hand in greeting. I shook it, trying not to notice her month-old manicure.

"Alice," I corrected. "And this is Thomas." I nodded towards the baby-carrier.

"Please sit down. I'm Patty, and this is Susan, Monica, and Debbie." Patty gestured towards an empty chair. "The coffee shop really prefers that we all order something, since we take up so much space," Patty said.

"Right," I straightened up from my half-sitting position and picked up the baby carrier.

"Oh, we can watch him while you order. Doesn't look like he's much trouble," Debbie said. The offer was friendly, but I didn't know these women.

"That's okay. We've already had some trauma today, I'd better keep him close." I smiled my corporate smile, but met only a host of raised eyebrows.

In need of something simple, I ordered a black coffee and returned to the group.

"You're not breastfeeding?" Monica asked me, looking concerned.

"N-no, I am." That seemed like a weird opening question.

"Well you can't have coffee if you're breastfeeding!" Debbie exclaimed. Her face still looked friendly, but I worried they were going to jump me to get the dangerous coffee away from my innocent baby.

"It's decaf," I lied.

"Hmmm…" Susan said. "You know that even decaf has some caffeine in it. I'm sure it'll be fine. I just wouldn't take any chances with my baby."

"I think we're getting off to a bad start," Patty said, patting Susan's arm. "Every mom is different, right?"

"Right," I agreed with relief. I took a defiant sip of my drink before setting it aside.

"Did you ever get that new Diaper Genie?" Monica asked, turning towards Susan.

"You know, I did some research and the reviews say that there isn't much difference between the name brand and the generic versions. They all stink after a few days."

"Well, I can tell the difference." Monica said firmly. "Of course, I empty it every day." A murmur of agreement passed through the group.

"Maybe I should try that," Debbie said. "Michael's bowel movements have been so foul lately, I've been putting my diaper genie out on the porch because I can't stand to have it in the house even if I do take it out every night."

"Has anything changed in his diet lately?" Patty asked.

"Well, I have been trying these new vitamin fortified applesauce cups, do you think that could be effecting him?" Debbie asked, all concern.

"Oh, I would never give Brianna apples!" Monica cried. "I don't know about the smell, but the amount of poop she has if she even has an apple slice is simply incredible. And it lasts for days!"

"Really?" Susan asked, incredulous. "Adding a little raw fruit to Patrick's diet has really helped with his constipation. Everything goes much smoother now. It's better than fruit snacks or applesauce cups."

I sat there as they continued to discuss the various effects and ramifications of stool deposits.

"Do any of you work?" I asked, inserting myself into the poop discussion. I'd held managers and labor officers down in meetings; I could handle a subject change in a mommy group.

"What?" Monica asked.

"Do any of you work?"

A very scary silence fell over the group as they all stared at me in blind shock. Patty was the first to recover.

"It's a common expression, but in this group we want to be supportive of each other's choices, and we all know that taking care of children is very hard work."

At once I was insulted, embarrassed, and wondered if Patty worked in human resources. She would be good at it.

"I'm sorry. How should I ask?" I tried my best to be pleasant and non-confrontational.

"We prefer you ask if we work outside the home," Monica said, a smidge imperious. Patty gave her a look.

"Do you?" I asked.

"Not in this group. There's a group that meets on the weekends with some working moms. I know Sharon goes to that group and she's single," Monica said.

"Oh. I'm married," I felt the need to add.

"Of course you are!" Susan exclaimed, patting my knee. Like I'd asserted that I thought I was pretty.

"Do you work outside the home?" Patty asked. At another time, her tone would be a bit condescending; at this moment it was downright kind.

"No. I've been thinking about looking for a job, though." I knew that idea would not be popular in this group. But if I was ever going to meet these women again, they should know whom they're dealing with. Maybe I could be their token feminist.

"Is the budget getting tight?" Debbie stage whispered.

"No, my husband is an established doctor," I replied. "I've just been feeling a bit…" My mind searched for a word. Bored wouldn't quite cover it, because I felt just as overwhelmed as I felt restless. "I'm not sure how I feel, but this isn't what I wanted my life to look like."

"It's always hard the first few months," Patty said, gently.

Monica scoffed. "Just wait until he's two! Wait until he's screaming his head off in the grocery store because they don't have chocolate flavored teddy-grahams."

"I hired a nanny for ten hours a week just to get a little break from Michael when he turned two. It's really been a life saver," Debbie said.

"You know, I've been thinking about doing that myself. I just need a few hours to collect my thoughts and not worry about anyone breaking the furniture," Susan put in.

"Can't your husband take the kids for a few hours?" I asked. They stared at me again. That was getting old.

"Of course it's important that fathers interact with their children as much as possible," Patty said cautiously.

"If I left my kids with my husband I would spend the whole time worrying about them," Monica said.

"Oh, that's too bad. My husband is really great with the kids," Susan said.

"So why do you need a nanny?" I asked.

"Oh. Well…I don't have one now, I was just thinking about it. Gerald is so tired when he gets home. I'd hate to leave him with the kids so I can go off and play."

I was not in the mood to listen to Susan talk about how tired Gerald was when he got home from work, not anymore. This experiment felt like a trip to the nineteen-fifties. So I stopped talking and just let the women continue their conversation about how difficult their kids were, how much they loved them, how Brianna was going to start piano lessons soon even though she was only three, how Michael was in bilingual Mandarin pre-school, the difference between two brands of car seats and how soon one should switch to a booster seat instead. After a half hour of that kind of talk I began to wish I'd brought a book. I gently kicked Thomas's baby carrier in the vain hope he'd give me an excuse to leave. Of course, now he was quiet and docile. His lips turned up a bit like a smile.

"Well, ladies, it's been a great afternoon. We'll meet again next week. I hope you'll join us, Alice," Patty said. Sadly, she seemed sincere. I tried to smile.

"Great to meet you, come back again," Susan said cheerfully as she departed, shouting over her shoulder for her kids to follow her. Monica was wrestling a toy train away from her son. Debbie just smiled before she left. As I rose to leave, Patty touched my arm.

"Do you have time to stay for a moment?" she asked. I checked to make sure the other women were really leaving.

"Sure."

I couldn't bear the thought of going home to the wrecked

house, caught between the jaws of apathy and raging discontent. And as much as I now loathed the whole idea of a mom's group, I had to admit that Patty had a little more substance than the others. So I settled back into my chair while she spoke a few words to Monica before that woman left, dragging her three-year-old son behind her. Remembering my coffee, I took another sip of the now cold black liquid. It still felt good.

"Hey, Alice," Patty said, choosing a seat a little closer to me.

"Where are your kids?" I asked, looking around. All the noise had left with the other women.

"Oh, my Angie is right over there," she said, pointing into the kids' room. Sure enough, there was a little girl in a pink T-shirt quietly playing with a plastic dollhouse.

"She looks like a very good girl."

"I just wanted to touch base with you. Susan, Monica, and Debbie have been in the same group for several years and they can be kind of hostile to newcomers. They don't mean anything by it."

I smiled, wanting to show Patty that I appreciated her sensitivity. "I don't think I would ever have gotten along with that group. I'm not like them."

"All mothers are different, and all kids are different. There's no right way to do this; that's why we need each other."

"That's great," I said. "But I don't think that I'm going to contribute much to this group. I really appreciate your warm welcome, though." *Being here makes me want to die, and you're not going to talk me into coming back*, I thought.

"Of course it's totally up to you. I just wanted to present the idea that you bring a new perspective into the group. If we don't understand other kinds of mothering, it's because we've never been exposed to them."

"That's a nice way to say it," I said.

"But?"

"I'm not..." I hesitated. "While I appreciate your saying I would add value to the group, I think I need to do something that's helpful for me."

Patty nodded. "I understand that. I hope you find something helpful. Feel free to call me if you need anything or just want to chat. And of course you're always welcome to try us out again."

"Thank you."

I knew she meant it, I knew the other women didn't mean to be hurtful, and I knew Peter would be home soon to help. Still, I cried all the way home.

·•·

After three sulky hours at home, half-heartedly trying to tackle the mountain of dishes in the 20-minute breaks Thomas gave me, I remembered that Peter would be at the homeless shelter today. While I was wondering if my life had any meaning at all, my husband was saving lost souls from the streets. Of course we discussed how much time he spent volunteering, and of course it was totally fine with me to watch the baby while he was out saving the world. Until now.

My vision focused, staring down the dark tunnel of my future where my big contribution to the world was watching Thomas while Peter did great things. Despite my iron grip on emotion, developed after years of working in an industry that saw hysteria behind every tear, I found myself trembling. Little hiccups of sobs bubbled up, shaking my whole core. Surely this was sleep deprivation having its way. It had to be, because this was not me. I didn't even like this person.

Lips trembling, I packed Thomas back up in the car seat. Unlike our last trip out, this time he wailed pathetically while I strapped the carrier into the back seat of the car. He let out rhythmic wails as I pulled onto the street and turned on my blinker. Tears spilling unbidden onto my cheeks made my skin raw and puffy.

I drove to the shelter. One thing I knew; Peter had to take the baby. I was losing my mind, and my son needed a safe parent. Handing him to his father felt right. If Peter would take the baby, I could go do...something. Anything to feel like myself again.

Usually I held an image of myself in my mind, gauging the reaction around me, making sure I was projecting an attitude of calm capability. I must have left that attitude back with my flat stomach, because I couldn't bring myself to picture how I must look to the woman at the front desk. Despite my mental anguish, I saw the faint note of surprise in her eyebrows.

"Mrs. Anders, nice to see you. Are you looking for Peter?" the woman asked. I think her name was Regina. She looked very vaguely familiar from the annual picnic.

"Um, yes. I don't want to...um...interrupt him...you know...if he's...well...with someone, I just...well..."

"I'll try to find him," she smiled. I wanted to smack myself for how stupid I sounded - just more evidence that I was not myself. I'd morphed into an incoherent mommy nightmare.

"Why don't you have a seat? It may take a minute," Regina said, gesturing at a chair. Apparently, she didn't want me staring at her with a screaming baby while she tried to find my husband.

I sat in an uncomfortable chair and rocked the stroller back and forth in a futile attempt to calm my child without touching him. I probably looked like a junkie, and I felt like one too. Regina made some discrete calls, and I saw her glancing at me before she turned away, keeping her words to herself.

After a few interminable minutes, Margot's lumbering form came through the big swinging doors. She was mid-fifties at least, but she slouched and stuffed her hands in her pockets like a sullen teenager. I didn't want to see her.

"H-hi, Alice," Margot muttered.

"Hi, Margot. Where's Peter?" My last nerve was fraying as I bounced my leg nervously, shook the stroller, and tried to speak kindly.

"He usually talks to me first," Margot said. I bounced a little harder, annoyed that Margot expected me to understand that. "He hasn't talked to me yet," she added.

"Right." I heard how rude I sounded. Tears edged my eyes, because now I was being rude to a mentally challenged person who came to talk to me after Regina sent up a flare. I could almost hear the PA system crackling, *Deranged woman in the lobby, please assist.*

"Can I hold the baby?"

"He's kind of upset right now," I said, feeling shifty. Half of me didn't want to hand Thomas to this mildly uncomfortable person. The other half would do anything to pass the burden of his screaming. Margot shrugged as if to say, *he's a baby, he's supposed to cry.* "Sure," I agreed.

Margot retrieved Thomas from his stroller, looking him over like a piece of cheese that might have gone bad.

"I know it looks awful, but I swear he's totally fine. I've fed him and changed him, and…" maybe I made a few more excuses, but they didn't seem to register with Margot. She shrugged again. Without ceremony, she tucked the wriggling, reddish bundle into the crook of her arm.

"Maybe Peter can talk to him. I used to scream a lot, too." Margot made this suggestion with blank sincerity, an expression I couldn't quite read. Was she teasing? Or did she really think that a psychiatrist could make a baby stop crying?

"Well, I was hoping Peter would at least take the baby for a while. The house is such a wreck since the baby's been born and I thought if I could get a couple hours I might…" I almost said, "clean up the house," but I had no intention of cleaning if I did get a break. Not that it mattered; Peter wasn't here. "I don't know. I guess

I got his schedule wrong."

For a long time, Margot didn't say anything. She looked at her shoes, at my shoes, and then down at the baby that was still thrashing against the world.

"I don't know about this baby," Margot said at last, handing him back to me. Taking him from her, I couldn't muster up even the slightest bit of affection for him. I held him loosely, letting him work his arms and legs in desperate circles as his back rested on my lap.

"But I do know about dirty houses. I clean them all the time. That's my job." When Margot said these words, she grew a little taller. How wonderful to take pride in a simple job like cleaning houses. For a second, I was distracted from my breakdown.

"I bet you're really good at it," I said. The second passed, because Thomas was working his way off my lap and I had to snatch him back before he fell off my knees. Margot said something else, and I nodded. Peter would tell me my listening skills need work, but he could be the damn counselor. I was trying to figure out motherhood.

"I'll make your house perfect too."

The last sentence sounded like a conclusion.

"What?"

"I'll clean up your house. Then there won't be trash and mess around. The windows will let all the sunlight in and all the dishes will be ready for food."

"Oh, that's okay. Nice of you, though." The words were out of my mouth before I'd given her offer a second thought. She couldn't be serious anyway, she was just talking.

"If your house is perfect, you won't be so sad."

Margot met my eyes for the first time. Her eyes were murky green, set deep into her face. Those eyes saw through me, and I felt like I was trying to cover my nakedness with a wet sheet.

"I can clean up my own mess." I clapped my mouth shut to cut off the sharp words. Margot's eyes dropped.

"Peter helped me. I didn't lose anymore of my toes. Peter is my good friend, and I want to make him happy, too."

How sad that she thought she had to scrub my toilet to be kind to Peter. I bit back my sarcasm, trying to breathe first. Even if I wasn't the same competent, efficient, controlled woman I had so enjoyed being, I shouldn't mock someone kind and innocent like Margot.

"Peter doesn't care about the mess," I said.

Margot shrugged again. I couldn't explain it, but every time she shrugged I felt a little release between my own shoulder blades.

"Peter loves you more than the sky. If you feel better, he'll be happy, too."

I gasped for breath, like she'd slapped me with those lovely words. How could she know anything about me and Peter? Yet I believed her like I'd never believed anyone. I felt heat around my eyes, and I tightened all the muscles in my face to keep from crying.

"It's okay, Alice. All the things will get better." Margot smiled sheepishly, and I couldn't help smiling back.

．•．

When Margot arrived she walked around the house slowly, taking it all in. Margot walked as if she were stalking a deer, placing each foot with precision. Her eyes touched each and every object in my home, one by one, as if she had all the time in the world. I held Thomas and rocked on the balls of my feet.

"I told you it was a mess," I said, blushing.

"A house is a puzzle. First I look at all the pieces, then I put them together." Margot leaned over to examine the pile of onesies at the foot of the stairs. "This puzzle has too many pieces."

A small laugh broke from my throat. That's exactly what I'd

thought since Thomas was born. So much stuff for such a little person, and a lot was still in the box it came in. Margot didn't hear my quiet agreement; she just kept mentally cataloging every item.

Watching her process calmed me, the slowness of it. This was not what it looked like when I cleaned. I would have music blasting, stuff in categorical piles, a rag tucked in the waistband of my crappy jeans, a bottle of multi-purpose cleaner hooked on my belt loop. That was the person I used to be, not this overwhelmed mommy. Now I was leaning on the help of a homeless woman while I tried to get my stubborn son to burp.

Peter agreed to Margot's suggestion without a thought. "Margot loves to clean things; you'd really be doing her a favor," he said with a wave of his hand.

A nice dry burp erupted from my son, and he rested his head against my shoulder and sighed as if his burden was just too much to bear.

"He'll probably sleep now. I'll put him to bed and then I'll come down and help you."

Margot shook her head without looking up from the junk on the coffee table. "No, I'm here to get the things right. This is a one-person puzzle."

"Okay." But I couldn't quite accept that. "Margot, I'm going to go a little nuts if I'm sitting around while you're cleaning the house."

Now she looked up at me, knocking through me with those blunt, murky eyes. "I can deal with the things. I can't...can't do lots of stuff, things with thoughts trick me. You can move planets and stars. You shouldn't want to take my work."

"Oh." Air escaped my lungs. How did she keep doing this to me? "Well. Maybe I'll use the rowing machine downstairs. I haven't worked out in a while."

Margot nodded solemnly like I'd told her I was going to work on my cure for cancer.

Thomas slept for a beautiful hour and a half. I worked out, took a nice long shower, and read news on the Internet. Strange and somehow wonderful that the world had gone on turning without me. While I was finishing up an article, the baby monitor started squawking. My shoulders turned away but my eyes clung to the last few sentences of a grown up world before I went upstairs.

When I emerged the living room was spotless, organized, and emanating the soothing aroma of lavender. A baby swing was set up next to the most comfortable chair, books were stacked and arranged by size along a shelf now free of several empty boxes. The coffee table was clear, except for a plump purple candle lit with a tiny flame.

"Oh."

"The things are better, aren't they, Alice?" Margot appeared in the doorway, wiping her ruddy hands on a dishtowel.

"It's beautiful."

"The kitchen isn't all the way solved yet, but this room is done." Pointing straight up she said, "bedrooms next."

Slowly, I nodded. "This is fantastic, Margot. You are really good at this."

Margot smiled, and her whole face glowed. When I got upstairs and picked up my crying baby, I was struck by how lovely he was. He quieted as I held him to my chest, and I loved the warmth of his small body.

"Mommy's here, sweetie." His big dark eyes looked up at me, and a hint of a toothless smile touched his tiny mouth.

∙•∙

By the time Thomas was six months old, we were more mobile. The less restrictive books I'd read said the benefits of breast-feeding ended at six months, and we switched to formula. There was more stink in the house after the switch, but it was worth it for Peter to be able to get up for some of the late-night feedings. Plus, I could travel without exposing myself.

By now I had a routine worked out with Thomas, so I knew the best times to get out of the house, and he had a better idea what to expect from the day. He was sleeping more consistently, and my brain felt less like mush.

I'd found lots of activities that would be a lot of fun once Thomas was older. At the moment, we mostly toured the parks of the Twin Cities. We'd been to Minnehaha Falls, and the sculpture garden at the Walker Art Museum. But sometimes I would just pack up and drive until I found a nice spot.

Today our trek took us to a little park with a baseball diamond and one of the little wading pools I'd found all over the city. The pools were only operational for three or four months of the year, and the water only reached my shins. Still, the neighborhood kids would splash in their turquoise ripples at all hours. Once I saw a couple teenagers lying down in the two feet of water in their string bikinis. Thomas was happy to have me tickle his toes in the water while I soaked my feet.

So I stopped here and unloaded from the car; first the baby carrier, then the huge diaper bag. Finding a shady spot, I spread a blanket on the grass and took a few toys out for Thomas to chew on while I ate my sandwich. After Thomas was happily smacking a light-up keyboard, I surveyed the park.

There were groups of moms who had lunches just like mine. If I wanted, I could set up a play date with Patty and her Angie. As much as I appreciated Patty, we had little in common. She sympathized with my discontent, but she did not understand it. Instead I went by myself. Sometimes I told myself I'd meet someone at the park. When I struck up a conversation with a mom, it felt just like that mommy group. Somewhere there were moms who struggled with their sense of self, wondered if supporting this one little life was their only purpose, and oscillated between rage and intense guilt. They were probably eating their lunches alone too.

Today the park was nearly empty. Unlike some parks with swings and slides, this park was just a baseball diamond, a long stretch of lawn, and a wading pool. Just as I was wondering why there weren't any kids in the pool, an ear-splitting screech answered my question. A plane flew overhead, soaring so low I could make out individual windows. I would gladly drive to the next park to avoid the hideous sound. Thomas didn't mind. He babbled, pointed at the sky, and went back to his toy.

The sound of a bus straining to a stop caught my attention and I turned to look. A tall, skinny man with dark skin and a piece of paper flapping in his hand got off, saying a few words to the bus driver as he did so. He just stood where the bus had dropped him, looking bewildered. I returned to my lunch. Not a moment later, I felt a tentative touch on my shoulder. When I turned, there was the man, holding the paper towards me.

"Excuse me, I am very sorry. Do you know how to get to here?"

Faking a smile, I took the paper and read it over.

Your appointment is at 11:15. Arrival after 11:30 will result in immediate seizure of your visa

Below these threatening words was an address on Airport Lane and a room number.

"I don't know, I'm sorry," I said. I handed the piece of paper back to him, but felt a pang of sympathy. His forehead formed four distinct wrinkles as he looked around.

"The bus man, he said this is the right stop for me."

Glancing at my watch, I saw that it was already eleven.

"Here, I can look up the address on my phone," I said, relenting. Pulling my phone out of my pocket, I tapped the GPS application and searched for the address. Clearly we were near the airport, but we were north of the terminal. That address was on the south side of the airport. "This is the wrong bus stop," I said, showing him the map.

"O-okay," he said. "I must go now, I must find this address. Thank you."

As he walked away I sized him up, wondering if there was any chance he was a serial killer or rapist. I could feel gravity sticking me to the ground, the dull weight of boredom. I thought about Margot carefully arranging books along my shelf, liberating my dishes from the stubborn sink. She would know what to do.

"Wait a second," I called, packing up the toys and blanket. "I can take you to the office." As I spoke, gravity snapped and I felt light. A ten-minute drive, interrupting a long, empty afternoon, would keep this man from being deported. Today I would use my resources for a purpose, for someone besides Thomas.

"O-oh." He looked uncomfortable. "It is okay. I will find on my own."

I shook my head, knowing my confidence had to compensate for the strangeness of the offer. "You won't make it in time."

"But it is your lunch, your child. I am an inconvenience."

"Just help me with this, okay?" I said, pointing to the diaper bag with the blanket stuffed in the top.

Seeing I was serious, he picked up the diaper bag and gave me a shy smile. "You are an angel for me today."

I didn't reply, wondering if this guy knew that a real angel would not look like a sleep-deprived woman lugging a fussy six-month-old. With a few clicks and straps I got Thomas's carrier latched into the back seat, and handed him a toy to keep him busy while we drove.

"I think we have to get on the freeway, just for one exit," I said, as I turned left onto an entrance.

"You are a very kind person, I think," he said.

"What's your name?" I asked.

"Muhammed."

"Nice to meet you, Muhammed. I'm Alice. That's Thomas." I pointed to the back seat.

"Alice and Thomas. Very lovely names."

"Thank you. How long have you been in the US?" Since I was helping change this man's life, I should know a little about it.

"I have been here nine months. After one year, I can bring my wife from Ethiopia."

"I can't imagine being away from my husband for a whole year."

"It is difficult."

"Do you have children?" I asked.

"Not yet. We have not been married long time. Her father let us marry after I find a job here in the United States."

"What do you do here?"

"I am on a fellowship at the University."

Following the directions on my phone, I found a tiny door marked 207 in the middle of a non-descript office park. Everything looked dirty and like it didn't quite belong. Planes zoomed overhead, even louder than at the park.

"Go see if this is the right place. I'll wait," I said, eyeing the door.

"Very good, I will go check." He hopped out of the car, closing the door carefully behind him. He disappeared behind the door and reappeared a moment later, waving and smiling. "It is good, Alice, it is good!"

After a friendly wave back, I pulled out of the parking lot and headed home. Thomas smiled and gurgled. "That was fun, huh, Tommy?"

Instead of the empty gnawing push to keep moving, I sailed along with new purpose. Thinking back to my dream job, I knew it never felt this good. I warmed with pride that a man named Muhammed with a wife he missed had a better life because I helped. It was so easy, too! Just a few extra miles, a little deviation from my plan, a little risk. What a difference all those little things made for that man, for Muhammed.

Thomas dozed, and I decided to drive for a while. My mind was whirring with possibilities, ways I could get this feeling again. Profit increase dominated my life for years, but now my eyes opened to how that focus could help people. I could fundraise, organize, streamline, optimize, do all the things I'd spent my life learning to do. Putting that kind of work into a non-profit like a homeless shelter or food shelf would amplify their effect on the world. I could make a difference every day. I laughed!

This was what Peter described when he went on that camping trip so long ago. When he'd left, I was planning on leaving him. Laura and I talked for hours on the phone that week, plotting out how I would get my old job back and build my life alone. But Peter came back a different person, suddenly able to engage at a depth that shocked and delighted me. He still had the gentle and subtle qualities I loved, but with a new sense of life radiating through his skin.

Maybe it was no more than coincidence. With enough objects floating in space and time, they were bound to collide. With enough collisions, something good had to emerge occasionally. Peter told me there was something on the other side of the silence, the emptiness. On the other side, there was an entity bigger and greater than a human mind could fully conceive. Somehow, Peter thought that being might care about our small lives on this blue planet. I thought he'd spent a little too much time outdoors, but it didn't sound so crazy now. Now I'd thrown my own impossible question into the void and received this transcendent reply.

Acknowledgements

For a book of such great multiplicity, thanks must go out in every direction. Thanks first to my wonderful husband, whose mere existence is a constant source of joy, and whose love brings me to awe. To Kim, my sister and friend. To Alice, who believed in me when I had no ability to believe in myself. To Heidi, who never lets me forget that I'm an artist with at least one awesome fan. To River Heights Vineyard Church, whose members claim me as their own and love me without condition, even when I make some of them really uncomfortable.

To Celebrate Recovery, for saving my life and breaking me out of a cycle of judgment and guilt. The women in my first 12-step group taught me to respect, admire, and love people I'd always scorned. Without them, I would not be the woman I am today, and this book would never be written. To Faith, Rachel, and James, whose honesty opened my mind and heart to the plight of Christian LGBT's, and whose commitment to our friendship conquered my cruel assumptions. To Izzi and Jacki, whose beauty and intelligence showed me the enormous capacity of children. To Jill, whose tireless work and willingness to share her experience lent some reality to the shelter system represented here. To Vivi, whose wonderful existence allowed me to understand what it is to care for a newborn.

To Barnabas, who saw the potential of these words long before they were finished. To everyone who read all or portions of this book and had the courage to tell me what they thought. To St. Albert's Church, for graciously allowing me to use their name. To Jamie Winter Dawson, whose incredible talent and commitment to her craft are a continual inspiration, and who created the artistry on the cover of this book. To Steve Wright and Double Pixel Publications, for giving me this incredible opportunity to get my work out in the world. Finally, to the God I follow, who loved me long before I could believe it.

Lauren Martinez Catlin is an author and poet who is committed to inspiring compassion through the written word. Her work has enhanced the efforts of A Minnesota Without Poverty, Breaking Free, Source Ministries, Justice4All, and A Beautiful Rescue. She graduated from the University of Minnesota in 2008 with a degree in English Literature. The Other Side of Silence is her first novel. She currently lives in Minneapolis with a very cute husband and a German Shepherd.

Visit her on the web at LaurenCatlin.com.

Made in the USA
Charleston, SC
18 October 2012